To John
met your daughter
in El Jo Bean
Mark [illegible]

Sons of a Citizen Soldier

Sons of a Citizen Soldier

a novel

Mark Abernathy

Deeds Publishing | Athens

Published by Deeds Publishing in Athens, GA
www.deedspublishing.com

Printed in The United States of America

Cover design by Mark Babcock. Text layout by Matt King.

ISBN 978-1-947309-91-3

Books are available in quantity for promotional or premium use. For information, email info@deedspublishing.com.

First Edition, 2019

10 9 8 7 6 5 4 3 2 1

This book is dedicated to all those who served our country in times of war and peace. To the men and women who so gallantly perform their duties at home and abroad, in the past and present. To the husbands, wives, and children whose lives will forever be affected by their sacrifice. To those who will hear the call and choose to take-up arms to defend the freedoms our forefathers dared to put forth. To the men and women who put their lives on the line every day, braving the mean borders and streets of modern America. To all of you, we thank you and your spouses and children.

Contents

Foreword

Everyone is a product of the chance merging of inherited genetic codes and environment. By the time we make monumental decisions, our natures are already formed. Free will is at best a whimsical notion. To each man, destiny is inherited.

Acknowledgments

Nothing is possible without God, conversely all is. Every member of my Mother's and Father's family of age served in World War II as army aviators or naval officers. Uncle Milton was shot down over France and captured. Uncle Jack survived a parachute fall into Hudson Bay. They were the best of human beings.

Without my athletic coaches, I never would have graduated high school, much less the Virginia Military Institute. Colonel Buchanan, barely a day goes by without hearing one of your truisms in my mind. "If it walks like a duck..." Thanks to my Brother Rats, Scott Shipp Hall and the path of least resistance (English Literature). To all the men and women I had the honor of serving with in Armor, Cavalry, and Aviation units of the U.S. Army.

To Salli, who tirelessly inspired, took dictation, helped me develop characters and events and oh yes, navigated the storms on land and sea.

To Phyllis and Charlie Atha, Bob Babcock, Jim Bentley, Janet Carlson, Stephanie Coates, Pete Cull, Ralph George, Paul Goodwin, Richard Lawrence, Rick Lester, Randy Miller,

Moon Mullin, Dave Richardson, Gary Seufert, Mike Tinney, Dianne VanBeek, Pam and Jim VanDenBerg, Cheryl Vespoint, Deborah Walsh, and Neal Zimmerman. All of you have inspired and supported my efforts to produce this book in ways you may or may not know. THANK YOU!

1. Elliott

Elliott barely felt his feet moving. He thought out loud, trying to rationalize his situation.

"I used to know exactly what I was supposed to do—get good grades, win a scholarship, go to college, it was all so clear. Now we have to police the world, win a war, stop the communists, worry about being defeated. It all goes back to the Industrial Revolution."

He hated the greed that motivated people to poison the rivers, strip mine for coal, and clear cut the forests. The whole system was screwed up, and Elliott didn't want to be part of it. He wanted to live life without anyone screaming at him or telling him to shoot people. Elliott was serious when he burned his draft card.

He stood on the side of the road with a backpack and his thumb out, trying to sing, "I feel free."

There was an art to hitchhiking. He didn't just stick out his thumb on the winding mountain road from Humboldt to Trinity. He had to pick the right spot. If he got bored and started walking, he might miss a ride if there was no place for the driver to stop. It was also better to see who was coming.

There were plenty of loggers who would beat his ass just for the hell of it, just for having long hair.

It was the element of the unknown that appealed to him. He could be picked up by hot chicks, beat up by rednecks, or propositioned by a businessman.

Two trucks passed without slowing, then he got lucky. A long-haired man in a VW rounded the curve, had to be cool. No one else would drive a 50 hp van in those mountains. It had to be someone who didn't care how long the trip took. He pulled up next to Elliott.

"How far you going?" he asked.

"Up to Denny."

"Great. I'm heading upriver, too."

"Toss your gear in the back and hop in."

The little German motor wound tight, as the driver skillfully shifted gears through the curves and steep grades of Highway 299 in Northern California's coastal range. The Trinity River raged blue-green below the highway on its race to the Pacific Ocean.

The driver pulled out a joint, passed it to Elliott, and they smoked to Crosby, Stills, Nash, and Young's *Four-Way Street.* Elliott felt good when he was high, but his heart was sick at the thought of disappointing his father.

His dad promised his deceased wife, Caroline, the boys would go to college. Elliott was conflicted. He wanted only enough money to buy the bare essentials, wanted to live close to the earth the way he was raised, hunting, fishing, and gathering. He didn't need college for that.

He couldn't stand big cities, great towers, or the smell of pulp mills. The thought of going to war for the American

Dream made no sense. He couldn't imagine that Vietnam was preparing to invade the United States. They didn't attack Pearl Harbor. There wasn't a single thing he needed or wanted from Vietnam, Cambodia, Laos, or red China. To hell with Kennedy, LBJ, and the rest of the congressmen who wanted American boys to shed their blood in Vietnam.

Elliott's ancestors fought in every war since the nation began. They shed blood against the English, fought to protect their homes during the Civil War, and defeated the Germans and the Japs. His dad almost died in World War Two, but Elliott would never go to Vietnam. That was their own civil war, north against south. If the communists landed at Coos Bay, Oregon, Elliott would fight, not before.

"Why are you going to Denny?" Elliott asked.

"Haven't you heard what's going on there?"

"No. What's up?"

"There's a whole commune thing. A bunch of people got together on government land and staked gold claims."

"They're mining gold?"

"No. They're growing pot. A whole community's living there and cops won't even go near Denny."

"That's a trip. Our family actually own gold mines on the Trinity River. We've been at it since World War Two."

"No shit? Ever find any gold?"

"Not much. We never struck it rich or anything, but it pays the tax man."

"They're growing green gold in Denny. Some Special Forces types were sending Thai stick back, killer buds tied to little sticks that damn near make you hallucinate. A friend got them to send seeds, and you can figure the rest. It's green gold."

"Wow. I'd like to try some of that."

"I can take you up there, as long as you're cool. You aren't a narc, are you? These people are dangerous. No bullshit."

Elliott was on an adventure. His new friend drove flawlessly through River Canyon to the turnoff and over the dirt roads to Denny. It was like an old mining town in the Wild West, and Elliott loved it. They were defying the establishment, claiming the land that belonged to the people, not the government.

The sun started setting, and the night would be chilly. When Elliott left his college dorm, he packed for survival, with Camp Trails freighter frame and backpack, a down bag, warm clothes, tent, stove, charcoal water filter, magnesium and striker, wrist rocket, and fishing tackle. He had everything he needed to survive, including maps, compass, and binoculars.

He pulled his fifty-pound pack from the VW bus and followed Gary to a campfire where girls and guys were drinking Mateuse wine from a bottle and passing a bamboo bong. They welcomed the newcomers into the circle to smoke and drink with them.

The pot was much stronger than the Mexican weed Elliott usually smoked. He watched the fire in a euphoric, timeless haze. The sun set, and darkness settled around them. He took his pack and found a place to roll out his sleeping bag. Laying on his back, staring at the Milky Way, he drifted off to sleep.

He was awakened by someone kicking him. Squinting into

the light from a Coleman lantern, he saw a pistol aimed at his face. Someone kicked him again. The word *LOVE* was tattooed across the fingers holding the gun.

"Where you from?" they demanded. "Where do you live?"

"Junction City, Junction City."

When Elliott told them he was raised in Junction City, that was all the information they lacked. They laughed, kicking Elliott until he was unconscious.

When the residents found Elliott the next morning and heard what happened, they launched a search for the culprits, but the pair vanished, taking Elliott's backpack, gear, and watch. He felt like he'd been used as a tackling dummy in football practice. Blood clotted his swollen face and scalp. Bruised ribs and hurt feelings infuriated him.

The girls from the circle insisted on taking care of him until he was able to leave. They took him to their tipi, undressed and bathed him with warm water. They had him drink powerful marijuana tea to help with the pain. He drifted in and out of dreamy consciousness.

The girls were uninhibited, kind, sensual, careful not to hurt him. They placed him in the middle of their bed and slept on either side. They were almost always nude inside the tipi. Elliott had never before considered being unfaithful to his girl, Janet, but, after a few days of healing, watching them, and sleeping with them in the nude, it happened repeatedly with both girls simultaneously in ways he never imagined.

As he healed, he wondered if given the choice, he'd take a beating just for the pleasure of convalescing.

Randy was driving across Highway 299 from Arcata when he saw two drifters hitchhiking on the lightly traveled mountain road. His Land Cruiser growled to a halt, and he offered them a ride.

They claimed their truck had blown its engine. The only thing they had of value was a Rolex watch, claiming they bought it from a kid on the coast.

Randy recognized the watch. It was given to the star quarterback of the Trinity Wolves Championship football team by his father, John Copeland. Cope, as he was called, was Randy's best friend.

He didn't believe the story, but he gave them fifty dollars for the watch and drove to the Copeland Ranch in Junction City. Cope had gone to Fort Rucker, Alabama, to attend his youngest son's graduation from Warrant Officer Candidate School and the U.S. Army Rotor Wing Aviator Qualification Course. Cope took his K5 Blazer, and Randy didn't know when he would return, so he left a note.

Cope,

I bought Elliott's watch from a couple of dirt bags I picked up hitchhiking on 299. Something smells fishy. I left them at the watering hole in Big Bar. They should be easy enough to find.

Have you heard from Elliott? Call me when you get this note.

Randy

Gary the VW driver, felt really bad about what happened to

Elliott. He offered him a ride after he completed his business in Denny. Gary bought a bag of Thai seeds intended to improve the quality of his marijuana in Mendocino. He dropped Elliott off at a Whitewater Outfitters in Burnt Ranch.

Elliott was now broke and needed money. Fortunately, he was highly skilled and had a standing offer as a whitewater guide for his friend's company. On some level, he wanted to go home, but the thought of facing his father was too much. His dad's judgment could be severe.

Elliott was an excellent guide. He was paid $50 per half-day trips, or $100 for a whole day. He loved it. He made even more money in tips from grateful customers than he did in wages.

Elliott and his brother grew up on the Trinity River. Both swam like fish and paddled a raft or kayak instinctively and gracefully. Elliott had mastered the art of reading the river and was at one with the water. All his senses and thoughts focused in an exhilarating presence of life and death. Sliding between boulders and cascading falls, going through eight-foot walls of water, that was his thrill, joy, and Zen.

After leaving college, he had great days on the river, but at night, when the thrill was gone, he was troubled. He sought to find his way in a confusing world, torn by the ethics of his staunch Christian upbringing and the wave of upheaval in the 1960s social revolution. Whenever he felt guilty for being unfaithful to Janet, he sang, "If you can't be with the one you love, love the one you're with."

A customer Elliott guided down the river gave him a card and offered him a job on the Stanislaus River as soon as he could get there. Elliott decided to take him up on the offer.

Burnt Ranch was way too close to Junction City and his father. He gave up on getting his watch back and revenge on his assailants. He bought new backpacking, camping, and survival gear, then he caught a ride with a group returning to Sacramento and planned to hitchhike the rest of the way to Angels Camp.

2. Graduation

Tears of pride flowed down Cope's face, as he pinned Army Aviator wings on his youngest son's broad chest. They were the same wings he wore to war at twenty-two, and brought him back a hero in the eyes of everyone who knew him. It wasn't just about how he conducted himself in combat. It was how he lived his life.

John Copeland was an honorable man, uncomplicated and predictable; for him, there were no gray areas.

That simple ethos was adhered to by all who came under his authority and love. The gospel according to John Copeland meant don't lie, don't cheat, don't steal, and don't tolerate those who do.

The staunch, stoic Cope felt overwhelmed, unable to control his emotions, which was rare for a man who'd seen what he did during World War Two. It was a joyous day, yet he felt underlying fear that Jack would be one of the boys who would pay the ultimate price. Helicopter pilots didn't have much life expectancy in the new airmobile warfare. A fearless young man, Jack would carry the family name to war the way his ancestors did since the beginning of time. There were always those who had to do it and couldn't hide from their calling. Men were called to defend. They started by whacking things as toddlers, making pretend weapons, and joining football teams.

Jack was one of those men. He chose to be an attack pilot. He didn't want to be just a target. He wanted to shoot back at the enemy. If his brothers were being shot, and he could help, that was for him. Like his father, he saw no gray areas. The Viet Cong were the enemy. He was going to Vietnam to kill the sons of bitches who were enemies of his country.

Then he got his orders. He was being sent to Vietnam in the 101 Airborne Division, where he would be a Cavalryman like his great-grandfather, great uncle, and the many heroes throughout history he admired.

Jack and Cope went to the Officer's Club to celebrate the graduation ceremony. For the first time in his life, Cope bought a hard drink for Jack, marking it as a rite of passage.

He looked his son in the eye. "Damn it, Son, you're a man now. The things you're about to see will change you forever. There will be no going back to the way things were."

Tears slid down the creases and across the scars on Cope's face, his steely blue eyes bright with intensity. Cope bought a round for everyone at the bar, then he tapped his Virginia Military Institute class ring sharply on the hardwood bar to get the men's attention.

"Gentlemen, a toast to the fine young men who graduated today and will carry on the proud traditions of the U.S. Army Aviation Corps."

"Here, here!" the others cheered.

They drank, and the barmaid tried to refill the glasses for the next toast.

Jack raised his glass and said, "To our fathers."

"Here, here!"

There was another chorus of approval. The Cavalry had a funny tradition. Though they weren't allowed to wear their Stetsons in the Officer's Club, they did it anyway, on special occasions. The price for such an infraction was buying a round for everyone at the bar.

A tall Colonel in his flight suit and Stetson walked to the bar, rang the bell, and nodded at the barmaid. Pouring continued. He served under Cope as a young man right after the war. Now he was gray. Cope could recognize every man in his command at 100 yards by the way he walked. He knew how many children each man had and where he came from. He passed on those leadership skills and many other things to the Colonel who ordered a round and said, "To the Cavalry!"

Though Cope's back was turned, he recognized the voice turned and asked, "How are you, William?"

"Fine, Sir. Just fine." They shook hands and embraced.

"You look great, Captain."

"I haven't been called that in twenty years. Cope's good enough for me, William."

"To me, you'll always be the captain. I heard you'd be here for Jack's graduation. I've been following his class to see how he was doing—without interfering, of course. Top ten isn't bad for a kid raised in the mountains hunting goats and chasing gold nuggets underwater."

"Great to see you, William. What brings you back to Mother Rucker?"

"I'm here to get this airmobile training program on the fast track. We're going forward with air mobility as the way to victory in this battle theater. We have to hit Charlie fast, whenever and wherever we find him. There aren't any battle lines. It's a different kind of war.

"Cope, can you imagine an enemy who doesn't wear uniforms, lives on a handful of rice each day, and sneaks through the jungle like a snake? They'll send a woman with a baby and a hand grenade up to a GI. What American boy will shoot a woman with a child? The GI figures it's a language problem. He says, 'Halt,' and she says something he doesn't understand, then she comes closer, and kaboom!"

"How will you defeat that, William?"

"I don't know. The smart people in Washington expect us to win the hearts and minds of the people, so some developer can build a new Disneyland in the Vietnam jungle."

"Hell. When did the Army get into public relations? That's not a soldier's job. That's for a social worker. Did we try to win the hearts and minds of the Japs or the Germans? Hell, no. We gave them Dresden and Hiroshima to think about. The politicians are too involved in this war. That's what scares me."

"They don't scare me, they sicken me. If they'd take off the gloves, we could bomb Hanoi into oblivion and get out of this guerilla warfare. The politicians seem to care more about public opinion and their reelection chances than the lives of American soldiers."

"Are they scared the Chinese will jump in?"

"They're already in, Cope."

"Yeah, like the Russians in Cuba. How much longer will you be Stateside?"

"I'm heading back in a month."

"I wish they'd let the military fight the war to win or just get the hell out. Godspeed, William. I need to collect Jack and feed him a big steak before I take him back to the barracks."

When Jack returned to his bunk, he found mail waiting for him.

Saturday
Dear Jack,

I miss you so much. I picked Bear up at your house and drove the Jeep to Hellhole. Both are fine. The whole gang was there. It was really hot, and the guys drank beer and tried to shoot Hellhole in inner tubes. No one's as good at that as you are.

Freddie went right into the big rock. God, I thought he was dead. After a few seconds, he came up without his shorts. It was so funny. We laughed, as he ran through the bushes. He went to the rocks and was bit up by mosquitoes. It's been hot and humid, with lots more rain than most summers.

Some kids from Redding showed up, and there was almost a big fight. I was a bit scared. Pete and Phil stood up to them, even though there were more of them. I knew what you would've done, so I'm glad you weren't here.

They were jerks. They threw bottles, and we yelled at them. That's how it started. Bear went crazy when they tried to come over to Janet and me. He chased one drunk jerk up into the rocks and stood there, growling and wagging his tail like he treed a raccoon. Everyone cracked up.

It was all over after that. Even his buds laughed at

him. I can't understand how people can trash such a beautiful place and disrespect the earth like that. Those guys should've had their asses kicked—if violence was OK, I mean. Maybe their mothers and fathers should've done it when they were little.

I walked downstream and checked your dad's dredge. It was still there. The cables seemed in order. I hope you two have fun at Fort Rucker. He bragged you up and down at the Moose Club. He's been showing off the picture of you in your dress greens, my mom said. I have that beside the one of you in your football uniform after the state championship game last year.

I miss you more than I can say. Sometimes, I worry. Whenever I hear a forest service helicopter flying around, I wonder what it must be like. Maybe when you get home, you can get a job with them and can take me flying. I don't know if I can stand the thought of you going to that awful place. I can't even watch the news without thinking of you there.

I wish you didn't have to go. Sometimes, I wonder if you really love, truly love me. If you did, you never would've joined. Then I know it's your duty. Your dad helps me understand. I love him so much. He's so cute with Bear. They ride all over town in the Willys. Bear rides shotgun, his head sticking out the window. Whenever I see them, I think for a second it's you.

Please come home soon and write me as soon as you can. I love you forever.

Love, Katie

PS. I went to our special rock by Hobo Gulch, waded up the creek, and thought about you. Janet and I went skinny dipping in the deep hole. The water was freezing cold.

Pressing the letter to his face, he inhaled the scent. It was like the sweetest flower God ever made, chocolate, ice cream, fresh cookies, sunshine, and rain on a hot summer day. He loved Katie from the day she first walked up the creek. They were thirteen, still kids unspoiled by life. That night, he dreamed of her, seeing a German officer tie her to a chair with instruments of torture on a table, files for teeth and surgical instruments, all waiting on a white cloth.

"You'll tell us everything we want to know."

A big woman in an SS uniform grabbed her hair. "You're so pretty. It would be a shame to cut up that pretty face."

"OK, OK, I'll tell you!" Katie said. "He went to Canada. Elliott went to Canada!"

Jack woke up screaming, "Elliott's in Canada!"

His bunkmate rolled over. "Who the hell went to Canada?"

"Long story, Dennis. What a weird dream. I dreamed about my brother, who said he'd run away to Canada if he lost his deferment and his draft number came up."

"Maybe he's right. The jury's still out."

"I don't see it that way. Neither could you and still do what you're doing."

"Sure I can, Jack. I didn't volunteer because I wanted to be shot at. I just didn't want to rot in jail over some silly bullshit."

"Could you keep it down over there?" someone called. "Some of us are trying to sleep."

"OK, OK." Dennis lowered his voice. "You see, Jack, I was kind of dating the mayor of Red Bluff's daughter. She tended to be a little on the wild side. Well, one night, one of the deputies caught me in her daddy's car in what you might say were not proper circumstances for a seventeen-year-old girl. The chief of police, the mayor, and the prosecuting attorney decided I could be convicted as a rapist and car thief or be a proud member of the U.S. Armed Forces. Helping free the world from Communist aggressors seemed like an honorable solution to a rather unfortunate turn of events.

"If Canada had been an option, I would've taken that over Southeast Asia with its yellow fuckers with AK-47s and missiles. I really don't care one way or the other about that part of the world. Hell, we don't even play Vietnam in football or baseball. Do they even play sports?"

"I never thought about it, Dennis. Maybe they'll cover that when we get there."

"Yeah. Seven days. I can't wait. What about your brother? What did your dad do when he found out how Elliott felt about the war?"

"He won't talk about it. He spends a lot of time in the river, dredging, or hiking in the high country. He works in his shop a lot, too. There's always plenty of work to do without saying a damn thing."

"If I were your brother, I'd never want to piss him off. He looks tough as hell for his age."

"He's tough for any age. I've never seen him unable to handle a situation. Sometimes, he does it without even raising his voice. It's all in the eyes and some carefully chosen curses. When he says something, it's best to pay attention. I saw him drop big men in the blink of an eye. It was so fast, they never saw it coming. Dad always said to strike fast, first, and furiously. Never tell someone you're going to hit him."

"I wish I had a role model like that when I was growing up."

"You'll get a taste of it this weekend. You can see how you like it."

3. St. George Island

Cope's K5 Blazer pulled up outside the barracks at exactly 0800 hrs. Jack and Dennis fell out of ranks from inspection in their dress greens, complete with blooded aviator wings and Warrant Officer bars. Changing into civilian clothes, they grabbed their bags for a weekend on the Florida coast.

Cope had prepared for the expedition, filled the cooler with clear little Miller pony bottles. He liked them, because a man could drink them before they got warm. It was 100 miles to St. George Island and Cope wasn't wasting any time on the highway.

"You boys can have a beer if you like," Cope said.

"Thank you, Sir. May I get you one?"

"I think not. The Alabama countryside is sliding by too fast. I never do more than one wrong thing at a time. If I get pulled over for speeding, the officer might let an old veteran off with a warning. If I drink a beer, I'm endangering the safety of the good citizens of the proud state of Alabama. We'd go see a judge, but we wouldn't get any time with him until Monday. That should be an object lesson in good judgment for you."

"Yes, Sir. I see your point. Never do more than one wrong thing at a time."

Jack turned his head to look at his friend in the back seat. "There's a lot more where that came from. Trust me."

Jack stared at acres of peanut farms. "I've never seen so much red, flat dirt in my life. How can these people live out here in those little houses? They don't even look like they have electricity."

"You'll see people living a lot more primitive than this, Jack," Cope said. "Some folks back home in Virginia like it simple. They have very few needs, less work, fewer complications, and fewer demands on their time. They stay busy with the basic needs of life.

"My people still had outhouses and wells into the forties and fifties. Hell, some people are still probably using outhouses and drawing well water today. I actually prefer that. There are no foul odors in the house, no pipes to break or freeze in winter, no electric bills, and lower taxes. Dennis, we have a large tank at the ranch. Water comes down from the mountain to fill the tank. It's all gravity fed, no pumps or electricity. It's the sweetest water you ever tasted."

"That sounds really great, Mr. Copeland."

"What plans do you have for us, Dad?"

"Considering the training and isolation you boys just completed, I thought about girls at the bars and on the beaches. However, your mother, rest her soul, always reminded me of my tentative relationship with the Almighty. I decided we would abstain from such carnal temptations and do the next best thing. We're going surf casting. We'll build a fire on the beach and can stay up all night fishing for reds."

"Would those be redheads?" Dennis smiled.

"That sounds great, Dad, but what's a red?" Jack asked.

"Red drum. They're great fighters and one of the best eating fish around. They can top the scale at over thirty pounds."

Cope called an old friend in the park service and got access to a locked gate at the end of St. George's Island. The road was closed for years except for foot traffic. It was a seven-mile drive through deep, loose sand paralleling the shore and along grass-covered dunes that formed a break between the Gulf of Mexico and Apalachicola Bay.

The road ended at the cut that connected the two bodies of water with a fast current. It was a high-energy place. The Gulf waters were so very blue against the white sand. It was exciting to see breakers crashing and birds diving on baitfish the predators chased to the surface. Spanish mackerel and bluefish cut the surface, while mullet performed acrobatics. The food chain was busy. If a person needed a meal, that was the place to go.

The island held alligators in small ponds, as well as rattlers, cottonmouths, snapping turtles, coral snakes, wild pigs, coons, and possums. The most-abundant life form however, was flying insects. A person could catch a few meals on the island, but he had to donate blood to voracious airborne units of no-see-ums, horse flies, and several species of mosquito. Those could be avoided by staying in the water where there was a breeze. That was the only sanctuary. The danger was that the current might sweep someone away, or a shark might be curious about the stringer of bloody fish tied to a person's waist.

The Blazer halted at the main gate of St. George's Park. A young man in a green uniform and a baseball cap with the

Florida Park emblem on it greeted them. When he saw the California license plate, he smiled.

"You must be the folks from Fort Rucker. I've been waiting for you."

"If you're here to open the gate to the end of the park, then I'm your man," Cope said.

"Yes, Sir. Just follow me. If one of you wants to ride in my truck, I'll share what I know about the recent catches."

"Jack, why don't you ride with the ranger and see what you can learn?" Cope asked.

Jack got into the ranger's truck for the short ride to the locked gate. Jack learned that the fishing had been excellent, and the place they were going always produced fish.

At the gate, they got out of the truck.

"You'll be on your own down there," the ranger said, "but it looks like you're prepared. The road hasn't been used in a while. A little rain would help. The sand's pretty soft."

"We'll be fine," Cope said. "We can't thank you enough for opening the gate for us. We'll see you on the way out if you're on duty."

Cope let air out of the tires until they were at fifteen pounds. The treads weren't too aggressive, so the tires wouldn't dig into the sand too much. Locking the front hubs, he went through the sand in low. The 300-horsepower small block sounded like a Harley-Davidson. None of them had ever seen sand so white or water so blue.

It took an hour and a half to go seven miles to the end of the island. Cope brought everything—twenty gallons of water, five pounds of dry ice, forty pounds of crushed ice, big coolers, beer, bait, smoked bacon, ham, watermelon, tomatoes, cantaloupe, and peaches. He even brought marshmallows and graham crackers.

It was like summer camp for adults with really good toys. They had nine-foot surf casting rods, PVC rod holders, and medium-action spinning rods.

When they reached the end of the island, Jack shouted, "Look! Birds and porpoise! Something's tearing up the bait!"

They arrived in time for a feeding frenzy. Equipped with spinning rods and silver spoons with steel leaders, the three men waded into the water's edge and cast among the feeding fish. The first cast produced a large speckled trout, and they got hits on nearly every cast.

The boys hooted and hollered, and Cope grinned while smoking a cigar. They could've filled the entire cooler if they wanted.

"If we don't want to be cleaning fish all night, we'd better quit now and make camp."

"You got it, Dad," Jack said.

Cope pulled out a four-foot two-by-twelve and rigged up a fish-cleaning table between two coolers. He worked like a machine. He grabbed the fish head with his left hand, slid the razor-sharp blade behind the head down to the spine and firmly back to the tail. Then he flipped the fillet over and pulled on the head to slide the knife between the fillet and the skin, leaving a beautiful slab of meat behind.

He rolled the fish over and repeated the process on the other side. Dennis watched him like an intern observing surgery for the first time. Jack learned to butcher from his dad when he was a young man.

"OK, Boys," Cope said. "The old man needs a drink. Your turn, Jack."

"Let me try, Jack," Dennis said.

"Have at it, Denny," Jack said. "If you don't get it right the first time, there's plenty to practice on."

"You boys don't fight over it. There's plenty to do if we want a cocktail with the sunset."

Soon, the fish were filleted and placed on ice, the fire pit dug, and wood gathered. There was plenty of fish, potatoes, and veggies wrapped in foil with butter, ready for the coals.

As the sun set against the western sky, Jack realized he forgot about where he was headed. At least for a few hours, he ignored the war. He knew the war would change the path of his life.

Looking into the Gulf of Mexico, he wished it could be like that forever, fishing at the beach with Dennis and playing horseshoes, watching campfires, and drinking cold beer.

Then he saw a small sailboat, with a man with curly blond hair and dark tan at the helm, beach on the lee side of the point. He came in just as the sun set.

Curious about the boat, Jack and Dennis went to investigate. Cope lit the fire, enjoying the wonderful sunset and eight-knot offshore breeze. The moon would be nearly full. The only way it could have been better was if he had both sons there, but he wouldn't let that spoil his time with Jack.

Rounding the point toward the catamaran, the boys were greeted by 100 squawking gulls protesting being rousted by a bounding yellow Lab. She barked and ran wildly, jumping headlong into the light surf, her tail straight up and ears flopping like Dumbo trying to fly.

The dog greeted them with respectful barks. The young

captain whistled once, and the dog streaked back to leap onto the trampoline of the lightly grounded vessel.

"Good evening," Jack said. "Can we give you a hand dragging her onto the beach?"

"No, thanks. She'll be all right here. The tide's going out until morning."

"Where'd you come from?"

"I left Dauphin Island about three months ago. I've been beach camping ever since with my first mate here, Clara Bell."

"That's a fine name for a dog," Jack said.

"She's an awesome first mate and my best friend."

"Do you hunt her?"

"Not lately, but I enjoy working a good dog. Are you guys in the military?" he asked Dennis, while Jack walked toward Clara Bell.

"Yes, Sir," Dennis replied. "We just finished Warrant Officer Candidate School at Fort Rucker. Our haircut probably gave us away. My name's Dennis." He offered his hand.

Jack wrapped his arms around the Lab's neck and realized how much he missed his dog and Katie, his girlfriend. Shaking off the thought, he turned and shook hands with Neil, their new friend.

They invited him to join them at the fire. When they arrived, Cope wasn't surprised. With two sons, there were always extra boys at mealtimes. Cope always made sure he had plenty of food. Jack introduced Neil to his dad.

"Pleasure to meet you, Son," Cope said. "We've got twice as much food any four men and a dog could possibly eat. Help yourself to a cold beer. Your ration is only six, because you arrived so late."

"You must be ex-military," Neil said. "Most people don't ration beer. Anyone else need one?"

The boys nodded, and Neil handed out beers from the cooler.

"In answer to your question, Neil," Cope said, "yes, but that was many years ago. How about yourself?"

"Yes, Sir. I answered my country's call." He sounded slightly bitter.

"You aren't very enthusiastic about it," Cope said.

"Well, Sir, I got mixed reviews when I came back from Southeast Asia. It seems a lot of people don't appreciate our service and sacrifice." He shook his head.

"That's probably the saddest commentary on our society I can think of," Cope said. "How could the citizens of a country turn their back on those who are willing to fight for them? I'll never understand it. I can understand disagreeing with the politics, but you can't blame soldiers for doing their duty. I sincerely thank you for yours."

"I appreciate that, Sir. Smells like you have a great meal going. This must be a good place to fish."

"It is." Jack put their spinning rods in the truck. "We could've filled the cooler. We kept enough for a minor feast. There's nothing better than fresh fish."

"Neil, a note of caution," Cope said, petting Clara. "We threw the carcasses of the fish we cleaned into the water over there. I wouldn't want to see your dog get bit by a shark."

"We have a big male black Lab at home. He sure would like this handsome girl. How old is she?"

"She'll be two later this year, and we never go into the water after sunset. Most people who grew up around the Gulf would agree, especially when fish have been cleaned. I saw a man attacked by a bull shark in only eighteen inches of water when I was a kid. We were flounder gigging at night. My dad beat the shark with his gigging pole. He saved the man's life, though he lost his leg from the knee down. It made quite an impression on me."

"That would do it for me," Dennis said. "You guys are giving me the willies."

"You think we could catch a shark tonight, Dad?" Jack asked.

"We'll definitely put out our rods. I'd like to see a big bull red, but there's no telling what you'll catch out here at night."

Cope forked potatoes to see if they were done, raised the grill on the tripod, and transferred the hot tin foil to the Blazer's tailgate. "Dinner's ready. No need to stand on ceremony. Everybody grab a plate and dig in."

The fish was poached in its own juices with butter and old Bay seasoning. It broke into white flakes that melted in their mouths. The four men barely spoke as they ate first and second helpings. Cope pulled half a fish from the foil to cool on a separate plate, which he brought to Neil once cooled.

"Would you like to give this to your dog?" he asked.

"She'll love that. You can feed her if you want."

Cope placed the fish down in front of Clara Bell. Drooling, she looked at him, then at Neil. Cope sat back down at the fire.

Neil gave Clara a command, and she stood and carefully ate the fresh trout. When she was through licking the plate, she sat beside Cope and placed her head in his lap. Patting her head, he felt the warmth of the fire, raising steam from her coat.

"What will we use for bait?" Dennis asked, rubbing his stomach. "That's the best meal I've had in a long time. You sure know how to cook, Mr. Copeland."

"Thank you. I enjoy cooking almost as much as eating. There's some mullet in the fish cooler for cut bait. You can get the surf casting rods and holders out whenever you're ready, Jack."

Dennis and Jack began baiting lines, while Neil relaxed by the fire with Clara and Cope. They sat without speaking, enjoying the fire.

"That's the best meal I've had in a while too," Neil said. "Thank you. Y'all made me feel right at home, more than a lot of people since I came back. I actually had people spit on me and call me a baby killer when I arrived in Seattle. It about broke my heart and made me angry at the same time."

"I'm sorry for you, Son. From one combat veteran to another, let me tell you I have the utmost respect and admiration for you and all the young men who chose to serve. It was very different when I went to war. The whole free world was against Hitler. He threatened the homeland of most Americans' ancestors. There was no moral dilemma. He had to be stopped, and every red-blooded American was duty-bound and hell-bent for leather.

"This war, though, will test the very fabric of American society. Soldiers will be called to duty, and politicians keep looking for advantage. These two boys just finished rotor wing qualifications and are on orders for Vietnam."

"I can imagine how proud you are of your son, but I can also imagine how afraid I'd be if he were my son. Until the politicians figure out if they want to let us fight this war, it'll be hard to win. We could've vaporized Hanoi like we did Hiroshima, and we wouldn't be in this guerrilla war. It's a damn mess over there. I never knew who the enemy was. They don't wear uniforms and refuse to confront in traditional battle. They fought like coyotes, sneaking around at night, so we used unorthodox tactics, too."

"Let's not talk too much more about this tonight. I want Dennis and Jack to feel like kids for a while. When they come back, they might not be able to."

"I understand, Sir. That's partly why I'm sailing the Gulf in a Hobie cat. I'm trying to get back to the person I used to be."

"It takes time, but you're going about it the right way. You need time to make sense of things. I wasn't the same person when I came back, but I made peace with the killing. What's the other reason you're doing this?"

"While I was gone, my dad disappeared in his shrimping boat. There was never any flotsam or mayday call, and no life raft, either. We come from generations of watermen. My dad wouldn't just disappear. It was rumored that drug dealers might be involved. I figured if I sailed the Gulf, there was a chance I could find out what happened. I don't believe he perished."

"I wish you the best of luck finding yourself and your dad."

Jack cast a hunk of mullet into the deep water of the cut, while Dennis opted for half a blue crab. They stood ten feet apart, watching the moon and its twin reflections against the rolling waves of the Gulf. Small crabs skittered around the Coleman lantern.

Suddenly, Jack felt a strong pull on his rod. He counted three seconds, then jerked the rod back and shouted, "Fish on!"

Dennis whooped and reeled in his line to avoid getting tangled in Jack's. Aroused by the excitement, Clara ran to the water's edge and chased the crabs from the light. Jack's rod bent almost in half, the line zinging.

"Should I tighten the drag?" he asked. "It's stripping me!"

"Just a little, Jack, not too much."

Neil grabbed a lantern and followed Jack, as the fish pulled him along the beach. His biceps and forearms pulled on the rod, then he cranked in line when he lowered it. He gained a few yards, then the fish moved again, stripping out more line.

Cope went down to where Dennis stood. "Let's get our lines in while they're moving down the beach."

Casting their lines, they stood near each other, waiting for Jack to either land or lose the fish. Jack and Neil were almost out of sight.

"Sir, what was World War Two like?"

"Son, it was a glorious hell, something that after a man walked through it, he never wanted to visit it again."

"You were a pilot, too, weren't you?"

"I wore the same wings that were pinned on you the other day. My old wings are now pinned on Jack. That's about as much as I want to say about the war."

Dennis' rod suddenly bent in half.

"Whoa, Son!" Cope said. "Be patient. Wait...wait...set it! Fish on!" Cope reeled in his line.

"Damn, it's a big one, Sir. He's stripping my line."

"Keep your tip high and tighten the drag just a hair. You can't horse him. Just play him slow. Work the rod up and down.

Try to reel in some line. You have to wear him out. That's all you can do."

Neil ran toward them along the beach. "We need a gaff. He's tiring out. We're starting to gain on him. He came to the surface three times and looks like a big bull red about four feet long."

Cope grabbed a six-foot dowel with a pointed piece of stainless steel bolted to it. "This ought to do the trick. You'd better take a couple beers. Jack will want one after that fight."

Ten minutes later, Jack and Neil came down the beach dragging a forty-five-pound redfish. Jack was ecstatic, still high on adrenalin.

"Now that's a fish, Son," Cope said. "How are your arms?"

"Like I boxed five rounds."

Laughing, Cope patted Jack's back.

"Do you think it's as big as the King Salmon Elliot caught at Willows on the Trinity River?"

Cope paused at hearing his other son's name. He missed him. "I'll bet he's every bit as big."

"What's Dennis got on?"

"Who knows? It looks big. It hit like a freight train. It might be a bull shark or a black tip. You never know what you'll get in these waters."

An hour later, Dennis landed another giant bull red. Neil caught and released a small shark while the boys relaxed by the fire. They basked in moonlight, watching falling stars, while Jack filleted the reds, iced down the slabs of meat, and yawned.

"Neil, where are you and Clara going?" Jack asked.

"No real agenda, just cruising and camping like I was a kid again."

"How long will you do that?"

"Long as I want, I reckon, as long as it feels right."

"That sounds great," Dennis said. "When I'm through with the Army, I'll learn how to sail."

"I'd like a bigger boat, though," Jack said. "I'd like something with room on it, a real sea-worthy boat you can live on. That would be too cool."

"That's exactly what I want to do," Neil said. "I'm looking at a center cockpit, shoal-draft ketch. I dreamed and studied about it the whole time I was overseas. By the time you get back, I'll have my dream boat. You'll have to look me up."

"How would we get hold of you?"

"If you go to Dauphin Island, Alabama, right after the bridge over the inland waterway, you'll see a seafood shop called Tinners. You can't miss it. That's my uncle's. We always stay in touch."

Jack fell asleep on his bag near the fire. Clara curled up next to him until he was sound asleep. Neil and Clara went back to the Hobie cat and left just before dawn.

Something about the smell of coffee and bacon on a wood fire calls people awake as gently and irresistibly as the caress of a woman's lips.

"Is it coffee yet?" Jack asked.

"It has been for half an hour, Sleepyheads. Putting eggs in the skillet right now," Cope replied.

They ate eggs over easy, fried fish, bacon, watermelon, French garlic bread, tomato juice, and coffee while listening to the rhythmic slapping of curling waves and the cries of sea gulls.

Cope had two ammo cans beside his chair and gave one to each of the young warrant officers without a word. Inside each can was a Ruger .22 caliber semiautomatic with silencer and 2,000 rounds.

"Men, this is your survival weapon," he said. "Learn to shoot it without aiming. The silencer will keep the enemy from knowing where you are. At close range, you can kill anything. It has no recoil and fires eleven shots as fast as you can pull. There are five clips with each weapon. This is the most-dependable weapon I know for a pilot. Go practice on those empty cans against a sand dune before it gets hot."

Jack and Dennis, opening their cans, examined the fine, stainless-steel pistols, resembling German Lugers. Jack hugged his dad and thanked him, then Dennis shook his hand.

They loaded five clips each and collected cans. With the silencer on, there was no front post sight, so they learned to point shoot like gunfighters. Within a couple hours, they were hitting cans at twenty feet without aiming.

The boys returned to camp very excited and pleased. They studied the schematics and meticulously cleaned their new pistols. After crushing the bullet-riddled cans, they opened cold beers to go with lunch. Ham sandwiches with tomato slices and dill pickles was a favorite of the Copelands.

"What do you want to do now, Dad?" Jack asked.

"That's entirely up to you boys."

"I'll look for some cool shells for Katie and walk the beach awhile."

"I'll come with you. Maybe I can find a Southern belle." Dennis smiled.

When they returned from their walk, the sun was low in the sky. Cope had three rod holders and surf rods in place. A tumbler of sour mash sat in his hand, as he waited for the sunset and the elusive green splash.

"What makes it splash green, Cope?" Dennis asked.

"I'm not exactly sure. It could just be a myth. I've never seen it."

"That doesn't give me much confidence in the phenomenon, Dad."

"I guess you'll have to see for yourself." Cope chuckled.

He left the boys talking at the fire at ten o'clock that evening. He was tired. They caught two sharks, a stingray, and three bull reds. It was a big night, and he was pleased with their trip. He hoped Jack and Dennis remembered it forever, as he would.

The following morning, their three-day weekend would end, and they'd break camp and head back to Fort Rucker. Dennis would go home for a short leave in Red Bluff before departing for Vietnam. Jack would go to AH-1G Cobra transition before he deployed.

"What happened to your dad in the war?" Dennis asked. "I know he got a Silver Star, but what did he do?"

"He never told me personally, but I heard the story from my uncle and read the narrative from the commendation. Dad was a B-17 pilot. They were bombing the German industrial sites along the Rhine River Valley when his plane was shot up. They parachuted into the waiting arms of the Germans and spent the rest of the war in a POW camp in eastern Germany somewhere.

"It was horrible conditions, and it got worse toward the end. The German soldiers were starving, so you can imagine how they treated the POWs. They ate rats and bugs and anything else they could find. There was plenty of death and starvation.

"The Germans randomly fired through the barracks walls at times. When the Russians were approaching from the east and the Allies from the west, the commandant went crazy. He lined up the POWs and walked behind the ranks, shooting men in the back of the head. He said it was retribution for the bombings.

"According to the citation, my dad was standing in ranks when the commander stopped behind him on his morning retribution. Dad dropped down and reached between his legs, grabbing the officer's feet out from under him. He recovered the pistol and shot him and the two sergeants walking with him.

"Other POWs grabbed the submachine guns. When they finished, every German in camp was dead. Some were brutally killed when they tried to surrender. I think that's why Dad won't talk about it. He weighed 185 when he left the States and returned at 110 pounds. He lost seventy-five pounds."

"Damn. That's incredible. I can't imagine going through

something like that. Now I understand why he gave us those pistols."

"Yeah. I don't think he wants anyone to go through what he went through."

"I'll sleep under the stars tonight, Jack."

"Me, too. It's so beautiful. Maybe there'll be a meteor shower."

"That would be cool. Where do you think Neil and Clara are right now?"

"Maybe fifty miles from here on a beach. Neil is probably looking at the Milky Way, too."

"I sure hope he gets that big sailboat. That would be the coolest thing. Wouldn't it be fun to sail around like that? When you get tired of someplace, you pull up the anchor and shove off."

"How can you shove off when you're anchored?"

"You got me there. Seriously, that would be a great life."

"I'd like to try it. Hopefully, we'll get back alive and have a chance to do that. I think Katie would love it. She always talks about traveling and seeing the world. She'd love cruising."

"Let's plan on it. When we get back, we'll find a boat on the West Coast and sail down to Mexico, Cabo San Lucas, and the Sea of Cortez. Hell, we'll sail the whole damn world!"

"Sounds great. Maybe I'll dream about that tonight."

"I might be too excited to sleep. What a plan."

Sleeping well, they were awakened by the rattle of pans and the aroma of brewing coffee. Cope cooked breakfast, then they broke camp. After all was secured for the trip home, they would shoot for a while and fish for speckled trout.

4. Dreamworld

"Mayday, mayday, mayday, Jack taking fire, going down, lots of Viet Cong."

Jack is in the front seat of a Cobra flying high cover, "I see you Dennis we're coming in hot"

"Shit they're everywhere, better hurry, Jack." The pilot in the back seat raises the nose of the Cobra, kicks in right pedal and the gunship dives straight down. Rockets and mini guns blazing toward hundreds of VC charging toward Dennis's downed helicopter. They pull up and execute a return to target expending their remaining rockets. The pilot in the back seat is hit. Blood splatter partially obscures Jack's visibility. He gains control of the Cobra from the front seat, coming to a hover over Dennis. He initiates a pedal turn, firing 40 mm grenades in a 360° protective ring around the downed ship. The cockpit fills with smoke and everything turns white.

When Jack woke up, he thought he saw a rotor blade overhead. Slowly, it became a ceiling fan. Everything around him was white and hazy. He wondered how long he'd been asleep and how many times he had that dream. At least he was in a hospital and alive. People came and went in the room, talking about him to each other. He felt like he was in a room down a long maze of corridors, a catacomb of confusion. How long was he out?

He wasn't sleeping, but he was somewhere in his mind when he heard the sweetest voice God ever made—Katie. When he opened his eyes, he saw her sitting on the edge of the bed, crying. Dad was there, too.

He could barely speak, but he managed to say, "I love you."

The two people he loved most in the world held his hands.

He learned they were in the naval hospital in Pensacola, Florida. When they left St. George's Island, they were in a terrible wreck in Cope's Blazer. He had a couple of cracked ribs and a minor concussion, while Jack's injuries were worse. He was unconscious for a week. He had a new steel plate in his head, and he was unfit for duty, which meant he would soon be discharged from the Army.

Dennis made it through the wreck without a scratch. He came in to see Jack before he shipped out while Jack was still in a coma. Jack thought it funny how life went. Katie and Cope spent every day for a week with him.

He finally began to remember. They were driving down a rural highway on their way to Fort Rucker when a pickup truck full of farm workers slid through a stop sign. Dad saved all three of them by avoiding being hit broadside. Unfortunately, he had to drive into the ditch to do it.

They rolled over twice and ended up back on the wheels. Cope was able to get to a phone, and a Medivac helicopter took them to Pensacola Naval Air Station.

Jack learned he would be out of the Army within sixty to ninety days. Cope and Katie had to return home to the Trinity Alps, where Jack would join them instead of deploying to Southeast Asia.

Believing it was his destiny to be a warrior, he wondered what he'd do with his life. Mail that had been initially delivered to Fort Rucker was rerouted to his hospital room.

Hello, Brother,

Sorry I haven't been in contact. I miss you and thought about you a lot. Wish you could be with me, but I know you're doing what you have to do.

I suppose I should explain what happened. I had a bad year statistically, and the coaches were under a lot of pressure to win more games. My scholarship depended on being a starter and maintaining my grade-point average. My shoulder was slow to heal from an injury, so they recruited a big, strong quarterback named Kevin something from Sacramento.

I didn't want to sit on the bench, and I knew my scholarship would end, so I took off. I wasn't coming home to wait for the draft.

I was hitchhiking across 299 when I got a ride going to Denny to score some weed. I ended up camping there, but unfortunately, some assholes beat me up pretty bad at gunpoint. I never had a chance to fight back. They took my watch, my pack, and all my gear. They were real mean bastards. I could've taken them if it weren't for the gun.

They were real slick. They sat around the fire with everyone, as people talked about the war. They waited till

I went off to sleep, then they jumped me. Oh, well. What comes around goes around. They'll get theirs someday. I'll always remember their faces.

After recuperating for a few days, I left Denny and hooked up with the rafting company at Burnt Ranch.

I guided a bit on the lower Trinity, then got an offer to go down to Columbia and guide on the Stanislaus River. It's really great down here. All the river rafters live together and run around naked—girls, too. There are always trips to make money, and the river is kick-ass beautiful. There's plenty of fish to catch, and there's probably gold to be found, too. I haven't had time to look.

There are Indian petroglyphs on the canyon walls. The top nine miles are pretty wild, and the bottom nine are gentle. I could spend the rest of my life here. It's an awesome place.

There are people here who are really cool, idealistic, and feel the same way I do about Vietnam. The only thing that could screw this up is some idiotic plan to flood the river for a bigger reservoir. They want to destroy all this beauty for subsidized water. I hope enough people fall in love with the river to want to protect it for the future.

When the season ends, I'm heading to the Florida Keys. I've been invited to go with another guide to treasure hunt and make money catching lobsters. What a trip, eh? I'll try to keep in touch, but I don't know where to write you, so I'll send letters to Kate for now.

I hope Dad doesn't hate me. I figured I'd be disowned for leaving college and all. I just had to go, though. I can't explain it any better than that.

Tell Dad I love him and sorry I quit. I'm being safe, having a blast. Watch your ass and don't get shot. We'll have some fun again when you're done. I always think about us as kids and the wonderful afternoons on the river with Mom and Dad. Damn, I miss you all. Is Bear doing OK? I miss him, too.

As always, your brother,

Elliott

Dear Jack,

I came over to water the garden today and hang out in your room. Bear wanted to go to the river, so we didn't stay long. He barks when I ask, "Where's Jack?"

The tomatoes are starting to come in, and so are the green peppers. The beans are hard to keep up with. Wish you were here to help. Janet's coming over tomorrow. We're going to blanch and freeze beans for your dad. She can take tomatoes, peppers, and squash home. The garden's great this year with all the rain. I hope you call soon.

My dad says there's trouble downriver. A bunch of people are camping at Denny, calling it a miner's claim and supposedly growing pot. Who knows what else? I went to the river and walked to your dad's dredge. Bear went crazy, sniffing around. I wasn't sure, but it looked like people were hanging out on the claim. It's probably just rafters or canoers pulling out to rest.

Oh, yeah. I saw a doe with two fawns in the orchard when I came up from the creek. They were so cute. Bear didn't even bark. He just looked at them and then at me, with a real intense stare as if asking, "Are you going to let them do that?" He's so handsome and smart. I'll write more later.

Monday

Well, I'm back. I hope you didn't get sunburned with your dad. Janet and I took Bear to the lost coast for a weekend of beachcombing and camping. I had you with me every single step. It was gorgeous—hot sun and waves crashing. Bear was body surfing and chasing seagulls down the beach.

We camped on the beach and had a big fire. Bear ate five hot dogs and would've eaten more if I let him. He was so hot, steam rolled off his wet fur. I could barely touch him.

I saw lots of beautiful falling stars and made the same wish each time. Unfortunately, when I woke up, you weren't with me.

Do you remember the day in the meadow, lying in the wildflowers, making pictures in the clouds and holding hands? We talked about us living to be 150 years old, because we had so much to do together. Then we would die together, so we wouldn't have to be without each other's love. I think I was fourteen. We promised that if one of us died, the other would live for both and celebrate every moment.

I'm trying to live in the joy of now, but it's hard with you gone. Write to me soon. I hope you had a blast with your dad.

Love you always,
Katie

After reading the two letters, Jack knew what he wanted to do with his life. He would marry Katie, build a home, and raise a family. He'd work the family gold claim for money. Dad still was certain there was a fortune under the boulders of the Trinity River, and Jack believed him. He would get Elliott to help.

The real problem with getting gold was its weight. It liked to hide in the lowest places it could find, as if the earth's center was its destination. Each day, the gold sought the lowest spot. Jack's job would be to move what was on top of it aside and get the gold.

He started designing, filling pages with drawings of large boulders, cables, and winches. The letter from Kate made him worry a bit about his dad being alone on the claim, but the fact that Bear was with him brought some comfort.

The day Jack was released from the hospital, his flight commander flew a Huey down to Pensacola to pick him up. He let Jack take the copilot's seat. Jack suspected that was the last time he would ever take the controls of a U.S. Army helicopter.

Jack was elated while flying, but, back in the barracks alone, the thought saddened him. He enjoyed flying. He had to wait for his separation orders to arrive.

He spent days exercising, planning, and doing research. Most nights, he was assigned as the duty officer at Battalion Headquarters. Jack kept his uniform pressed, shoes polished, and hair neat. He was proud of his wings and uniform. In some ways, he envied the new warrant officer candidates, though he sometimes wondered how many would survive. Maybe Elliott was right. Maybe there wasn't anything in Vietnam worth dying for.

Jack couldn't afford to let himself think like that. Duty was duty, and he was a Copeland.

5. Trouble Downriver

The men who called themselves Johnson and Spider weren't veterans. Neither served time in the military, but they'd been guests of the state's penitentiary system. Spider grew up on the hard streets of Los Angeles. His father was an over-the-road trucker who came home periodically strung out on speed and addicted to downers to sleep. Spider went on the streets during those visits to avoid his father's beatings. His mother wasn't so lucky. Spider stole to survive and soon found an outlet for his anger in the drunken bums who slept on the street. Johnson, his partner, hadn't fared much better.

The second of five sons, Johnson was raised on the Olympic Peninsula by his father. The boys' mother left when he was eleven to work the Alaskan pipeline boom. Dad and his brothers lived in a frame tent when Dad wasn't logging. He spent most of his time in the bars, trying to cure a broken heart. The boys did the same, washing dishes, mopping floors, and doing whatever they could to survive.

Johnson and his older brother did five years for killing a drunk Indian in a robbery attempt in a bar parking lot. Johnson and Spider met in the drunk tank in Portland, Oregon. It was the perfect partnership—two angry miscreants with no moral compass.

They decided to make the mountains of northern California their destination and left a trail of petty larcenies and burglaries behind. Campers were their favorite targets.

Sneaking in at night when the campers were asleep, they took food, gear, booze, and even a Smith and Wesson .38 from under the seat of a pickup truck. At first look, they appeared to be veterans wearing fatigue jackets and jungle boots, but a closer examination showed both men were creepy. The jailhouse tattoo of a black widow on Spider's neck and a bleeding heart mom on Johnson's arm, combined with their shifty eyes, made people nervous.

Rabbit was suspicious about their story of buying Elliott's watch. The attack on Elliott was an escalation of violence in the partnership that began in Portland. The idea of a big score brought on the attack. Once they started, they found they enjoyed inflicting pain. When they heard Gary talking about the Copelands' gold-mining operation, they had a destination.

They planned to rob the old man and buy an RV, like all the rich people in the campgrounds they hated and stole from. Elliott gave them the final piece of information they needed. Armed with the .38 pistol and fresh provisions from Big Bar, they left for Junction City. Accessing the river from the campgrounds at Big Bar, they went upstream on foot to find the dredging operation. Moving upriver slowly, they enjoyed the swirling pools and turgid rapids. It was fun for them.

"Spider, what will we do with the gold? Will it be heavy?"

Yeah, but not too heavy. We'll take only what we can carry

and bury the rest. We'll go to Reno to cash in and stay in one of those fancy hotels."

"Yeah. We'll be high rollers and buy some pretty whores, three at a time, snort cocaine, and party like rock stars. I want a round bed with mirrors on the ceiling. I'll dress like Mick Jagger, eat lobster, and drink Jack Daniels."

"Shut up. I fucking hear something."

They grabbed their gear and went behind a rock, as a motor boat approached.

Randy Running Rabbit, as his parents named him, or Rabbit to his friends, was a legend among the locals. A barrel-chested Scots-Indian mix, he was both fierce and gentle. He loved rabbits and kept them fed, letting them run wild on his property. His lucky charm, they served him well.

A trained scout pilot, Rabbit survived being shot down three times in the Vietnam jungles in an OH-6 helicopter. Randy felt he was being watched as he navigated upstream. It was an instinct that made the hair on the back of his neck stand up.

He noticed footprints on a sandbar just above a big flat. There were two sets and an old campfire on the sand bar. It wasn't unusual for people to camp on the bar, but footprints that disappeared into the Manzanita bush a quarter mile downriver from his claim worried him. There was no good reason for anyone to leave the easy going on the riverbank and enter the tangled Manzanitas unless they were hiding.

Spider and Johnson watched from cover, as Randy stood in the center of his aluminum John boat, steering with an extended tiller made from PVC pipe clamped to the throttle. He was so close, they saw his scars from bullet wounds. He wore a .44 Magnum Smith and Wesson revolver in a holster on his hip.

"Spider," Johnson whispered, "that's the dude in the hotrod FJ-40 who gave us a ride to Big Bar."

"I know. He bought the watch for fifty bucks, but he's not our guy. Our mark is an old man, not that crazy son of a bitch."

"Man, he's crazy to go through the rocks that fast. That's a big damn pistol, too. He's nobody to fuck with."

"Yeah. We should stay clear of that one."

After the sound of the motor was long gone, they crept out of the bushes and continued upstream. Soon, they heard what they thought was a chainsaw, but it wasn't. They saw a big pontoon boat cabled to the shore high above the riverbank. A big engine sat on the rear of the deck with thick hoses going in and out and what looked like a sliding board at the rear. Smaller hoses, a weight belt, a wet suit, a snorkel, and a mask lay on the deck. The big guy was on the banks, running something that looked like a chainsaw with a cable attached.

Randy wasn't just courageous. He was ingenious, too. He engineered a mobile winch from a chainsaw and a hydraulic pump. He was in the process of winching Volkswagen-sized boulders from their resting place, certain gold lay underneath them.

Once the rocks were moved, he would suck what lay under them with a four-inch hose, the water going across the baffles of his sluice box. Though he worked with a sense of purpose, something bothered him.

He felt there was something malevolent about those footprints on the shoreline. Maybe it was his Pictish ancestors warning him, or maybe it was his Indian blood. Maybe it came from his combat tours, but Rabbit knew danger was close. He might have caught the glint of metal or glass earlier, and he definitely got a whiff of cigarette smoke, but he didn't let on. If someone was watching, he wanted to keep the element of surprise, not let the bushwhackers know he was on to them.

Johnson and Spider climbed high on the ridge to get around Rabbit's claim on the south side of the river. They heard Rabbit shut down his dredge. The only sound was an occasional car on 299 to help mask the bandits' passage.

When they crossed a section of loose shale, a small part of the hillside cascaded down. Rabbit grabbed his AR-15 and sent thirty rounds of forty-grain .223 bullets across the hill-side. There was no reason for anyone to be up there. He fired in a Z-shaped pattern across the top of the ridge, down to the left, and across to the right.

Spider and Johnson were caught by surprise. Johnson wet his pants when a bullet impacted one foot from his head. Spider laughed silently. Like when he robbed and beat hobos in LA, the thrill of danger pleased him.

The two remained silent for what felt like forever until Randy started his dredge again. He wasn't sure if anyone was up there, but he knew he sent a decisive message. He set his .44 Magnum pistol on a nearby rock, hidden by bushes near the water's edge.

Putting on his wet suit, snorkel, and regulator, he disappeared into the water. He reemerged at the water's edge where he left the pistol to investigate. It didn't take long to find the trail of the two men wearing jungle boots. They were gone, trying to escape the crazy man who shot at them.

Randy went back to work underwater, making a mental note to talk to fellow miners about the incident. Thinking about Cope's dredge, he wondered if he was back from Alabama.

Cope shoved a small pack containing his clothes and ditty bag into the plane's overhead compartment. He logged a lot of flight time in a B-17, and he loved flying. Combat, however, added a dimension of danger to it that he could have lived without.

Relaxing in his seat, he ordered a Jack on the rocks and closed his eyes. What a roller coaster of emotions he'd been through. First was flight school graduation, the vacation, the accident, the coma, and recovery. He was finally headed home. He thanked God he had Katie and friends to watch over Bear, his ranch, and to tend the garden.

He thought how airplanes had turned to jets in such a short time. Takeoff always had the greatest element of intensity for him. The best chance for a mechanical problem and an unplanned return to ground with a full tank of fuel happened at takeoff. There was exhilaration in it, too, which he never tired of.

The plane soon leveled off at 20,000 feet, and he drifted to sleep to the engines constant drone. He thought of his childhood on Chesapeake Bay in the Virginia Tidewaters. As a child, he watched seagulls, osprey, and eagles and wished he could be one of them. He wanted to fly above the seas, to soar and dive without effort, fall out of the sun headlong into the water to snatch an unsuspecting fish. He relived memories of crabbing and collecting oysters and clams. They always had Labrador retrievers around. They were an intrinsic part of Tidewater life, in the boats, onshore, and beside the bed. He suspected he spent more time with his dogs than any other human.

Sometimes, he spoke to Bear as if he were human, not talking so much as communicating, the way two people did who worked together without saying a word, bonded in a sense of purpose and understanding. Cope was thankful for Bear, the last genetic connection to the family of dogs he grew up with. He hoped Bear would sire puppies for his sons to choose from. He considered Clara as a possible mate. She was a fine-looking dog.

His last conscious thought was the memory of walking on the beach with his dad and his dog.

Cope had a vivid dream about his grandpa, dad, and two uncles hunkered down in a duck blind. The morning was totally obscured. It was a winter storm on Chesapeake Bay, wet snow turning to freezing rain.

The air was rich and pungent with wood smoke, wet dogs, tobacco, and whiskey. Fog and low clouds hid even their decoys. There was still no visibility, long after sunrise. Ducks and geese were heard but not seen.

Something troubled the water, and his wife's face appeared on the surface. She had something in her arms. When he looked closer, he saw Elliott and Jack. As she rose from the water, she pulled them up.

"You'd better keep a better eye on my boys."

Startled, he woke and realized where he was. A woman in the seat across the aisle stared, and he realized his heart was pounding.

"That must've been a powerful dream," she commented.

Cope nodded while folding down his tray for the upcoming meal. The vision of the two boys haunted him as he ate. He knew the dream was a message, a connection his family always had with the unseen. In his childhood, the family called it "the sight," when future events were revealed in a dream. Dreams were often as important at breakfast as the day's plans. In the predawn glow of the fire, Grandma and Cope discussed their dreams, hoping to interpret their meaning. He didn't care whether this dream was created by his own mind or was planted by a spirit. He couldn't ignore his feelings.

His boys were in danger. Other than the dream, his flight was unremarkable.

Katie was waiting for him at the airport when he arrived. Cope saw Bear sitting on the front porch as they ascended the gravel drive. He perched at the top of the eight-foot-wide staircase like a sphinx guarding the deck that went around the front of the place. The sixty-foot porch was made of long, old-growth Redwood posts and beams, covered with a metal roof. Two six-foot porch swings complemented rocking chairs, a ten-foot picnic table, and benches. It was the focal point of family life for most of the year. The porch commanded a captivating view of the surrounding terrain and approaches to the ranch. Cope enjoyed rocking there with his evening cigar and whiskey.

He purposely oriented the house for the inspiring view,

referring to it as "the grandeur of God's creation." He enjoyed watching the deer that frequently appeared at sunset. His deep love of nature came from his grandmother when he was a small child. She held a Zen-like philosophy that included creationism and moral integrity.

Giant redwoods were one of his favorites. He salvaged old-growth redwood from abandoned mining operations and homesteads to build his house. It was laborious and sometimes dangerous, but he loved being surrounded by ancient trees and detested the idea of letting their wood go to waste.

Bear came to his feet, barking frantically when Cope got out of Katie's car. Two bounds, and he leaped from the porch, touching his nose to Cope's and licking his forehead. He overlooked this minor infraction of etiquette and grabbed the big dog under the forelegs and around the chest.

Katie laughed in delight, as Bear shagged around Cope, leaping into the air to do 360-degree turns called "whoop-de-dos." The two alpha males gave a rare display of total adoration. The more she laughed, the more Bear performed.

When Cope ascended the five steps to the porch, he found Randy's note and read it. The celebratory mood was dampened by the sudden furrow of Cope's brow and the fierce look in his eyes. It scared Kate. She didn't want to see it again.

"Come inside, Kate. I need all the information you can give me about Elliott. This note from Rabbit tells me he might be in real trouble. Some drifters Rabbit picked up sold Elliott's watch to him for fifty dollars. Something's very wrong."

"I agree. He loved that watch way too much to ever part with it. I can't imagine anything short of fearing for his life would make him give it up."

"If Elliott's been in touch with anyone, it's Janet. Let's go visit her after I call Rabbit."

He dialed and waited. "Hello, Rabbit? I just got back and found your note. I hope you didn't say anything to anyone about this. The fewer who know, the better. Gear up and meet me here. I want to talk with Janet and see if she's heard from Elliott."

"Roger that, Cope. Say 1800 hours?"

"Sounds about right. Make yourself at home if I'm not back yet."

Katie quickly called Janet, who was waiting for them when they arrived. She worked at a new pizza shop that shared the name of the riverside village just downriver from Junction City, called Big Flat Pizza. Janet, in tears, handed Cope a Dear-Jane letter she received from Elliott, then she and Katie walked away to talk alone.

Dear Janet,

There's no doubt I will always love you. I had to make some decisions that will take me away for a while. I had to quit school at Humboldt State. I can't go home to face my dad. He expects too much. I have to follow my heart. I'm going to be a river guide down near Angels Camp.

I had a bit of bad luck and was bushwhacked by some mean assholes and ripped off for everything I own. They got my pack, watch, binoculars, compass, and fishing tackle. They even took my clothes.

I planned to come see you, but my ride south made that impossible. It's probably better this way. I'm so sorry to tell you this, but I was unfaithful. I didn't mean for it to happen, not at school, but after I was robbed and beat up, I got high with some girls, and it just happened. It didn't mean anything from my heart, but it breaks my promise to you, something I never wanted to do. Please forgive me if you can.

You have your senior year to come and your whole life ahead of you. Please forgive me. I'll love you forever.

Elliott

PS. My address is me in care of Stanislaus River Adventures, PO Box 311, Angels Camp, California.

Cope finished the letter and approached the girls, who sat at a picnic table outside the restaurant.

"Janet, I'm sorry for the way my son behaved. He can't be in his proper mind right now. He's making bad decisions at every turn, and no good comes from poor judgment. Thank you for sharing this very private letter with me. Please call me if there's anything I can do, Sweetheart.

"If you hear from Elliott again, call me. Do me a favor, girls, and keep this business about Elliott private, including the part about being robbed. No one needs to know family business or get involved in private matters, especially if these varmints are still around. We don't want them to know we're looking for them. I don't want taxpayers to feed them in jail or pay them to be represented in court. There are better ways of taking care of people like them."

"You have my word, Mr. Copeland." Janet hugged him, and he was as rigid as an oak tree, barely able to pat her shoulders.

Every muscle in his body was hard as a rock. He was like a ticking bomb—controlled, poised, and rational, but a predator on a mission.

Spider and Johnson weren't totally lost, although they didn't know where they were. The panic created when thirty rounds impacted near them sent them on a reckless trek into the wilderness. It could have meant their demise, but they were lucky and found a trail. They figured it had to end somewhere.

They drank water from creeks and ate some of the dry rations from Elliott's pack. When they ate the jar of venison, they didn't know what it was, but it tasted delicious. They laughed, remembering how much fun it was to kick the kid and see the look on his face. They relished his expression when they would pull back the hammer on their gun, spin the cylinder, and talk about blowing holes in his head.

That made them laugh even harder. Cowards find great pleasure in hurting others, probably because they've been hurt, too, and know what it's like to feel vulnerable.

Cope found Rabbit waiting on his porch when he got home. Rabbit told him what he knew and described the two men, including their gear, boots, the tracks in the sand, rocks falling, a glint of something on the hillside, firing shots, and the trail he cut up the hill from his dredge.

"What do you want to do?" Rabbit asked when he finished.

"I intend to catch those bastards and recover my son's things. If need be, I'll send both of them to hell. I could tie them to a tree and whip the hide off their backs, then add some pine tar to the wounds before I walk away. They're no good."

The two men prepared to leave. Bear watched with growing intensity as Cope pulled on his boots. Rifle and pack in hand, they loaded up in the FJ-40. Bear knew they were going hunting, but he didn't know it was human prey.

They parked at Big Bar and started upstream on foot. The rain had washed away any footprints, and they found only a couple of dirty campsites with empty cans of smoked oysters, Elliott's favorite trail food, that must have come from the stolen pack.

They hoped to find new signs above Rabbit's claim toward the Copeland claim, but there was nothing. They searched the riverbank until dark, then returned to the ranch where they sat on the front porch to eat. Cope poured whiskey for conversation and planning.

"Maybe we should go upriver tomorrow," he said. "If these two come out to the water like any rational person, we should be able to find them."

"Maybe we should go back to my claim first, to their last known whereabouts."

"That's probably a good idea. We can see if Bear's nose is any good on a cold trail. That's a better plan, in case they doubled back and went downriver. That may be why Indians make the best scouts."

The following morning, Cope let Bear out the front door just as Rabbit's tires cut the gravel up the driveway. Cope saw the distinctive close headlights long before he heard the dual exhaust of the 327 Chevy engine with headers. He had bacon and egg sandwiches and two thermoses of coffee prepared.

The ride to Rabbit's claim was quick. They sat on the dredge, waiting for more light. Bear marked the perimeter, and then watched in silence.

Finally, the men hoisted their packs and reached for their rifles. Bear became all business. He walked at Cope's side unless signaled to go ahead. Cope was good at reading Bear's movements. If the dog stopped, so did Cope, and vice versa. They moved as one, utilizing the dog's excellent nose and hearing with the man's vision and logic.

In less than an hour, they reached the loose shale that gave away the two men's location. Cope found a Manzanita split by a bullet from the AR-15. Bear sniffed around without finding a clear trail. Rabbit found a pair of soiled underwear and a pair of Levi's 501 jeans.

"You must've scared the piss out of that one," he commented. "Looks like he had to change clothes."

Cope rolled up the jeans and tied quarter-inch parachute line around them, then tossed them and let Bear retrieve them. The dog quickly understood and took point as they climbed uphill.

At the top of the ridge, the trail headed south. Like sheep and lost children, the two men they were after followed the easiest terrain, trying to put as much distance between themselves and the bullets as fast as they could.

They followed the trail for four hours. The sun overhead, combined with climbing the steep terrain, warmed the hunters. They hadn't planned for an overnight hunt and wondered if they were walking into an ambush. Cope always liked having an edge, like the element of surprise or overwhelming firepower. Climbing up and down hillsides while being exposed to observation and sniper fire didn't appeal to either of them.

"What do you think they're doing?" Cope asked.

"They're moving, but where? They definitely aren't going back to the river. They must be running from the law, staying away from the road and civilization. There are plenty of freaks and fugitives on the lam in the national forest. Hell, you could walk from Old Mexico to Canada and never see anyone if you didn't want to."

"I hope they don't hurt anyone else. Mark my words, they aren't here for the mountaintop experience. Unless God Himself reveals a burning bush or something, there will be other victims. Men like those two are dangerous to decent folks."

"All right, Cope. Let's cut back to the river, cool off, and head back to the claim."

"Sounds good. Bear, back to the truck."

The dog, understanding the command, soon swam in the Trinity River and drank from it. Cope and Rabbit sat near the water to talk.

"Randy, you met them," Cope said. "Why in the world would they head across such rugged terrain?"

"They definitely didn't strike me as the wilderness type. I don't think they have a destination. Maybe they're just scared and moving. If they had a map and sense of direction, the only place they could be going is Hayfork or Hyampom. In either place, they'll sure stand out. I might drive over Ray's Peak to Hyampom on Saturday and talk to some people I know, find out if anyone's seen any strangers. There are plenty of logging trails they could've taken, too."

Spider and Johnson heard heavy equipment in the distance. Soon, they were close enough to see the skidder pulling logs to the landing. They heard the faller's chainsaw and the sound of crashing trees.

An old man was loading the trucks at the landing. Unseen, the two men snuck around to where the crew parked their personal vehicles. Johnson stood guard, while Spider went through the nearest truck.

He found a model 94 Winchester .30-.30 in the Easy Rider rack, a box of shells, and a bag of Red Man chewing tobacco in the glove box. Under the seat, he found a fifth of Ten High whiskey. The back seat in the crew cab had a cooler full of cold cuts, soda, and beer.

Suddenly, all sounds ceased. Johnson ran up.

"Something's going on! I think they're quitting. Let's get out of here."

They stuffed the food and drinks into their packs. Spider shouldered his pack and raised the rifle in triumph. He didn't fear anything now. That rifle was his equalizer.

They headed back to the ridge overlooking the log landing and trucks. Spider wanted to watch what happened when the driver returned to his truck. The man's anger would be pleasant.

Every day when the fallers came back to their trucks, they talked about the day over beer. Luke, the crew boss, known as the Bull of the Woods, gave assignments for the following day.

They used an old Willys Jeep to bring the fallers back to

the trucks at the landing. Luke went to get a beer from his cooler but found only a couple left at the bottom. He knew he put in an entire case that morning.

When he reached under the seat for his whiskey and found it missing, his blood almost boiled. He calmed himself in case it was one of the men playing pranks and turned to them. They gathered around his truck as usual.

"What the hell, Boys? I don't mind sharing my beer. I love y'all, but I'd like a taste of my whiskey now. Let's give it up before I get angry."

Looking at each other in confusion, no one had a clue what he was talking about. They knew about Luke's temper, and no man willingly crossed him. Twenty years of climbing steep hills with a chainsaw and falling trees had made him a tough man.

The newest man in the crew made the wrong comment. "You probably drank it last night and don't remember."

Luke's fist struck like a cobra, hitting the man so fast the others only saw the effect, as the young man went up and over, knocked out cold.

"Anyone else got any smartass comments?" Luke asked.

"Luke, we're all drinking Bush. You drink Hams beer. None of us took your whiskey or beer. I was first back. Weren't nobody messing with your stuff. Ain't nobody on this crew that crazy."

Luke quickly checked the cab and found his food, chewing tobacco, beer, and whiskey gone. "Goddamn it! My rifle's gone!" He was furious. "Some motherfucker will get the life beat out of him if my shit ain't back in one minute!"

He cursed all the men individually and searched their trucks, including the loader. Maybe one of the log truck drivers had taken his stuff. He planned to visit the mill and get the names of the drivers for the day. He'd visit each one at home that night unless he caught them all at the bar in Hyampom.

Luke's cousin, who rode and worked with him for fifteen years, knew it would be one of those nights people would talk about for years.

Luke spoke with the dispatcher, who knew all the drivers, but they were longtime residents and family men. Luke couldn't imagine any of them stealing, especially from him. That rifle belonged to his father. Everyone in town knew Luke and his dad. Joe, Luke's cousin, went to the bar with him, where they sat to drink beer and shots. Scrappy, an old man with a limp who ran the loader, came in and pulled up a chair at their table to talk.

"Luke, I want to talk, but no matter what I say, you got to remember I'm an old man. You can't go using my bones like you did with that kid at the landing, OK?"

Luke nodded.

"I don't think anyone we know stole your rifle and stuff. There was never any vehicles over there. I loaded the rigs, and they chained their loads and left right from the landing. You know damn good and well, none of your men stole from you.

"I believe we got a human coyote sneaking around in the woods. Maybe it's a tree hugger or a dope head cull from San Francisco. I had a feeling I was being watched today. Call me crazy, but I think we got a thief in our woods."

"You know something, Scrappy? That makes more sense

than it being one of our own. Shit. I should've seen it. I wish that boy hadn't opened his mouth."

"He's comin' in the bar right now, but by his expression, I think he wants more than an apology."

"You son of a bitch!" the younger man said, walking in. "Don't no one get away sucker-punching me like that. You stand up and fight me like a man."

Luke stood and faced him. The young man swung a haymaker that Luke caught with his left hand, engulfing his fist. He picked the man up by the neck with his right hand and lifted him off the ground.

"Boy, I'm sorry I hit you like that, but don't you ever sass me again, understand?"

The boy nodded as best he could, as Luke set him on his feet.

"Let me buy you a drink, Kid. You got salt. I'll give you that. I'm real sorry I hit you. You just got to learn to keep your mouth shut."

Young John's actions earned the respect of everyone in the bar and the whole logging community. No one ever called Luke out. He stood six-feet-five and weighed 250 pounds. He used to be called One Punch Luke in his wild days. Luke hired John, because he liked the kid, and now he felt respect for him, too.

The kid was only five-feet-eight and maybe 170 pounds, but he had enough pride to stand up for himself. His self-respect overcame his fear of an ass-whipping. A lot of people ran their mouths, but when it came down to it, they didn't have the stomach for a fight.

Luke circled his hand in the air to get the bartender's attention.

"Tomorrow's Saturday," Scrappy said. "I say we go coyote huntin'."

"Good idea, Scrappy," Luke said. "I'll meet you tomorrow at four-thirty. We'll take the Willys. Hopefully, we won't get shot by my own rifle. That would be hell, wouldn't it? I've worked these woods for twenty years, and I never had anything taken from my truck. It's the damndest thing."

"You think if we find 'em, they'll just hand that rifle over?"

"More likely we'll pry it from the lifeless hands of some son of a bitch who died of lead poisoning from my .30-.06."

Laughing, they raised their glasses in a toast.

Spider almost had a coronary when Luke punched John and started screaming and cursing the rest of the men. He had to bite his hand to avoid giving away their position. He rolled, laughing silently until tears streaked his face.

When the trucks drove off in a cloud of dust, Spider and Johnson drank their first cold beer since Big Bar. Spider kept repeating the story of Luke's knockout and rage. He loved it. The more whiskey he drank, the more he wanted to be like Luke or his abusive father, able to hurt people and make them feel his pain.

He ranted about the gold and the old man, too. Johnson just wanted to make Rabbit pay for making him piss his pants. Spider laughed about that, too. They two acted like a pair of mad dogs, drinking whiskey and hopping around their campfire like Indians in a Hollywood movie, chanting and doing a war dance. When the two finally collapsed beside the fire, they slept deeply.

At six o'clock Saturday morning, Rabbit put his overnight bag and cooler in the back seat of his FJ-40. His AR-15 sat between the passenger seat and the console. A couple extra clips went into the console box. He gave the vehicle a quick inspection before putting on his .44 Magnum in a shoulder holster.

He thought about the girl in Hyampom. Sarah could've been the one for him if there could be just one girl. However, one of anything wasn't his favorite. If one was good, more was better. He remembered her long, golden hair, her scent, and the way she smiled at him the last time they made love on a sandbar. Despite thoughts of her firm breasts and long, tan legs, Rabbit was on a mission.

When he turned off Highway 299 toward Ray's Peak, he remembered the primary reason he was heading through the mountains to Hyampom.

Johnson was the first to wake up when Luke and Scrappy arrived in the big red pickup. He shook Spider gently, who slept with the .30-.30 cradled on his chest.

"Shit, oh shit!" he whispered. "We got trouble."

They watched from their hidden vantage point as Scrappy and Luke loaded up in the Willy's Jeep with their rifles and drove off.

"Let's go see what they brought us today," Spider said.

"Not me. I'll watch. You can go down there if you want." Spider came back with doughnuts, peanuts, and a bag of venison jerky.

The two men planned to go back to Junction City, steal

Copeland's gold, and head for Reno. The maps and compass in Jack's backpack were invaluable. Johnson learned land navigation when he was sent to Outward Bound by a caseworker when he was a juvenile. Spider couldn't believe a pussy like Johnson had such a skill.

They'd been lucky for months, leaving a trail of victims everywhere they went. They left camp and headed north, back toward the river, while Randy Rabbit circled to the south.

Luke and Scrappy searched the logging roads and skid trails. Rabbit saw a logging road and muddy tracks left by recent trucks, he was watching the shoulder for boot prints when he suddenly met Scrappy and Luke coming the other way down the switchback.

Rabbit drove the Land Cruiser into the bush to avoid a collision, while Scrappy bailed out of the Jeep, as it went over the side. It stopped when it struck a lone red cedar, just before it would have taken a 200-foot cascade into a ravine.

Rabbit got out and met Scrappy, who slowly stood.

"You all right?" Randy asked.

"Yeah, yeah. I've been limpin' like this for years. Hello, Luke. You all right?"

"Nothing hurt but my damn pride. I'm afraid to move, though. I'm in a bit of a tender situation. This little ol' tree seems a mite fragile."

"Luke, it's me, Rabbit!"

"Rabbit, you son of a bitch. If you get me out of here, I might not whip your ass too bad."

"That's awful mean talk from a man who's about to roll

down a ravine. Besides, you haven't given me much incentive to help you."

"Yeah, well, Rabbit, that's about the best I can do in this situation."

"Just sit tight. I'll get a chain and my winch cable. Scrappy and I will have you out of there in no time."

"Hell with that! Get me a rope and fuck this Jeep! Tie off a rope and pass it to me!"

Rabbit grabbed a 100-foot line he kept in his gear and tossed the end to Luke. Luke tied it off and jumped free of the Jeep. Rabbit lowered a chain on his winch cable, while Luke attached it to the Willys Jeep. He climbed back up the hill hand-over-hand on the rope, with his Winchester bolt action .30-.06 over his shoulder.

"I already lost one rifle this week," Luke said. "I don't want to lose another."

The comment went unnoticed, as Rabbit focused on pulling the Jeep up the ravine. When that mission was accomplished, Luke and his old friend, Rabbit, shook hands and gave each other bear hugs.

"What in the Sam hell are you doing in my woods?" Luke asked.

Rabbit told the two men his story, then Luke told his. They returned to the log landing to see if they could identify the thieves by the boot prints. Scrappy found something almost immediately.

"Looky here," he called. "Someone's done been in your truck today, Luke, while we were huntin''em. Can you imagine that?"

Rabbit grabbed his AR-15, and the three men followed Spider's trail to the site of their abandoned camp.

"Son of a bitch," Luke muttered. "There's my empty whiskey bottle, some beer cans, and even some Beanie Weanies. I see there's two of these guys."

Rabbit confirmed the tracks were the same men he was hunting. They also found empty .38 and .30-.30 casings from the two men's drunken target practice.

The trail went south, back toward Junction City. Rabbit wished he could tell Cope about it.

The other thing Cope didn't know was that Katie received a call from Jack on Friday; he finally received his terminal leave. He wanted to surprise his dad by showing up Saturday unannounced.

6. Homecoming

Katie's mom let her make the five-hour trip in the Pinto to Sacramento to pick up Jack. She wore a blue-jean skirt made from a pair of Jack's 501s and a white peasant blouse open at the bottom and low-cut enough to expose the top of her shapely breasts. Jack requested the outfit, saying he always dreamed of her that way, asleep or awake.

Arriving on time, they embraced and kissed. Jack wore his dress greens for the last time, as they waited at baggage claim. Two punks with long hair and peace-sign T-shirts began making baby killer comments loud enough for Jack to hear. They made the mistake of following him into the rest room to continue the harassment.

"Hey, Baby Killer, you like shooting women and children?"

The boy grabbed Jack's shoulder from behind. Jack instinctively brought his left arm back and over the boy's arm in a classic overhook takedown, but there was no wrestling mat, so the boy's face connected with the urinal. His companion cringed when he saw his friend's teeth break, and blood filled the receptacle.

Jack grabbed the second boy in a sleeper hold and put the

two of them in one stall. One boy sat on the other's lap, both out cold. Jack washed blood off his hands and face, hoping no one outside heard the noise.

He and Katie left in a hurry, just as airport security was summoned to the scene. Jack didn't want to waste time in explanations. He wanted to spend it with Katie, who didn't know what happened and didn't care. After so many months and tears, they were finally alone.

Jack could barely control his passion. His blood pounded, and he felt dizzy, as Katie caressed him and kissed his neck. Jack exited I-5, driving the little car over grass-covered slopes to the west until they were atop a hill overlooking the interstate.

The blanket and lunch in the back were perfect. They made love on the blanket and green grass. The first time was quick and clumsy. The second was slower and more controlled. The third time, they climaxed together.

They ate lunch in the car, feeling whole, content, and happy to be in love. Jack wanted to marry her and wished he could propose at that moment, but he didn't have the ring.

The reality of being in Northern California hit home when he saw the snow-covered peak of Mount Shasta. They took Highway 299 west out of Redding. Jack pulled the Pinto over at the peak of Buckhorn Summit, where they had a glorious view of the Trinity Alps.

"This really is God's country, isn't it?" he asked.

They continued through Weaverville. The little Pinto struggled up Oregon Mountain, its barren hillsides the legacy of the monitors who washed away the earth. They pressure-washed every bit of topsoil down to the bedrock into sluice boxes for the gold. The soil ended up in the Trinity River that cascaded through the gorge below on its way to the Pacific Ocean.

They stopped again on the one-lane bridge leading to the Copeland ranch. Jack was very happy to be back.

When they turned up the long drive to the ranch, Jack saw his dad's K5 Blazer for the first time since the wreck. He bought it from the insurance company and had it shipped to California.

Cope sat on the porch with Bear, enjoying his rocker while drinking lemonade and smoking a cigar. When he saw Katie's car, he wondered who was with her.

He realized immediately when Jack got out. At least one of his sons was home safely. Bear's tail thumped the deck harder and harder, as Jack neared. He gave two bounds down from the deck and leaped into the air to touch the tip of his tongue to Jack's nose. Jack held the dog in a big hug. They had a fun time, the dog circling and shagging, even barking a few times, which was rare. Dad and son went from handshake to bear hug, in typical Copeland fashion.

"What's your Garand doing on the porch, Dad?" Jack asked, eyeing the gun.

"I had it out for varmint hunting."

"What kind of varmint would you shoot with a .30-.06?"

"It's a long story. I'll tell you later."

"Kate told me about the letter and the two drifters who beat and robbed Elliott. Have you found them yet?"

"Not yet. Rabbit went to Hyampom to see if they showed up there, but there's been no word."

The three sat on the porch talking until almost dark. Jack, worried about Elliott, wanted to catch the assailants. He held Elliott's watch in his hand, which Rabbit had returned.

"I'd like to get my hands on the sons of bitches who beat my brother," he said softly.

Katie, feeling his anger, squeezed his hand. Jack walked her to the car and kissed her good-bye, because she had to be home by dark. As Jack walked back to the porch, he kicked at rocks, wishing he could hold Katie all night long.

He sat in a rocking chair beside his dad and cradled Bear's head between his hands to rub the dog's forehead. Looking at Dad, he saw a glimmer in his eye.

"Dad, I want to marry Katie."

"You'd be a fool if you didn't. I believe she'd make a fine wife. That's why I want you to have this." He handed Jack the engagement ring he gave Caroline, Jack's mother, after World War Two.

"Really, Dad? Are you sure?"

"Your mom would have wanted Katie to wear it."

"Thank you, Dad. I hope she says yes, but I want her to finish school first. We won't marry until next summer."

"What about college? What if she wants to go and earns an academic scholarship?"

"I don't know what we'll do. Maybe I'd go to school, too. I have the GI Bill. I just know I want to be with her the rest of my life."

"I understand how you feel, Son. Are you hungry?"

"Oh, yeah. I almost forgot to tell you about a little trouble at the airport. A couple little pricks called me a baby killer. They followed me into the restroom, and one grabbed my shoulder, so I shoved his head into a urinal. That knocked him out and busted up his mouth pretty good. I put the other one in a sleeper and stuffed both of them into a stall. We left in a hurry. I didn't tell Katie about it."

"Hurry is a loaded word, Jack. What happened, exactly?"

"OK. I was pulling down my fly with my back to the door, facing the latrine, when I heard people come in behind me. One of the kids said something like, 'Hey, Bitch, I was talking to you.'

"I felt his hand on my left shoulder and overhooked his arm with my left and gave it hell. It must've caught him off balance. He had no idea and hit his face in the pisser beside mine. It knocked him out and also knocked out his front teeth and messed up his face a little, though it wasn't that bad. He was holding a drink from the fountain, so after I stuffed him and his buddy in a stall, I put the teeth on ice. Maybe they could be put back in like you once did for Elliott."

"Whoa! What did you do to the other kid?"

"I grabbed him out of preservation instinct and put him to sleep."

Cope rocked for a minute, thinking it over. "Jack, this may come home to Junction City. It won't be that hard for the airport authority to track you down through the flight manifest. Let's not borrow trouble, though. Those boys might feel lucky you didn't kill them."

"I didn't have time to think about getting in trouble. I reacted instinctively."

"That's the way it is with people like us, Jack. When action is required, there's no time to calculate. Hesitation can be the difference between life and death. When the boy grabbed you, if he intended to stab you, your reaction would've saved your life. Don't second guess yourself on things like that. Leaving, though, might be a problem, if anything comes of this."

They rocked in silence for a while, enjoying the cool evening.

"Have you got any idea what's going on in your brother's head?" Cope asked.

"Not really, Dad. I just know how he's always been. He has his own mind about things and likes to do things his own way. Take his play calling. If conventional wisdom was to run on third and three, he rolled right and passed left. Sometimes, he's brilliant. Sometimes, he's reckless."

"I know all about being an individual. I encouraged you boys to think for yourself and to stand up for what's right. Elliott's behaving erratically. I suspect he's caught up in the new drug, sex, and rock 'n' roll business."

"He's always been curious about everything. He questions everything and has his own opinion about the war, but his heart was always good. He's always been a good brother to me and a good son to you."

"I agree, but if he was in his right mind, he would've come home and told me what's going on. Haven't I always been there for you boys?"

"True, but you have to admit you can be a fierce critic of things you don't agree with."

"Fair enough. I'll own that. I'll have to pray Elliott has the wisdom to do what's right. Do you have plans for tomorrow? I'm going down to the claim at first light."

"Great. I've been longing to kayak down the river. I've been working on new ideas to move the boulders and can't wait to show you my ideas. Let's pack a lunch, and Katie and I will paddle down to meet you for a picnic."

"Will you propose to her tomorrow?"

"If it feels right, I will. Have to see how my courage is doing."

"We need to stay vigilant about security. Let's keep Bear in the house at night. You need to have a firearm handy at all times, and pay attention. These men are dangerous."

"Roger that, Dad."

7. The Bushwhacking

Sunday morning was the best of Jack's life. He cooked breakfast and packed a picnic lunch. Cope and Bear drove to the claim downriver. When Katie arrived, Jack flipped some eggs for her, too.

They went to Jack's room and sat on his bed. Then he pulled a box out of his nightstand, knelt down, and proposed.

Katie laughed at first, then she realized he was serious. "Yes, of course!"

He slipped his mother's ring onto her finger. When Katie looked at it, she cried.

"If I thought this would make you cry, I wouldn't have asked," Jack said.

"Shut up, you big brute."

They stayed in the house for an hour. The kayak trip was awesome, more beautiful than ever before or ever would be. Soon, they heard the dredge over the turbulent waters.

Jack was in front when he first saw the claim. He immediately turned his kayak into the bank and motioned Katie to do the same.

What he saw terrified him. Cope's hands were tied behind

his back. Bear lay unmoving on the gravel. One man held a rifle on Cope while another pistol-whipped him.

Jack eased into the water and vanished. It took only seconds, but it felt like eternity to Katie. Jack quickly surfaced at the boulder where the man with the rifle stood. He jerked his feet out from under him from behind. Spider never heard Johnson's face hit the boulder or saw him being pulled under, where Jack's six-inch knife went into his kidneys repeatedly from behind. Water turned red around them both. Jack came up for air, took a deep breath, and swam underwater to the dredge.

Spider never saw him coming. He was having too much fun to look around. Jack grabbed Spider's arm with the pistol and wrapped it around his neck with his left arm. Reaching to the front with his free hand, he inserted the blade under Spider's ribcage and sliced across his torso. Spider went limp, looking at his guts spilling out from the gaping hole where his stomach had been. A moment later, he collapsed.

Cope was still conscious but bleeding badly from multiple scalp wounds. Jack cut his hands free and rolled him onto his back, holding the bloody head in his hands. Cope was still in his wetsuit with weight belt on.

Katie, screaming, ran toward them.

"Get the back of the Willys open!" Jack shouted, lifting his dad in a fireman's carry to the utility wagon. Finding Bear still alive, he placed him beside Cope.

Cope slowly sat up to caress the dog's head. Katie attempted to stop the bleeding on Cope's head with gauze from the first-aid kit as Jack got behind the wheel and drove them toward the doctor's house.

The doctor had retreated to the mountains from Southern California. He was a qualified emergency-room surgeon who bartered his services to the local residents. He was just returning from his five-mile run when the Willys arrived.

Cool and calm, he took care of Cope's lacerations with twenty-three stitches to the scalp. He had a possible concussion and maybe cracked ribs.

Bear's prognosis was also good. Katie was holding Bear when he regained consciousness. Her heart melted when he looked into her eyes and licked her hand.

It turned out Cope had been underwater on his hookah when the bandits arrived. Bear was on the dredge's deck, watching from above. The .38 bullet meant to end Bear's life penetrated the skin on his forehead and glanced off the front slope of his skull, exiting behind his ears. His hard head saved his life.

Doc gave both patients a prescription for antibiotics.

"Doc, can I use your phone in private?" Cope asked.

"Sure."

Cope dialed and waited.

"Sheriff's office. Hi, Cope. How are you doing? Haven't seen you in town lately. No, the sheriff's in Douglas City."

"Can you reach him on the radio?"

"Hold on. I'll try. Base to Sheriff. Come in, Sheriff."

"Yeah, Debbie? I'm here."

"Sheriff, Cope's on the phone for you."

"What's that old polecat want?"

"Cope," Debbie said into the phone. "I got him on the radio."

"Ask him how soon he can meet me at the river claim. This is real serious."

She relayed the message.

"Tell them two hours, Debbie," the Sheriff said.

Rabbit arrived at the claim soon after the others left. The dredge was still running, so shutting it down was his first step. He tied a rope to Spider's body and winched him across the river and up on the shore, and then he fetched Johnson in the same manner.

After unfolding a tarp, he unceremoniously chucked the two lifeless bodies in the back of his Toyota. The .38 pistol went in the glove box and the .30-.30 went on the floorboard. With a five-gallon bucket, he rinsed the blood from the dredge, then he shoveled the bloody gravel from the bank into the river where he beached the bodies.

He stopped at his school bus to pick up some C-4 and blasting caps. He knew how to get rid of trash. Driving hard, he accelerated over the Oregon summit and turned onto Highway 3. He took a right onto Rush Creek Road and stopped at the Lewiston Hotel, an historic old building with a rich history dating to the 1800s. It functioned as a seasonal tourist bar with a buffalo in the yard.

Joe, the owner, bartender, and cook was already pouring drinks for himself and the few fishermen who gathered at the riverside watering hole.

"Hey, Rabbit," Joe said. "How you doing?" He handed him a shot of tequila and began preparing a margarita, listening to the fishermen talking trash about each other's skills the way they always did.

Another fisherman walked in.

"What can I get for you?" Joe asked.

"I'll have a draft, please. Say, you know who owns that Land Cruiser?"

"That would be me." Rabbit's heart rate increased a bit.

"Looks like you're leaking something red out of the back."

"Just a little hydraulic fluid. Joe, I'll take my drink to go. I'm late on my way to Redding."

He walked outside and scuffed dirt over the red stain before driving up the dusty trails to an abandoned mineshaft in French Gulch.

Two hours over rough dirt roads and a plume of dust, he locked in his four-wheel drive and crawled the last leg to the mine entrance.

He dragged Johnson and Spider to their last resting place, chucking them into a deep, dark hole before setting off an explosion that buried them under tons of rock. As he walked away, he wondered how Cope was.

Jack drove the Willys back to the ranch from Doc's place. Cope asked Katie to stay there with Bear and keep him calm.

"If the sheriff needs a statement from you," Cope said, "we'll come get you, but I'd prefer to keep you out of it."

The drive was made in silence. When they arrived at the claim, they were further rendered silent by what they didn't see when they got there.

"Are we dreaming?" Jack asked slowly. "Was this a nightmare, or is it a miracle?"

Cope walked around to look, shaking his head before walking back up the trail off 299 to the claim. "I think I know who's been here, but it's only conjecture. When the Sheriff arrives, all I can tell him is what I know for a fact."

The Sheriff arrived and listened quietly. He walked around a bit and spat tobacco juice occasionally. He didn't want to cross the river where the alleged killings took place. He went to his cruiser and got a bulletin he received about a series of thefts, including a firearm, by two vagrants. The description matched Spider and Johnson perfectly.

"OK, now," the Sheriff said. "Let's see here. Cope, you got a good knock to the head, right? Your boy here was just released from the Army with a knock to the head. When I got here, there's no witness, no bodies, no weapons, and no evidence of a crime. Matter of fact, you boys are wasting my precious time. Unless you've got something else, I suggest you get some rest. I'll see ya around."

He ambled back up the trail to his cruiser, crumpling the bulletin in his hands. As he drove off, he spat out the open window. He just saved the citizens of Trinity County a whole lot of money, not to mention a ton of paperwork for himself. As far as he was concerned, Jack did the citizens a great service. Why punish a good family with a bunch of reporters, lawyers, and trouble? It was as clear a case of self-defense as any he heard. Justice was served, and no crime was committed.

Rabbit drove down Lewiston Road to Highway 299 West toward Weaverville. He stopped at the car wash and washed the dust and blood off his Land Cruiser, working his way from top to bottom.

He was just cleaning the wheel wells when he saw the Sheriff's legs on the other side of the cruiser. The Sheriff respected Rabbit for his military service and knew all too well his propensity for impulsive, rash behavior.

"Rabbit, you been busy today? Debbie got a call from a tourist, a fisherman who said he saw a blue Toyota Jeep with what he thought was blood dripping out the back. That was the second strange call I had today.

"Your buddy, Cope, got a blow to the head and told a wild tale of claim jumpers and all sorts of nonsense. You been downriver today?"

"Sheriff, I've been a lot of places today."

"I see you have a couple rifles in the cab there. Expecting trouble?"

"You know that sometimes a fellow might see a varmint while out on a ride."

"If a person like yourself were to shoot a coyote or some other varmint critter, he probably would put it in his rig and dispose of it somewhere it wouldn't stink and be offensive."

"That's affirmative, Sheriff, someplace deep in the ground, so deep no dogs or kids would find it."

"I sure hope no varmints show up in my county that could cause a stink."

"Absolutely not, Sheriff. You can count on that."

"That's good. You might wash that rear end a bit more. Watch your speed through town tonight, you hear?"

The Sheriff got into his cruiser and drove away. Rabbit walked to a nearby pay phone and called Luke in Hyampom.

"Luke, it's Running Rabbit. You busy?"

"No, just taking it easy, sharpening some chain and then

going to play horseshoes with the boys at the bar. Why? What's up?"

"Why don't you skip that game and meet me in the Barn in Douglas City for coffee? I got something I need to talk to you about."

The Barn, a mom-and-pop restaurant near Douglas City, was famous for its homemade pies. The place didn't have a liquor license, but the owner was known to serve real mean Irish coffee with the pies.

Rabbit had two cups of coffee while he waited for Luke. When his friend arrived, he ordered pie and more coffee.

"What's so important you had to talk to me in person?" Luke asked. "Sunday horseshoes is pretty important."

"Let's go out to my rig."

Rabbit led the way and opened the passenger door. He handed Luke his dad's model 94 rifle.

"I'll be John Brown!" Luke exclaimed, inspecting the rifle carefully. He held it like it was the Holy Grail. It was the most-important possession he owned.

"Rabbit, IOU big time. How the hell did you get it back? Who had it?"

"It's best you not know anything about it. Did you report it to the police?"

"What the hell for? Besides, I don't talk to the law unless they already got me in handcuffs."

"I understand, but this is real important. I took a big risk today returning this to you. Can you promise not to say anything?"

"Rabbit, you got my word on my daddy's grave. Not a word to anyone. How can I repay this favor?"

Rabbit recalled seeing an old FJ-40 parked in the field beside Luke's house. "What would you take for that old FJ-40 in the field?"

"That thing has a seized engine, some of that damn Jap crap. I won't ever do anything with it. It was towed to a gas station and left there two years ago. I got it for $200, and you can just come take it from my field. How does that sound?"

"Luke, you just made a young man a hell of a present. John Copeland's son doesn't have a rig, and he's always admired my FJ-40. He just got back from serving and needs a rig."

"I heard he was discharged after a bad accident. Is he all right?"

"He'll be fine. He's as tough as his dad. I'll bring him over to get that Land Cruiser if you don't care about it."

"Just remember to close the gate when you leave. I'll put the title in the glove box. Tell them Copelands I said hey. Thanks again for getting my rifle back. I was damn near sick over it."

"Oh, I forgot to tell you. It was underwater for a bit. Thank you, too."

After they parted ways, Rabbit drove to the Copeland ranch.

John Copeland saw plenty of death and killing while a prisoner in Nazi Germany. The horror of it calloused his heart. Caroline, his wife, helped him open his heart again, and her death closed it back up. If it hadn't been for his love of the boys and his promise to Caroline, he might've shut down completely.

He loved his boys as much as he loved Caroline. The beating he took that day made him remember the brutal treatment he and the other pilots received from the SS officers. None of the men ever gave in, and John Copeland carried the scars from those interrogations.

Jack, astonished at the Sheriff's actions at the claim, couldn't understand why he did what he did. He kept quiet and let his dad do the talking. Cope and the Sheriff knew each other for twenty-five years. Both men had a keen understanding of how things worked in the county.

Jack drove Cope to the ranch where they found a worried Katie sitting on the porch, her hand on Bear's back, as he lay quietly at her side. His tail began thumping long before Katie heard the engine.

Cope and Bear were most likely alive because of Jack's actions. Katie, though horrified by the bloody spectacle, was also proud and happy that Jack saved their lives. The two feelings conflicted her.

Bear gave a low, slow greeting, when the two men walked toward the porch, and Katie flew into Jack's arms. Cope was pleased to see Caroline's engagement ring on Katie's left hand. He slowly settled his tense body into a rocking chair, wincing with pain when he leaned over to pet Bear. He leaned back his head to close his eyes, imagining grandchildren on the porch until he smiled.

"How about something to drink, Dad?" Jack asked.

"Sure. Make it strong."

The couple went into the kitchen and poured lemonade from the pitcher in the fridge. Jack added whiskey to Cope's.

Returning to the porch, Katie asked, "What will the Sheriff do?"

Cope sampled the lemonade before answering. "Katie, you're the closest thing I've ever had or will have to a daughter. Sweetheart, what happened today was terrible for you to see. Jack did what had to be done, taking their lives to save mine. The men he killed would've killed me and him, and there's no telling what they would have done to you before killing you, too.

"These were the same men who brutally beat Elliott. They represent the worst side of human nature. Jack's actions represent the best side—a willingness to attack in the face of danger to save people you love without thought of your own safety. Jack's actions were righteous in the eyes of man and God."

Katie held Jack's hand, looking deep into his eyes. "What did the Sheriff say?"

"Someone came to the claim while we were at Doc's," Cope answered. "He removed the bodies and all evidence of what happened. The Sheriff listened to our account and said we weren't reliable witnesses, because both of us have had recent head trauma. There was no evidence, so there couldn't be a crime.

"He was right. It was clear self-defense, but it would become a big drama if it went public. We'd have lawyers, reporters, and public opinion intruding into our lives, changing all of us forever. People would want to come out here to see the scene of the killings. The Sheriff had our best interests in mind when he made his decision.

"We need to keep this quiet. Can you do that, Katie? We need to forget it happened."

"I know I can keep quiet, but I don't know if I can ever forget. I see it over and over in my mind. I was so scared for you when I saw you tied up and being beaten. Then Jack dove into the water and went after the man with the rifle. I prayed to Jesus at that moment. It was all I could do."

Cope reached out and took her hand in his two strong ones, his deep blue eyes watery and soft with sincerity. "I believe your prayer was answered. Now I pray you'll keep today's events a secret between us."

Katie threw her arms around Cope's neck, and he held her while she sobbed.

"I'll never say a word. I promise."

Jack joined the embrace.

"It's been a long, long day, Kids," Cope said. "I'll go to bed after I finish this drink."

"I should go home, too," Katie said.

Jack walked her to the Pinto.

"I really don't want to be alone tonight," Katie said.

"I don't want you to go, either. Dad, is it all right if she spends the night in Elliott's room?"

"Call her mom. It's OK with me, as long as there's no hanky-panky. You love birds aren't married yet."

Cope was still sitting on the porch, sipping his lemonade, when he heard and saw Running Rabbit approaching. He loved the sound of the 327.

"You've been a busy man today," Cope said.

"You're the second old codger to tell me that. The Sheriff stopped at the car wash while I was washing out my rig and asked me the same damn thing. Why do you think that was?"

"Probably has to do with your tires. They leave a deep, distinctive tread signature in the sand."

"Yeah. I guess that's true. Did you see my tracks?"

"I don't know when you were there or what you saw and what you did. I have my suspicions, but suspicions can't get anybody in trouble."

"The Sheriff knows what happened. A fisherman called in my rig for leaking blood. The Sheriff doesn't seem to care as long as it doesn't surface in his county."

"We had a real problem. I was underwater on my hookah when your two buddies cut off my air. They shot Bear in the head and damn near cracked my skull when I surfaced. They were interrogating me when Jack emerged from nowhere to end their lives with his dive knife. Katie saw it all."

"Damn. Jack's always been tough, but that took a lot of grit, facing two guns with a knife. Damn."

"I'm sorry he had to do it, but I'm sure they would've killed me if I gave them my gold. They thought I had a treasure chest hidden around here somewhere."

"How's Jack taking it?"

"He just proposed to Katie this morning. It'll probably bond them closer than ever. The Sheriff wanted it all to go away, like it never happened. He's a wise man."

"I can't figure it, Cope. Why?"

"He knows how the news would impact our little community. It might ruin Jack. Then there's the money he saved by not involving state police, coroners, prosecutors, lawyers, judges, funerals, a grand jury, and more. There's no telling how much time and money would be spent on an investigation like this. He's applying a little horse sense to law enforcement."

"I get it. It's like his policy of transporting vagrants across the county line. Not to change the subject, but I need to borrow your sixteen-foot trailer tomorrow."

"Rabbit, you can borrow anything I have except my chainsaw, my truck, or my...." He caught himself before he said, "wife."

"Great. Where's Jack?"

Cope hollered for Jack, then grimaced in pain. Rabbit opened his arms when Jack and Katie came onto the porch.

"Congratulations," Rabbit said. "I wondered how long it would take you two lovebirds. Jack, I got something for you today, but I'll need your help tomorrow morning to go get it."

"No problem. It must be something big if you need my help. What is it?"

"It won't be a surprise if I tell you.

"OK. I'll get up at six to make breakfast."

"Wait a minute, there. I'm a chief warrant officer. I didn't just get out of training. I'll be here at nine. I need my beauty rest."

8. Jack's Chevota

Jack, up at dawn, went into Elliott's room and climbed into bed with Katie. After a couple minutes together, she teasingly pushed him onto the floor with her strong legs. She didn't want their passion to get them in trouble with Cope.

Bear and Cope heard dishes rattling and came into the kitchen, moving slowly and brandishing bloody bandages. Cope took his coffee to the table, and Jack poured sausage drippings on Bear's dry dog food. He lay down with the bowl between his front feet and chewed slowly.

Rabbit arrived just as the biscuits were coming out of the oven. They ate eggs and sausage gravy over biscuits. Katie would take Cope and Bear to see Doc at ten.

Jack guided Rabbit, as he backed up his Land Cruiser, and attached the sixteen-foot trailer for their trip to Hyampom.

An hour later, they arrived at Luke's pasture. Jack opened the gate, then jumped back into the Land Cruiser. Rabbit pointed at the other cruiser in the field nearly covered by brush.

"What do you think?" Rabbit asked. "It's yours."

"You're kidding! Holy crap! Are you serious? Why is it out here?"

"It needs an engine, but supposedly, everything else is good. It belonged to a hunter from Los Angeles who was up deer hunting. It was brand new when he hydro-seized the engine a couple seasons ago and abandoned it. George has the tow truck contract with the U.S. Forest Service. Luke bought it from him for $200. He said he'd never do anything with it and wanted you to have it. Hopefully, all you'll have to do is either rebuild the Toyota engine or put in a Chevy like I did."

"It's beautiful. Holy Shit, Rabbit. I can't believe it. You know I've always wanted one. I even ordered a new one when I was at Fort Rucker, but I had to cancel it. I didn't have enough money and was out of a job. This is much better. Holy shit, Rabbit. Thanks so much."

"You got it, Jack. Don't you ever call me Shit Rabbit again. Let's winch it onto the trailer before you try to kiss me."

Thirty minutes later, the Land Cruiser was chained to the trailer and locked down with binders. Rabbit's rig had no trouble pulling the trailer across the field. Jack closed the gate behind them, as they left.

The trailer was a bit tricky to pull, because of the Land Cruiser's short wheelbase. They took it slow going down the highway.

"I returned the model 94 Winchester to Luke," Rabbit said. "It was his dad's, and it meant a lot to him."

Jack said nothing.

"That was one hell of a brave thing you did, Kid."

"I guess you were the one who cleaned up and got rid of the bodies."

"I must've gotten there right after it happened."

"How'd you feel the first time you killed someone?"

"I felt fucking lucky. I was glad to be alive and happy to go back to the little stinking shack called the Officer's Club and get drunk."

"You had an Officer's Club in the field in Vietnam?"

"Yeah. Most units had their own clubs. We were the Jokers. We had a little clubhouse to come home to and try to drink away the death. That's how most of us handled the stress. We lost pilots almost every day. We were almost afraid to get close to anyone. Are you doing all right?"

"Yeah, I'm OK. When I close my eyes, though, I can see the guy's face. His guts fell out, and he had a weird smile on his face. There was a creepy spider tattooed on his neck that looked evil. He reminded me of Charles Manson."

"You know, now that you mention it, he did look like Manson. He sat right where you're sitting when I picked him up hitchhiking."

"Stop, stop! Let me out!" Jack shouted.

The sudden outburst caught Rabbit off guard, and Jack started laughing.

"Gotcha!"

They laughed for five minutes. Jack did the joke again, and they laughed some more.

"You know," Rabbit said, "fuck those two assholes. I felt good when I dumped them into that hole and blew them up. I wished I could've been the one who stuck them. I might've done it slow, Indian style, stake 'em to the ground and pull their guts out a little bit and let the coyotes eat 'em alive. It wasn't enough that they beat Elliott, though he probably needed his ass beaten for being in Denny in the first place, but that's another story. Beating your dad and shooting Bear, though, the way I see it, they got off easy."

"I understand what you're trying to do, but I really don't feel bad. It happened so fast. I know I did the right thing. I had no choice."

"No shit, Jack."

They stopped at the Diggins for a beer and burger. Everyone was happy that Jack was back in town. They'd been proud of him for joining the Army and extremely happy to see him back whole, not maimed or killed in Vietnam like so many other young men.

Finishing their meal, they climbed the steep grade over Oregon Summit and down into Junction City, across the Trinity River, and up the gravel road to the ranch.

They unloaded the forest-green cruiser into one of the shop's empty bays, filling the building, which housed the tractor, the wrecked K5 Blazer, a Willys utility wagon, and Jack's 1971 Land Cruiser. They jacked up all four wheels putting jack stands under each axle.

Rabbit and Jack were both competent mechanics. Rabbit's knowledge of his own FJ40 made him invaluable. He'd taken his Land Cruiser completely apart down to the frame, then he reassembled it with a Chevrolet engine and transmission.

Jack and Elliott helped Cope rebuild the Willys and anything else that broke. Jack knew his way around a shop and understood that the first place to start was with the wheels, especially if a vehicle had been submerged.

Katie brought Cope and Bear back after their visit with Doc, then she went home to share the news of her engagement. Cope and Bear came down to the shop with fresh dressings on their wounds.

"How are you feeling today, Dad?" Jack asked.

"I'm glad to be alive and thankful for the son who made it so. A scripture came to mind last night while I was praying. 'Blessed be the man who has children in his youth for they shall be as arrows in his quiver.' That certainly came true for me." He hugged Jack.

"Look what Randy got for me. Can you believe it? It's only got a few thousand miles on it. A doctor from LA abandoned it after he hydro seized the engine. It's beautiful. I even have the title."

"I like it, Son. These are good four-wheel-drives. Toyota bought manufacturing rights from Chevrolet in 1955 to start producing these. Most of the drive train is a duplicated American design."

"It's a fact, Jack," Rabbit said. "I read about that when I first started working on mine. Most good designs come from the U.S., and the Japs just copied them."

"It's funny," Cope said. "If you asked me during World War Two if I'd ever have a Japanese vehicle on my ranch, I would've laughed at you. Things sure have changed since then. Germany and Japan are now our allies, and we're in a cold war with China and Russia. In a little over two decades, our friends became enemies, and our enemies became friends.

"These Land Cruisers are good, solid rigs, with stronger

running gear than the Willys. The 327 engine and transmission in the Blazer are yours if you want them. They barely had 15,000 miles on them when we wrecked."

"Wow. Thanks, Dad. I can't wait to get started."

"I'll tell you what Grandpa told me. If it didn't go together with a hammer, it doesn't come apart with a hammer."

They laughed.

Rabbit went to his FJ40 and brought back a shop manual and parts catalog. A company in Chatsworth, California, called Spectre, specialized in aftermarket parts and conversions for FJ40s. Jack would need an adapter to join the Chevy transmission to the Toyota transfer case. Rabbit offered to help him when he reached that point.

Jack ordered the adapter and spent the next week in the shop working on the project. Katie handed him wrenches and helped clean parts. Cope and Bear came down to supervise daily. Bear had a cute habit of catching someone when he couldn't move and licking his neck or ear. Jack always acted offended, but Bear knew he liked it and wagged his tail even harder when he protested.

Bear was back to normal, with just a couple of scabs where Doc sewed the entry and exit holes. The swelling in Cope's face went down, and his stitches were removed. His sore ribs were getting better.

The land Cruiser was getting better, too. All moving parts were lubricated, and fluid systems were flushed. Jack put Never Seize on the brake adjusters, because they were rusted from water in the creek.

Rabbit said that was normal and suggested the lubricant to prevent it in the future. The original engine and transmission were removed, and the Chevy power train was suspended from the engine hoist, ready to go, when the rural route carrier came down the driveway.

Jack called Rabbit and said, "The package from Spectre is here!"

He previously removed the radiator and grill assembly to make it easier to install the new engine and transmission. The only welding necessary for the conversion was motor mount brackets to the cross member in the engine compartment.

Cope, Rabbit, and Jack installed the new engine and tranny. Cope sent Katie to Big Flat Pizza to buy food for a party to celebrate giving the Land Cruiser an American soul. He said it was part exorcism and baptism, but it was definitely cause for pizza.

They celebrated starting the engine with pizza and beer. Cope presented Jack with a Chevrolet bonnet insignia to put on the grill and a pair of rally flags from a 1962 Corvette for the sides of the hood. Jack had always been a Chevy man. He cracked a beer bottle over the front bumper, and, in his best English accent, proclaimed, "I name thee YO."

The others laughed and applauded. Rabbit and Cope watched as Jack took Katie out for a test drive. The engine sounded strong. They went only as far as the bridge two miles away.

"Shall we initiate the Land Cruiser?" he asked with a devilish smile.

"Why, whatever do you mean, Sir?" Katie asked in her best

Southern accent, as she climbed in his lap to tease him. "We have to go back before they start to worry."

She laughed at his expression, always enjoying a good tease. She had tortured Jack since she was fifteen, when they first became romantically involved.

9. Stanislaus River

Elliott always had good luck when carrying a backpack and using a sign when hitchhiking. People seemed to trust someone who they thought was trying to get somewhere. A backpack was symbolic in many ways of adventure and carefree travel. Maybe the drivers were intrigued by the romantic image or thought it would break the monotony of their drive to have interesting company. It didn't hurt that Elliott was handsome, with his shoulder-length golden locks and muscular physique. He stood at the exit ramp off Interstate 5 to Highway 16, his piece of cardboard reading, *Angels Camp.*

An old Volvo wagon pulled over to the shoulder, the driver resembled Santa Claus. A thick layer of dust on the rear window evidenced that the car had seen heavy travel on dirt roads. A peace sign, the words *Save the River,* and *Wash me,* were scrawled in the dust by someone's finger.

"Angels Camp is a fine place to be in the summer for a young man in his prime like yourself," the driver said. "I'll go right through the town on my way home."

"I sure thank you for the ride."

"You betcha. A downside for you is that you'll have to

listen to an old social anthropologist talk about the evolution of modern society."

"That sounds very interesting, especially if it includes a little local knowledge."

"What's your name, Son?"

"I'm Elliott Copeland. My nickname's Otter. Your name, Sir?"

"You, Otter, shall not call me Sir." The old man slapped his leg and laughed. "My friends call me Nick."

Elliott, chuckling, relaxed into his seat. "It's my first time here. I'm going to work for a rafting outfit out of Angels Camp. What's it like around here?"

"That's a big question. I left Berkeley in 1948 to write my doctorate on the gold rush. I'm still studying the gold country phenomenon. It seems to be an ongoing process. Every time I think I've got a handle on what's really going on, something new comes up. People keep coming up with new ways to profit from what was put here—gold, trees, rivers, and even the land itself."

"Gold is something I understand."

"That's a pretty bold statement for someone your age."

"I grew up helping my dad get gold from the river where we live. We have several dredging claims on the Trinity River. I've worked on the claim since I was old enough to walk."

"You'll feel right at home here, then. There are many similarities between the two areas. There's a lot more tourism and development here, due to our proximity to Sacramento and San Francisco. A lot of people want progress, and a lot of other people want to preserve things the way they are. Some real conflicts are brewing over the river."

"We have conflicts occasionally on the Trinity, too. Some people don't like the brown water that comes out of the back of our dredge. They think we're destroying the river. The fact of it is that in most cases, we're cleaning up the mess left by the monitors on Oregon Mountain and the massive erosion caused by clear cutting in the fifties."

"As I said, Elliott, or Otter, I couldn't disclaim or support that theory. I'm more a student of social behavior, not environmental science, but it sounds good."

"Really, Nick, it's true. Our dredging loosens up all the compacted dirt and clays, and it separates the gravel. We produce nice, clean, loose gravel for migratory fish to spawn in. I've watched salmon and steelhead gather in our tailings of loose gravel to lay their eggs."

"There's a little of that on the Stanislaus. The rafters hate the dredgers due to the cables they use to hold their dredges, not to mention that the noise spoils their attempts to commune with nature. The miners think the rafters are a bunch of spoiled hippies and city slickers who should go back to San Francisco. There isn't much common ground."

"Does it ever get violent?"

"Not usually. It's just yelling and taunting. Sometimes someone cuts a cable loose, and there might be a fight in the bar, but that's as far as it's gone. The real battle is yet to come."

"What else is going on?"

"You'll find out when you raft the river. There's fifteen miles of wild river left. The Army Corps of Engineers has already built thirteen dams on the river. You talk about conflict! There were people's homes, entire towns, beautiful canyons, and untold wildlife habitat put under water in the name of progress."

"That doesn't sound like progress to me. Couldn't people stop it?"

"Oh, they tried, Son. Some died. I imagine more will before this is over. There's big money in federal dam projects, what with producing electricity for the urban populations and water for agri corporations. You should enjoy the remaining fifteen miles, my boy, like there's no tomorrow. Change is the only certainty that weaves the path of human existence."

Elliott was silent, thinking over Nick's words. Many things troubled him about the world, but he would try very hard to enjoy the Stanislaus River. He liked Nick and his thought-provoking conversation.

Nick turned the Volvo south on Highway 49 through Dry Town, Sutter Creek, Jackson, San Andreas, and in to Angels Camp. He stopped and took Elliott, whom he called Otter, into his favorite restaurant for a burger. Elliott called his new employer while they waited for their food. A driver in a red CJ 5 would pick him up at the restaurant in half an hour.

Elliott had one of the best burgers and fries of his life. Nick told him the lunch was his treat, just as the Jeep arrived, and Elliott left. He shook the old man's hand, then he grabbed his pack from the back of the Volvo and loaded it into the Jeep.

The driver was an attractive woman in her early twenties, who wore a white T-shirt with the company logo and a pair of short khaki shorts. With her hair in a ponytail, she was very pleasant to look at.

"You must be Elliott," she said. "I'm Lucy. I work in the office."

She extended her hand, and they shook. Elliott got in the front passenger seat.

"My boss tells me you're a top-notch rafter. You'll love the Stanislaus River. We have a lot of fun here. We're more like a family than a company."

In a few moments, they arrived at the office that looked like the front of a country store, with a porch and shed roof stretching across the front of the building. A long counter inside the front door was ready for customers to sign up for trips.

Ferg, short for Ferguson, was the man who hired Elliott. Welcoming him, he asked him to fill out the standard forms—job application, W-4, and a short description of company policies that everyone had to sign. When Elliott finished, Ferg introduced him to Steelhead.

"Steelhead will get you situated and take you on a couple of orientation trips before you start taking paying clients," Ferg explained. "With your skills, it won't take long. You'll have to follow the other guides before you start leading trips on your own. That's how everybody starts here."

"I appreciate that. I wouldn't want to be thrown to the wolves."

Steelhead took him on a tour of the facilities, talking the entire time.

"If you can handle a raft half as good as Ferg says, you won't have any problem. Just familiarize yourself with the river. Water levels in the summer are obviously low, and the river slows down considerably. We run eighteen miles of river. We call it the top nine and bottom nine. There are tons of beautiful caves and side canyons, with Rose Creek, South Fork, and the biggest fig tree in the world.

"The lower section is a relaxing run. I'll show you the

Mi-Wuk Indian petroglyphs at Horseshoe Bend. There are a couple spots we have to scout, like Death Rock Rapid, Devil's Staircase, and Widow Maker. Those are menacing names, but they're not that scary in the summer. It's a whole different animal in high water, though. We'll do plenty of sightseeing to give you the full tourist treatment. We'll camp at one of my favorite spots, the beach just above Razorback. It's a great place to build a sweat lodge. I'll get you a chart to study."

"That sounds great. Thanks, Steelhead."

"You can stay at my place until you're settled somewhere. It's primitive, but I like it."

"Awesome. I really appreciate it."

"OK. Let's go look at the rafts. I'll show you around. Tomorrow is an overnight, so it's a little more involved with all the food and camping gear, but you already know that. Ferg will probably start you with day trips. That's what he normally does with new guides. You'll fall in love with this river and will have plenty of fun, too. The showers and bathroom facilities are back here with the gear."

Elliott had never seen so much rafting equipment in his life. It wasn't a simple mom-and-pop operation. There were at least thirty rafts and too many kayaks and canoes to count. He saw a parking area with painted buses and trailers for ferrying people, rafts, and supplies. Everything was orderly, clean, and seemed well-maintained. It was apparent that the crew took pride in their jobs.

"Crew accommodations are back in the field of live oaks," Steelhead said, pointing.

"Are we camping?

"Sort of."

Elliott was amazed when he saw the carefully crafted tree houses within the oaks. Frank Lloyd Wright would've been enchanted. Elliott followed Steelhead up the ladder to his tree house.

"Say, do you have any other name? Elliott's kind of dorky, you know, not very hip. Everyone here has a nickname. Most people either come with one or get named here."

"I'm called Otter by my family and friends."

"Otter it is, then. I'll introduce you to everybody that way. It's a fitting name for a river man."

"My dad gave me that name when I was two-years old on the Trinity River behind our house. He was panning out some fines from the dredge and turned his back for a second. He said I went in and looked like a puppy the first time, my head up, and I was splashing. By the end of the summer, I swam like a fish or an otter, so the name stuck."

"Wow. That's a great story. Does your dad still have the dredge?"

"Yeah. My brother and I worked the claims with Dad since we were old enough to pay attention."

"We have something in common. I do a little treasure hunting myself. It's not dredging, but it's similar."

"What kind of treasure?"

"When the rafting season ends, I go to the Florida Keys and look for Spanish gold."

"Wow. That sounds too cool. What's the best thing you ever found?"

Steelhead, taking a wooden box from a chest, handed it to Otter. It was full of gold and silver coins, along with a few emeralds and rubies.

"This is amazing. There must be a fortune in here. How long have you been treasure hunting?"

"I started six years ago as a teenager on family vacation. I got consumed by it. I'd do it full time if it weren't for this place and the rafting. I divide my time between Angels Camp and the Keys."

"My brother and I spent a lot of time looking for gold, too. In the summer, Jack and I kayaked the Trinity, sniping and fanning where we thought there might be gold. We did all right, had some fun, and learned a lot. I want to hear more about your treasure hunting in the Keys. I always thought it would be nice to look for gold where the water wasn't so dang cold."

"We fan for gold, too, but we don't use our hands. We redirect the prop wash from the boat's propeller straight down with a big, ninety-degree pipe. The current washes away the sand and leaves the heavy stuff, but we'll have plenty of time to talk about treasure hunting. All the guides meet at Amigos at six. They've got the coldest beer in town and free hors d'oeuvres."

"That sounds great. I guess if it's safe enough for you to leave your gold here, I can leave my pack. I'm a little shy after having all my gear stolen."

"Not to worry. Nobody's ever had anything stolen from here."

Amigos was busy. It was the meeting place of the River Rats, as they were called. Happy hour was crazy, with pitchers of beer selling for only one dollar, while tacos were a dime. There were at least as many athletic, attractive women as men. Otter loved the outdoors, athletic type, without makeup, perfume, and stockings. He knew he had found his niche.

Steelhead introduced him as Otter to the other guides from the commercial rafting companies. If the Stanislaus River was half as beautiful as the people, Otter knew he found a place where he could be happy. He couldn't remember all the nicknames, like Skeeter, Twister, Snake, Wormy, but he could definitely remember River Goddess. She was hard to forget. The other rafters received him well, and he enjoyed the evening.

He took his first trip down the Stanislaus the following morning with Steelhead. He fell in love almost immediately. The river fulfilled his expectations, and the job would be fun. He enjoyed his days and nights on the river and with the clients.

Soon, he qualified to lead trips down the river alone. He was having the best summer of his life, and he was stockpiling a nice amount of cash for the winter.

10. Boulder Gold

The FJ40 performed well. Jack drove it to the claim every day. Up every morning before dawn, Jack and Cope started at daylight, working underwater around a large boulder in ten feet of water.

Cope held and directed the six-inch suction hose, and Jack moved the rocks that were too big to pass through the hose. It was like a giant vacuum cleaner, sucking up all the loose gravel and overburden from the riverbed. Jack was always encouraged when they saw gold sucked up. He was still amazed after all those years how shiny it stayed, flashing in the sunlight, as it was caught in the suction. A good day saw them bring in three to four ounces, along with a few jewelry-quality nuggets.

Katie arrived at noon with lunch and stayed for the afternoon. Jack liked knowing she was up there when he was in the water. She snorkeled with Bear and watched the men work from the surface. Periodically, she checked the washboard-like riffles in the sluice box for large nuggets. When she saw color, she dived down to give Jack and Cope a thumbs-up sign.

Cope gave Jack the signal to surface, and they came up beside the dredge.

"Tadpole, I think this is it," Cope said.

"Tadpole? You haven't called me that since I was ten."

"That's because I haven't been this excited since you were ten."

"Excited, you? What's wrong?"

"You'll see. Come on." Cope turned off the dredge and moved a few rocks off the riffles, showing gold.

"See the edges of this boulder? This is the one we've been looking for, the one that hasn't been moved. Our fortune is waiting under this boulder."

Jack looked around cautiously to make sure no one but Katie was there. "I see it, Dad. Oh, my goodness, I see it, too!"

Cope released the latches holding the riffle in place and raised it on its hinges. They rolled the carpet on which the gold collected and placed it in a five-gallon bucket. Jack had never seen his dad so excited. It was clearly a big strike. They'd been looking around and under boulders for twenty years, hoping to find the one that hadn't moved in thousands of years and had a fortune of gold under it. The rock was the size of an elephant on the surface, with no way to tell how big it was, because the rest of it was surrounded by smaller rock.

Cope drove Jack's Land Cruiser to the ranch with the bucket, while Jack rode with Katie in the little Pinto.

"I've never seen your dad like this," she said. "You think you found it?"

"I don't know, but look how he's driving my rig. He just burned rubber, damn it! I never should've let him take my Land Cruiser."

"I guess you forgot how you used to drive his rigs when you were sixteen."

"True, but I was only a kid."

"Besides, who gave you the engine?"

"Yeah, yeah. I shouldn't care. I've just never seen him drive like this. He's usually so cautious. Look at him go. He's already out of sight!"

"I think he saw a lot of gold go into the dredge. That's what I think, Jack Copeland."

"Well, hurry up and put your spurs into this Pinto."

When they arrived, Cope had already taken three home brews from the fridge. He saved them for special occasions. They gathered at the shop to pan out the day's find, as usual, and Jack had never seen so much gold in one day in his life. Neither had Cope. They had over seventeen ounces of flakes and nuggets, probably another ounce or two in sand, like fine gold. The fine gold was stored in fifty-gallon drums for future processing. The flakes and larger gold went into the safe.

"We did good today, Jack," Cope said. "Real good."

"I'd say so. You think we can get under that boulder? What I meant to ask was, *how* will we get underneath it?"

"We'll keep going the way we are, moving everything around it away, sucking up everything we can until it stands alone without anything wedging it."

"OK. I see what you're thinking, but what if it shifts or rolls from water pressure?"

"That's what we eventually want it to do, just not when we're close. We'll have to cable and chain it, as we move the overburden from around it. It depends on how deep it goes. We don't know how far down the bedrock is. This thing could be ten feet down in a hole. We'll have to take our time and work our way down, expanding the excavation around it so there's a gradual drop off."

The look they exchanged was telling. Both thought about Caroline, who died in an accident when a boulder crushed and trapped her underwater. The two men were somber for a moment, then Cope raised his beer.

"Jack and Katie, a toast to Caroline, the finest woman I ever knew. She would want us to do this, Jack. This was her dream, too. She loved the adventure and knew the danger involved in moving a large rock. If she were alive today, she'd tell us how to move it." He smiled, though a tear rolled down one cheek.

Jack drank, trying to wash away the lump in his throat. Somehow, he managed, "Here's to Mom."

Katie loved both men and hurt for them.

Cope used a tweezers to pick up two nice nuggets. "Here, Katie. You might get some nice earrings from these two."

"Really? Thank you! They're beautiful. Are you sure?"

"You bet I am. You'll get more than that before this is over."

Jack smiled, knowing how his dad appreciated everything Katie did around the ranch.

They walked to the house together, then Jack started a hardwood fire and cleaned the cooking grate on the grill. Cope seasoned the steaks, and Katie made a nice salad. Bear sat at the edge of the kitchen, carefully watching in case any trimmings fell to the floor. Supper was almost always eaten at the picnic table on the front porch during summer.

Cope was excited, already designing a way to expose the massive gold deposit under the rock. He certainly was prepared. He had already made 3/8-inch welded chain bridles to wrap around the boulder's girth. The bridles were made from two thirty-foot chains connected every three feet with a twelve-inch length, like a giant tire chain. In theory, the bridle would wrap around the boulder and hold it in place, or it could be used to move the boulder through winching. He and Jack would have to survey the dynamics of the surrounding rocks carefully. The situation always changed whenever a single rock was moved.

As he ate, Cope drew and talked. "A body at rest wants to stay at rest unless acted upon by another force. It's the force, Jack, that will get us. That's the current of the river pushing against the boulder. As well as the weight of the water, we've got gravity pushing it down. Those forces on the boulder will exert pressure against all the rocks around it. Even the upstream rocks are loaded against our boulder.

"The whole thing is hard to predict. The situation is fluid. Just moving one rock can trigger an underwater avalanche. It all depends on how big and deep the boulder is."

"We have to be real careful, Dad."

"That's an understatement. Gold isn't worth dying over," Katie added.

"We have to use the force of the river to our advantage," Cope continued. "The first thing we'll do is wrap two bridles around the boulder and secure cables at forty-five degree angles to the opposite sides of the river."

"What will we attach them to?" Jack asked.

"We'll set two-inch eye bolts twelve inches down in bedrock. One would hold a boulder that size, so we'll set two. We can survey the bank tomorrow morning. You can start exposing the bedrock, while I go to borrow a gas-operated rotor hammer in Weaverville."

"OK. What do we do once it's secured?"

"We should start fifteen feet downstream from the boulder, moving rocks and dredging down to bedrock. That will tell us how big the boulder is. We'll prepare a crater big enough for the boulder, then we'll work our way to its base, cleaning out all the cracks and crevices in the bedrock."

"What's to stop the force of the river from pushing the boulder over on you?" Katie asked. "Oh, yeah—the cables. It sounds dangerous."

"It's more than just the chains," Cope explained. "All the rocks on the sides have the boulder bound up, too. Until we remove all that rock and overburden from the sides, the boulder can't move. There's an untold amount of force against the sides of that boulder, holding it steady."

"OK, Dad," Jack said. "We secure it and make a place for it to go downstream. After we work the sides from front to back, then what?"

"Once it's all exposed on the sides and back, we cut the cables and let the river roll it over. Depending on how it's shaped, we may have to use the cables to pull it downstream. Once we move it, we'll find out what's under it."

"How long do you think this will take?"

"Your guess is as good as mine. Depending on how deep the bedrock is, it could vary greatly. Let's estimate one day to secure the boulder, one day to dig the hole behind it, with a day on either side. Then there's a day working in the front, and a day to move the rock. After that maybe two weeks to carry the gold home."

They laughed while Bear thumped his tail at the sound. He got up, barked once, and put his head on Cope's lap.

"Damn it, Dad. I sure wish Otter was here to help."

"You and me both, Tadpole."

"That's the second time today."

"You didn't used to mind."

"Yeah, but it's a kid's name, wouldn't you say?"

Katie laughed. "What should we call you now? Bullfrog?"

Cope slapped his leg. "That's it! It's Bullfrog."

"Anything's better than Tadpole," Jack said. "I'll take Bullfrog over that any day. In all seriousness, we really could use Elliott's help."

"I know, especially since he has a stake in this claim. It's shared three ways. That's the deal we agreed to."

Katie went to the kitchen picked up and dialed a number on the phone. "Janet? Hey, it's Katie. How are you doing?"

"Beat. I worked all day at the pizza shop. It's really hot in there lately."

"I can only imagine. Getting lots of tips, I hope?"

"Yeah, it's been pretty good. The best tips come from the ones who drink beer with their pizza."

"That's funny. I guess if they can afford beer, they can afford to tip. Hey, Jack really needs to get hold of Elliott. Have you heard from him lately?"

"His last letter said he was going to Angels Camp to work for a rafting company. I haven't heard anything else, so I assume that's where he is. Sometimes, I hope I never hear from him again, and other times, I can't stand not hearing. I'm not sure what's worse. That damn Copeland boy is driving me crazy!"

Katie smiled at Jack. "I know what you mean about the Copeland boys."

Jack threw his hands up to show he didn't understand.

"All right, Janet. I'll tell Jack. When you have your next day off, let's do something."

"You think you can stand to be away from Jack for a day?"

"Yeah. He's getting too used to having me around."

Jack, throwing his hands in the air again, grinned at his dad. Cope smiled and raised his arms, too. Bear tipped his head up at them and sighed, then set his head down, though his ears remained pricked.

"I've got tomorrow off," Janet said. "You want to do something?"

"I'll see you around ten. We'll go to the gulch or something."

"See you then. Tell Jack and Cope hi for me."

Katie hung up and relayed the information.

"You've got a place to start, anyway," Cope said. "Why don't you drive down to Angels Camp tomorrow in your Chevota, or is it a Toyolet?"

They laughed.

"You can take Bear with you if you want," Cope added.

"No. It might be too hot if he has to stay in the Cruiser. Besides, someone has to keep an eye on you."

"I'll pick the garden before it gets hot. Then I'll go to town for that rotor hammer and make sure we have everything."

"Janet and I can help pick tomorrow," Katie said.

"You can ask her, but I'll bet after all the hours she spends at Big Flat Pizza, she won't want to pick tomatoes."

"I'll be here at seven whether she comes or not, to make sure some sleepyhead gets an early start." She playfully punched Jack's arm.

"What do you think, Dad, six or seven hours each way?"

"That sounds about right, but you have to find him and see if he wants to come home. You might need to spend the night."

"He won't be that hard to find if he's working for a rafting company. When he hears what we found today, he'll know what to do, unless he's lost all his marbles."

"I believe you're right. Take his watch to him just in case."

Cope sat on the porch in his rocking chair, enjoying a cigar and whiskey. He and Bear watched Jack and Katie hold hands as they walked to the shop where her Pinto was parked. He hoped they were abstaining from sex, but he prayed even harder they were being careful. A pregnancy would be wonderful, but not yet.

He made a mental note to have the conversation with Jack again. Maybe he should talk to both of them together.

The couple kissed in the shop for a few minutes before Katie left. Jack reminded her not to mention the gold to anyone, but he didn't need to. She was wise about such things.

Bear greeted Jack at the top of the stairs with a woof and a lick on his nose. Jack hugged the dog and sat beside him.

"God, I love this old dog," Jack said.

"Me, too, Son. He sure has a big heart."

"You having a drink?"

"You can have one if you like. One won't hurt."

"Thanks. You think we need Rabbit's portable winch?"

"Not unless we get all the overburden away and still can't move the boulder. Then we might."

"Yeah. It could be like an iceberg, with more hidden below than what we can see."

"We'll go forward carefully and make adjustments to the plan as required. All we have is a plan. There's something else on my mind that I might as well say. I don't want to pry into your personal relationship with Katie, so I'll say this as delicately as possible. She's seventeen. That's too young to be tied down with babies."

"Holy cow. What's this about?"

"I know that you know what it's about. Don't play naïve with me. I wasn't born yesterday. She's beautiful and sexy, and you two are in love and engaged. Making love is a normal, natural progression. I don't want to know if you have or haven't, and I don't want to think about it or talk about it again. Do the right thing by her. Help her finish high school and go to college if she wants."

"Of course. I want what's best for her. I love her with all my heart."

"The bottom line is, if you can't control it, make darned sure you're covered up."

"Dad, we had this talk when I was fourteen."

"Some things can't be said too many times. I don't want you kids to have kids before you have a chance to live. Make sure you're right for each other and ready for the commitment."

"Thanks. I appreciate what you're saying."

"Enough said. I'm going to call it a night. Come on, Bear. Let's go in. I want you to take $500 from the cash box for the trip in case you have to stay the night or have trouble with your rig."

"I'll get it in the morning. I'm right behind you, Dad."

"All right. Good night. Love you, Son."

"Back at you."

Cope was up first the following morning and made coffee, sausage, grits, eggs, sliced tomatoes, and toast. The girls arrived, and all ate breakfast together. Jack left for Angels Camp, while Janet, Kate, Bear, and Cope went to the garden to harvest vegetables. When they finished, the girls left with plenty to share with their families, and Cope went to work in the shop.

11. The Investigators

Cope was cleaning rust off the eye bolt anchors when Bear raised his head and growled softly.

"What's the problem, Buddy?"

He followed Bear, who had his tail up and hackles raised, from the shop. Cope heard tires on the gravel and saw an Army green Maverick coming toward him. It had government tags, and two men in suits sat inside.

When the car pulled up, the passenger window rolled down, and a man asked, "Is this the Copeland place?"

Bear walked stiff-legged, growling around the car, and peed on the front tire. He stared at the man through the open window. Cope identified them as FBI or CID.

"Who are you?" Cope asked.

"Does the dog bite?"

"You always answer a question with a question?"

"It looks like I do as much as you. Let me start over, Sir. I'm Chief Warrant Officer Graham with the Army Criminal Investigation Division, and I'm looking for the Copeland residence, Sir."

"That's better, Chief. Now my dog won't bite. Bear, heel."

Bear walked up to Cope's left side and pressed his shoulder against Cope's calf.

"I was just going up to the house," Cope said. "You can drive up or park here and walk. I need a cold drink."

The men drove the little green Ford Maverick up to the porch and waited for Cope. When he arrived, they got out and walked up to sit on the swinging chair to the left of the door. Bear lay down between them and the door. Every thirty seconds, he growled a little, never taking his eyes off them.

Cope returned with iced teas. The men stood when he came out the door, and Bear sprang between them, showing his teeth.

"Don't mind him, Boys," Cope said. "He's just protecting an old man."

"Sir, I know a little about you. I doubt you need a dog."

"A compliment, then," Cope said. "I must be in trouble. To what do I owe a visit from the CID?"

"Captain Copeland, Sergeant Brown and I are investigating an alleged assault on two civilians by a soldier in uniform at the Sacramento airport."

"Boys, in case you haven't noticed, I haven't worn a uniform in over twenty years."

"We realize that, but your son, Warrant Officer Jack Copeland, traveled from Fort Rucker to Sacramento the day of the alleged assault. Would it be possible to speak to him? Is he here?"

"Do you have a warrant for his arrest?"

"No. We're on a fact-finding mission. Our job is to interview all Army personnel who went through the airport the day of the incident."

"It must've been a horrific assault to merit this much attention."

"Not really, Sir. The issue is more who alleged the assault. The boy who got his bell rung was a congressman's son. The congressman got his panties in a wad and wants heads to roll. He's a big Democratic antiwar politician."

"That sounds about right, with politicians running the show."

"That's only half of it. We interviewed three witnesses who saw the boys heckling the GI in question, calling him a baby killer and more."

"Sounds like the two boys might have instigated the trouble."

"Is Jack around?"

"Sorry. He's not here."

"When will he return?"

"Can't really say. He's off to join his brother, who's on a whitewater rafting adventure."

Bear turned his head toward the drive, lifted his ears, and barked once. He looked at Cope, then back toward the river. Someone was coming up the drive.

Thirty seconds later, Running Rabbit's FJ40 came to a stop. The chief and sergeant hoped it was Jack. They hadn't been completely forthcoming with Cope, but that was about to change.

Bear greeted Rabbit with a couple of woofs and a wagging tail.

"Who the hell are the suits, Cope?" Rabbit asked. "Army tags?"

"Hey, Rabbit. These are Army investigators looking for a

GI who allegedly assaulted some congressman's snot-nosed brat in the Sacramento airport."

"Hell, I wish I could do that. There's a whole passel of the little bastards on educational deferments who need their asses kicked."

"Did you call him Rabbit?" Chief Graham smiled.

"Is that really you?" Rabbit asked.

"Who the hell else would it be?"

Rabbit smiled. "Graham, you flat-headed SOB."

The two men hugged. They were helicopter pilots in the same unit, and both were Jokers. Graham lost partial use of his left arm and was permanently grounded from flying. He was given the option of going to CID to finish his twenty years.

"Cope, this calls for a drink," Rabbit said. "I haven't seen this guy since a field hospital. Both of us were shot up pretty bad. It was an extraction gone bad. Viet Cong were waiting for us and popped green smoke when we arrived. All hell broke loose. That's when I took a .51 caliber through the cockpit."

"I'd love to have a drink with you," Graham said, "but we're on official business. Maybe another time."

"The hell you say. What are they going to do, send you to Nam? Graham, you're getting stiff in your old age. The sergeant here won't tell on you for having a drink. He'll probably have one, too. Lighten up, Old Buddy."

Three hours later, Graham, the Sergeant, Rabbit, and Cope opened the second jug of sour mash. Cope requested and received keys to the Maverick. Court was convened on the porch.

Cope told Jack's full story as he heard it. Graham read the

accusers' false statements. The sergeant read eyewitness statements that corroborated Jack's side of the story. The congressman's son would be taken to task for lying.

Randy Rabbit volunteered to make a quiet trip to Sacramento and put dope in the kid's car. The boy would end up in jail on drug charges and lose his credibility as a witness. Case closed.

Cope knew it was bullshit and just the alcohol talking. He showed the men where to sleep and retired to his room with Bear. The young men would have to finish the party without him. He had important things to do the next day.

Another of his laws was, *Never let tonight ruin your tomorrow.* The case against Jack was weak and easily handled through proper channels. Cope wasn't worried. He believed in the military justice system. It was fair.

Bear woke Cope with a low growl at 3:15 AM. Cope listened and heard the guests laughing as they stumbled to bed. He smiled. He knew how they'd feel at seven o'clock when he called them to breakfast.

"It's OK, Boy," he said. "They're going to bed now."

Bear sighed, putting his head back on his paws.

12. Charlotte Harbor

Neil and Clara Bell traveled east across the Panhandle, then south along the Florida coast. He was more determined than ever to find a real sailboat with sleeping quarters, so he could cross open ocean. He sailed past the entrance to Tampa Bay and continued south. Constant thunderstorms and incessant mosquitoes took their toll.

He entered Boca Grande Pass heading for Pelican Bay, a small, protected anchorage at the mouth of the Charlotte Harbor. Tarpon rolled, and a pod of porpoises crisscrossed in front of the catamaran, rolling on their sides and looking up at Clara. Pelicans dove on a large school of thread herring that was chased to the surface.

A small isthmus separated the entrance to Pelican Bay from the estuary, a perfect place for Neil to slide the cat up onto the beach for the evening. He grabbed his cast net, as he did most evenings, to catch their meal. He saw plenty of mullet jumping, then a redfish just off shore.

He was cleaning a large fish when an elderly couple holding hands approached. Clara Bell's welcoming smile stopped them in their tracks.

"She's just smiling at you," Neil said. "That's the way she grins."

"That's a scary grin."

"Trust me. She's happy to see you. She won't bother you."

"That's a nice dog. Sweet puppy."

The couple petted Clara, and she wiggled before running in circles, kicking up sand.

"That's a beautiful fish," one of them said.

"Would you like half? There's more than enough for us."

"Oh, we would love some fresh fish. Unfortunately, I haven't been able to catch any. Are you day sailing in the Hobie?"

"One day at a time. We left Dauphin Island, Alabama, three months ago."

The couple looked at each other in amazement.

"Three months?" the woman asked. "My God. How can you stand the bugs and no shower? You must come aboard. We'll cook on our boat tonight."

"You can take a hot shower," the man added, "and we have cold beer and ice."

"It's terribly kind of you," Neil said, "but I have Clara."

"Nonsense," the woman said. "You bring the fish and her along. She's lovely, and dogs are welcome on our boat. This is our last trip out, and we miss having a dog aboard."

"Is your boat secure for the night?" the man asked. "Where are my manners? This is my wife of fifty years, Betty, and I'm Fred Miller, originally from Calvert Cliffs in southern Maryland."

"My name's Neil Tinner, from Alabama, and this, of course, is Clara Bell. My pleasure. The little cat will sit just fine here on the hook."

"Good enough. Let's dinghy off before the mosquitoes come out," he said. "I feel a cocktail coming close."

"Neil, you must excuse my husband. If he had his way, there would always be a cocktail very close. He always has a glass in his hand."

"Now, Betty, that's not true, and you know it. I only drink when we have company or we're alone." He laughed, and Betty gave a half-approving grin.

Once all were in the dinghy, Neil told Clara to load, and they pushed off. The little Johnson outboard started on the first pull, and they motored out to an Irwin 42. Neil saw the name *Sally Jo, El Jobean, Florida,* on the transom.

Fred offered Neil a hot shower, cold beer, and a comfortable cockpit. *Sally Jo* was set up for Bahamas cruising. She was a shallow-draft ketch, comfortable and forgiving, and the hull was almost bulletproof.

Betty made a fresh salad, black beans, and rice, while Neil and Fred grilled the fish with onions, peppers, and Old Bay seasoning. That was Neil's favorite way to cook redfish after eating it on St. George's Island with Cope, Jack, and Dennis. He thought about Jack and Dennis a lot, hoping they survived.

The evening was a delightful change from Neil's Spartan lifestyle. They sat in the cockpit listening to Dorsey, Miller, and other Big Band greats after watching the sunset.

"You get lonely?" Betty asked.

"No. I have my girl." Neil patted Clara, stroking her head.

"Aren't you afraid of being alone, in case something happens, like you get injured or sick?"

"Not really. This is a pretty hospitable environment compared to some places."

"Like a jungle in Southeast Asia?"

"Exactly like that, Fred."

"Probably like what I saw on Guadalcanal and the rest of those godforsaken islands fighting the damn Japs."

"Please, Fred, not tonight. Let's not talk about the war. It's such a beautiful evening."

"You're right. You aren't leaving tomorrow, are you, Neil?"

"No, Sir. I don't really have a firm schedule."

"Wonderful! Fred and I can take you and Clara exploring," Betty said. "We've been coming here for years. We know this area like the backs of our hands, and love sharing with first-timers."

"Sounds great. We'd love it. There's nothing better than having someone who knows show you around. I like what I've seen so far. There's a lot of sea life."

Fred went into the salon to play his favorite Glenn Miller tape.

"We'll take you to the manatee hole, through Lover's Lane to the Gulf. It's absolutely enchanting," Betty said.

Neil nodded, his foot tapping uncontrollably to the Big Band tunes. Clara was on a cockpit cushion with her head in his lap. Fred and Betty sat close, still deeply in love after fifty years.

They sipped wine, watching the stars. Lightning flashed in the distance over the Gulf, and muffled thunder clapped an afterthought. Neil admired the couple and wondered how much tribulation they survived. He thought about what Fred had endured in the South Pacific. It was inspiring to think about a man surviving such horrors and still having a loving relationship with a woman. Maybe there was hope.

Thinking about Jack and Dennis, he wondered what they were doing.

13. Double Trouble

Jack pulled into a Mom-and-Pop place beside an old Volvo wagon that looked like it was never washed. Bumper stickers covered the bumper, and they were covered in so much dust, he couldn't read most of them. One that was wiped clean read *Hay Duke Lives.*

Jack wondered who the hell Hay Duke was. The rest of the parking lot was full of work trucks and crummies.

Entering from the bright sunlight, Jack was momentarily blind in the dark restaurant.

"Otter, you got a haircut!" a loud, frail voice called.

Jack knew he was in the right place. Squinting, he looked for the source of the voice.

Nick called again, and Jack walked to the old man sitting alone at a table.

"Sir, I'm not Otter."

"Well, you sure as hell look like him. You answered when I called."

"I'm his younger brother."

"Well, you look enough like him. No milkman can lay a

claim to you." He laughed. "Sit and share dinner with me, Son. What would your name be?"

"Jack Copeland."

They shook hands, and Jack sat at the table.

"I've come on some urgent family business."

"You still have to eat, don't you? The cheeseburgers here are the best in the country. Draft beer is only fifty cents at lunch. You can't beat it. The crowd can get a little rowdy, but they never bother an old salt like me."

It was a large dinner crowd of loggers, miners, contractors, ranchers, and, more recently, surveyors for the Army Corps of Engineers. Jack felt he would fit right in, though his brother not so much.

Jack ate while Nick gave him an overview of the local politics, resource management, renewable resources, gold mining, water management, the dam, and the efforts to preserve the Stanislaus River. Being an anthropologist gave Nick an interesting perspective on the situation. He understood the value of tourism and the value of rafting a river that had been used by man for thousands of years. He also understood the conflict that would arise when people perceived their livelihoods were being challenged.

A different conversation occurred on the other side of the room. A well-dressed man bought drinks for a group of men in working clothes, getting them worked up about the long-haired hippie communist tree huggers, dopers, and rafters trying to block flooding of the Stanislaus Valley. It would take food off their tables and water from their farms and cattle.

It reminded Jack of a scene in a Western, when the locals get fired up and form a lynch mob. He felt trouble brewing.

He finished one of the best cheeseburgers he ever ate and washed down the last of his French fries with a final swallow of beer. Jack insisted on paying the tab and he left the restaurant with Nick.

He wasn't surprised to see Nick drove the old Volvo. Jack decided to read the rest of the bumper stickers and wiped dust off them. *We the unwilling, led by the incapable, are doing the impossible for the ungrateful.*

The next was, *Nuke the gay unborn communist whales.*

Jack laughed at that one. "Who the hell is Hay Duke, anyway?"

"Jack, you'll have to read the book, *The Monkey-Wrench Gang*. Don't let it go to your head." The old man laughed as they parted ways.

Jack followed the directions to the rafting company office. Ferguson, the owner, immediately saw the resemblance to Otter. He gave Jack a map to the takeout point where the old bus was parked. Jack would have to wait a few hours for Otter and his party to arrive.

Jack followed the map down a winding dirt road that paralleled the river, which twisted below like a snake. Jack gunned the engine when he crossed small creeks and threw water over the roof and out thirty feet on both sides. Smiling, he thought about his brother's face when he would see him.

Jack was having fun. He loved driving his Land Cruiser in a new, wild, and beautiful place. The trail finally ended abruptly at the water's edge. An old, round-nosed bus sat parked by the trees.

He saw a gravel beach and turnaround space for several other vehicles. Jack parked beside the bus under a big oak and removed his boots and shorts to go swimming. Tadpole was a fitting name for him. He was at home floating and swimming underwater for long periods of time. Studying the river with a trained prospector's eye, he knew where the gold would be. Fanning was done by waving a hand beside the silt and exposing the gold deposited by the rushing waters.

He spent several hours fanning until he was thoroughly chilled, then he unrolled a sleeping bag and fell sound asleep in the warm sun.

The sound of a truck approaching on the gravel woke him. He recognized the truck from the restaurant. The crew cab and bed were full of people. It seemed the mob had arrived, complete with a keg of beer.

When the truck stopped, Jack pulled his hat over his eyes and decided to play possum, but it didn't work.

"What do we have here?" Billy asked. "It must be Rip van Winkle."

The others laughed wildly.

"No, no. It's the boy we saw with the old faggot who drives a vulva."

Another chorus of laughs erupted.

"Wait!" Billy said. "I thought a vulva was a pussy. Why would a fag have a pussy? Faggots don't like pussy, they like ass. Ain't that right, Boy? Hey, Boy! Rip van fucking Winkle, I'm talking to you."

Jack got up and took his boots from the Land Cruiser,

ignoring the drunks. They yelled a few more insults, as he put on his boots. There was nothing worse than trouble in bare feet.

The older man who drove watched Jack carefully and noticed his jungle boots, short hair, deep tan, and a wrestler's muscles. He had the quiet, resolute motions of a man who was confident, not someone to mess with. He knew that from experience.

Unfortunately, Billy had no such experience and continued his endless baiting. "How about you, Rip? Are you the old fag's new boy?"

"Better leave him alone, Billy," the driver said. "He looks like a veteran to me."

"Maybe he just stole them boots and got a haircut in jail after being caught in a rest area sucking off truckers."

They all laughed except the old man.

Jack seethed on the inside, but on the outside he remained calm. "No, Boys, you don't know me. I'm just passing some time here and don't want any trouble. I will tell you, though, that I am a veteran and not a homosexual. What I do know about them is that it takes one to know one."

Billy's audience was confused at first, then they laughed at Billy.

"Hey, fuck you, Rip Van Winkle!" Billy replied.

Jack waved and lay back on his sleeping bag with his boots on. He knew the odds would soon change dramatically. The mob would be drunker, and things might get ugly. Jack hoped they left before his brother arrived, but his gut was in a knot, like he sensed there would soon be trouble.

He got up after a few minutes and put his bag in the back

of the Land Cruiser. He had his .22 pistol, but he didn't want to use it. He settled on an aluminum pipe he used as a cheater for his four-way lug wrench. It could cause lethal injury, but, if it was needed, it was better than shooting someone.

Billy and the mob greeted the group of rafters who passed with rude gestures and insults. They pulled down their pants and exposed themselves to the girls and invited them to drink beer and fuck. The situation was getting ruder and uglier, and they completely forgot about Jack in the back of his cruiser.

Thankfully, the raft continued downstream without further incident. The out-of-control surveyors were still laughing when Steelhead came into view with three teenage girls on his raft. The girls were immediately worried. They knew what it was like to dance with drunk jocks at frat houses, but the men on shore were older, in their twenties, and the girls were frightened. Steelhead jumped into the water ten feet from shore and dragged the raft by its bowline.

Billy rushed Steelhead, as he tried to climb the bank. Instead of being shoved backward, Steelhead sidestepped and jerked Billy's arm, sending him head-first into the water. He held onto the man's wrist and put his knee and all his strength into Billy's back, pinning him underwater.

Seeing Billy in trouble, four of his friends joined in to free him. Steelhead landed a few punches and took out a few of the men before he was overwhelmed. One got him in a choke hold, and two men held his arms, while he kicked at the other two.

Elliott dived off the bow of his raft, toppling Steelhead and the three men holding him. Getting to his feet, he struck the nearest assailant with his palm, driving his head violently back and spreading his nose like a ripe tomato. He clutched his face and fell into the water, bleeding.

It was close-quarters combat in waist-deep water. Elliott caught a feeble blow to the head and returned the favor with a devastating elbow to the temple that ended that man's part in the fight.

The next surveyor to fall received a flurry of blows to the head and quickly retreated. Steelhead caught Billy as he tried to climb away and escape up the bank. He rolled, trying to kick Steelhead, but he caught the man's leg by his boot and rotated it until it snapped.

Two more watching from the bank dove on Steelhead, knocking him off Billy. Otter moved toward him when the older man fired his shotgun into the air. He hadn't seen Jack slip up behind him.

The man in the suit, who'd been buying the others drinks at the bar, pulled out a 1911 .45 pistol. Jack's pipe crashed down on the older man's arm and snapped it like a pretzel. A second blow to the head laid him out. Jack snatched the shotgun before it touched the ground, chambered a round, and took aim at the man with the pistol.

"Drop the pistol, Asshole.

"I'm an officer in the U.S. Army, and you're under arrest," the man said, though his lips trembled, and fear showed in his eyes. There was nothing more harrowing than staring down the barrel of a shotgun.

Jack walked toward him, the 12-gauge aimed at his head. When Jack was two feet away, the man finally lowered the pistol.

He was rewarded by the shotgun butt striking his mouth. Teeth cracked, and he wailed in pain.

The last two men immediately raised their hands, nearly crying in fear.

"You'd better get those guys out of the water before they drown," Jack told them. "Hurry up before I change my mind and shoot all of you. Load them in the truck, then get in with them. Move!"

Jack smiled at his big brother. The look on his face was better than anticipated. Steelhead grabbed the bowlines and dragged the rafts to the bank. The five girls from the charter were aghast.

Elliott didn't speak, as Jack slid the .45 into his waistband and shot out the truck's front tire with the shotgun.

"That'll slow you down a bit," Jack said, "just in case you decide to cause more trouble. Whoever isn't hurt can change the tire after we leave and drive to the hospital. The next time you decide to have some fun, you should find a better way to do it.

"You." He looked at the older man. "If you are really an Army officer, you're a disgrace to the uniform."

He turned. "What about you, Billy Bigmouth? You aren't so tough any more, are you? You're lucky I didn't get my hands on you."

Jack stood guard with the shotgun, while Steelhead and his brother loaded the girls and rafts into the bus. A truck approached from a distance.

Ferguson, the owner of the rafting company, pulled up, hoping to witness the family reunion between Otter and Jack. He took one look at the situation and got slowly out of his truck with his hands in the air.

"What the hell's going on here? My God. These men are

hurt bad. They need to go to the hospital. Who did this? How did this happen?"

"Hey, Ferg, these drunk idiots attacked us for no reason when we got to the pullout. The keg of beer in the back of the truck might be a clue."

The Army engineer couldn't speak, but the older man with a broken arm and a knot on his head said, "These no-good river rats are felons. They assaulted a federal officer with a firearm while he was performing his duties. We're surveyors on official government business, and these boys jumped us. Tried to kill us."

"That's a bald-faced lie!" one girl shouted. "They attacked us for no reason and damn well got what they deserved. Otter and Steelhead kicked their butts, and then those two pulled out guns and started shooting. That's when the guy over there," she nodded at Jack, "showed up and took their guns away. Thank God! They might've shot us all. They're drunk out of their minds."

"That's a bunch of bull! We've got eight men who'll swear to that. Besides, who will you believe, a bunch of hippies or Major Carol of the U.S. Army Corps of Engineers? His word is as good as that of a cop. You river rats have done it this time. You'll go to jail until hell freezes over.

"See, boys, I know the law in these parts, and my uncle's a judge. You know how they feel about you drugged-up hippies running naked and spouting Mao Say-Tongue and Malcolm X. You just wait till I get to the sheriff's office. He'll be on you boys like stink on shit. There won't be a hole in this country big enough to hide in."

Ferg looked at Steelhead. "You'd better take your group to

the office. I'll meet you there. It doesn't look like we'll settle anything here. I'll meet you back there as soon as I can. I'll make sure these guys get out of here. It's obvious what happened."

Jack led the way in the Land Cruiser, so he wouldn't have to eat dust from the bus. The ride out wasn't nearly as much fun as the one in. He'd been through almost constant trouble. First, it was at the airport, then the bushwhackers, and now the unfortunate reunion with Elliott. He wondered why he kept getting into such terrible situations. He didn't know if he should go to the law or get the hell out of town. There was nothing he could do until he was back at the office and gathered his brother. That was the reason he came, after all.

He drove carefully out the dirt road along the river, keeping the bus in sight behind him. When they came to the first hard-surface road, he stopped and unlocked his hubs. Elliott got out of the bus and climbed into the Land Cruiser with his brother.

"Wow, this is a great rig. It was a great time for you to show up, too. Good to see you, Brother. I never expected seeing you today. I thought you were in Vietnam by now."

"That's a long story. I was medically disqualified."

"You look pretty good to me. We could be in a lot of trouble. That old man was telling the truth about how the establishment feels about us. They look for any opportunity to hassle us. This place is beautiful, but there's a war about to erupt here. There's a lot of money riding on building a new dam, and there's a lot of people who want to save the river. That battle today was just the beginning. We might just be some of the early victims.

"The guide I was with, Steelhead, says there's no way we'll get justice. The whole county government, including the law, is behind the dam. We're just an obstacle. He thinks the only way out is to run like hell. He's loading his car and planning to head to the Florida Keys."

"Man, you just said a mouthful. How the hell are you? You've got Dad worried half to death. He was afraid you'd gotten hooked on dope and lost your mind. Anyway, back to what's going on here. Do you think Steelhead's right?"

"He's been here a long time, and he knows what's going on. I want to clear out my gear and get the hell out of Dodge. The Florida Keys sound pretty great to me. He invited me to come down and go treasure hunting in the ocean, looking for Spanish galleons and pirate ships. It couldn't be any worse than the frigid waters of the Trinity and tumbling rocks."

"Elliott, there's been a lot of trouble you don't know about yet. The two people I consider taking advice from are Dad and Rabbit. I don't know Steelhead, but I'm not saying he's wrong. We'll get your gear and find a safe place to call Dad. Do you know anywhere we can hide?"

"I think so. There's an old man named Nick who gave me a ride into town when I was hitchhiking. He'll help for sure. Steelhead knows him. He's a legend around here."

"Does he look like Santa Claus and drive an old Volvo wagon? I met him in a restaurant on my way to town. He told me where you were. I liked him. He definitely knows his shit."

"All right. Let's get my gear."

When they got back, Steelhead was right behind them. He started loading his gear into a little Japanese pickup. He wasn't waiting for Ferguson to return, and neither was Otter.

In less than thirty minutes, they were leaving. Steelhead drove toward the Florida Keys, while Jack and Elliott were going to Nick's. It wasn't easy to find. After several wrong turns, they eventually found the low-water bridge marking the beginning of Nick's driveway.

Genuinely happy to see them, he greeted them with a big smile.

"Well, I'll be John Brown. If it isn't the twins. How the Sam hell did you find this place? No one comes here by accident, so there must be a reason. Is the world coming to an end and you came to tell me about it?" He laughed.

When Jack and Elliott recounted the battle at the take-out, Nick thought it was a grand story. He thoroughly appreciated the fact that the bullies were put in their place by some good citizens, namely Jack and Elliott. In his view, it was his civic duty to protect them and assist them in evading any possible actions by what he considered a corrupt local government.

He agreed with Jack that their first step should be to call their father and apprise him of the situation. They hid the Land Cruiser behind the barn at the back of the property. Elliott stayed behind and waited while Jack went with Nick to use a telephone in a secure location. Nick said they could use the phone of an activist who thought the Monkey Wrench Gang was the New Testament. Jack was able to use the phone in private.

"Dad? Can you hear me?"

"Yes, Son. I can hear you. How are things going?"

"The good news is, I found Elliott, and we're together. The bad news is, I don't know if we should come home quite yet."

"What on earth is going on?"

"Unfortunately, there's been a little trouble. We need your guidance. I don't know what to do."

"OK, Jack. Let's do this the way we always do, one step at a time. Exactly what happened?"

"I found Elliott's workplace, and they told me where to meet him at the raft takeout point. I was waiting there when a truckload of drunks arrived with a keg of beer. It wasn't the first time I saw them.

"I stopped at a little restaurant for lunch and saw a guy in a suit buying them drinks and getting them all riled up about people who were protesting building a dam. He looked a little older, probably forty, and something about the situation struck me as odd.

"They harassed me at the takeout point and tried to pick a fight, but I ignored them. Nine to one wasn't good odds. The drunker they got, the worse they were. They exposed themselves to girls in rafts and hurled insults. When Elliott and the other guide showed up with a load of clients, the men started a fight. Big brother is still lean and mean. He and his partner really put it to them.

"Then the old man in the group pulled out a shotgun and fired it into the air. The other guy, an Army engineer, drew his .45. I broke the shotgunner's arm and laid open his head with my cheater bar, then I took his shotgun and leveled it at the pistoleer to disarm him.

"I busted his mouth for his trouble. Maybe that was a mistake, but he sure had it coming. I loaded them all into the back of their truck at gunpoint and flattened one of their tires. The two who weren't hurt in the fight would be able to change the tire and get to a hospital before too long.

"All in all, they weren't hurt too bad for what they did, threatening deadly force on innocent civilians."

"Jack, if the other men started the fight, and you have the rafting customers as witnesses, it seems like a clear case of self-defense. You should immediately go to the local police and report the incident, so those men will be arrested. Is there something you aren't telling me?"

"The local authorities are behind the dam. They don't like the rafters and love the Corps of Engineers. A lot of prominent citizens stand to make a fortune not only on the dam construction but in selling their land. Apparently, justice in this environment doesn't have much chance. The one whose arm I broke says his uncle's the judge, and we're all going to jail."

"I see your point. Where are you now?"

"I think we're OK for the moment, but they might be looking for us already. I have my Land Cruiser hidden behind Nick's barn. He said we could hide with him until I talk to you and we had a plan of action."

"Sounds like you're caught up in a bad situation. I believe you did the right thing. We'll get this taken care of. Do you have the names of any of the men involved?"

"Yeah. The guy I think is the engineer is called Major Carol. He's the asshole with a busted mouth. Other than that, we don't know any names except for Billy. They're all supposedly part of a surveying crew. I assume they're working for Major Carol on the dam project."

"You boys sit tight. They won't search door-to-door,

especially in a rural environment. If you stay put, there's little chance they'll find you. They would expect you to run, so they'll cover all the exits from town.

"I'll set up a phone conversation through Nick in the next couple hours. I know you boys will watch out for each other. Let me talk to Nick."

"Hello?" Nick asked. "This must be the twins' pappy."

"Hello, Nick. I can't tell you how much I appreciate what you're doing for my sons."

"I can't tell you how much I appreciate what they've done for the community. I could tell they were good boys the first time I met them. You should be proud of the way they conducted themselves."

"I only wish the local authorities felt the same way. I'm led to believe there's no chance of a fair shake for them?"

"No, Sir. They don't have a snowball's chance in hell of a fair shake. If they turned themselves in, there's no telling if they'd live through the night."

"I need to make some inquiries on my end. Is there a number where I can reach you at a specific time? I could probably make some headway in a couple hours. Could I call you at six? By the way, Nick, my name's John Copeland."

"That sounds good, John Copeland. I'll be at this number at six PM—916-623-1848. I'll feed the boys and keep them safe. I'll come back alone, so we don't risk their being seen. I'll put Jack back on now."

Jack took the receiver.

"OK, Jack," Cope said. "It's all set. You boys hang tight. I'll call back at six. Nick will take the call and relay all messages. Do you trust him?"

"Yes. All is good. I love you, and thank you. Sorry about the mess. Check out Carol. I know he's bad."

The call ended, and Nick drove them back to his place. Jack lay in the back seat in case they passed a sheriff during the ten-minute ride back to Nick's house.

Cope called Randy, who said he'd come over in twenty minutes, then he called the Trinity County sheriff for information. The sheriff gave him bad news.

"If your boys crossed the wrong people," the sheriff said, "they might never leave the county. Do whatever is necessary to get them out safe and worry about the repercussions later."

Worried, Cope hung up. When Randy arrived, Cope said, "Glad you're here, Rabbit. The boys are in trouble down south. We might need to mount a rescue mission."

"I already heard about it."

"What? How? I just heard about it."

"My CID buddy from Vietnam called me after I spoke with you."

"That doesn't sound good."

"Hear me out. It seems there's a Major Carol down there who's been under investigation for being a little too friendly with the local business and contracting community in Calaveras County. He's suspected of taking bribes, corruption, ethics violations, and lots of unsavory personal behavior. Apparently, the boys who had him under surveillance said he was a real mess at the hospital. He got his front teeth knocked out by the butt of a twelve-gauge shotgun. They thought it was comical, the guy's a real piece of shit."

"That throws a little more light on the subject. What about my boys? I don't want them in jail."

"The CID boys got a copy of the police report and said it was a laughable fabrication. Major Carol said they were on a surveying operation when they were attacked by three drug-crazed hippies and beat up at gunpoint. The local sheriff put out an APB on a green Jeep, no tag number."

"What does CID want?"

"Officially, they'll launch an investigation of an alleged assault. Unofficially, they want the boys to stay unreachable. They want Carol to continue his corrupt ways, albeit without any teeth for a while. They plan to call you here soon. I'd try to get a little witness-protection money or some help from them. Maybe a vacation in Cabo San Lucas or something. Anyway, I hope this is good news. It seems the boys were dealing with a real piece of shit."

"You know the asshole pulled a .45 on them? He could have shot one of my boys. This guy's a loose cannon. I hope they put him away for a long time."

Cope stretched the phone cord out until the phone was near the front door, then he sat on the steps. Bear walked over and lay beside him with his head in Cope's lap.

"You seem to know exactly how I feel, ol' buddy," Cope said.

"That dog's smarter than most people," Rabbit said.

"I think you're right. If more people acted like dogs, the world would be a better place, or at least a lot simpler. I wonder what the boys from criminal investigation will say."

"I don't know. It seems to me that your boys are witnesses to a lot of crimes. When you think about it, they should probably be in witness protection. They don't want to spoil the investigation of a major corruption and conspiracy case for a simple assault. They'll probably want to keep that as their ace in the hole and keep trying to catch the bigger fish."

The phone rang.

"Hello, John Copeland here. Hello, Neil. This is a surprise. I was expecting another call. No, not really. Hopefully, it won't be too bad. My boys got in a little conflict. I'm trying to figure out how to get them out of harm's way. No, he didn't go. He got a medical discharge after we had a bad car accident on the way back to Fort Rucker. He's all right, but he's not fit for the Army. Dennis didn't get hurt. I haven't heard from him in a while. What about you and Clara? Where are you?"

"I found my boat," Neil said. "I met a wonderful older couple who were getting ready to sell their boat. Clara and I feel like we died and went to heaven. She's a beautiful Irwin Ketch with a shoal draft, perfect for cruising Florida and the Bahamas. I was eating redfish with peppers and onions the other night and thought about you guys, though I assumed Dennis and Jack were in Vietnam."

"Neil, I'm really waiting for an important call from CID. Have you thought about a crew for your boat? Really? There might be a solution that would work for all of us. OK, then. Call me back in a couple hours. You may have your crew coming in from California. No, I'm not kidding. All right. Until then, take care. Good to hear from you."

Cope hung up. "Just when you don't know what to do, a solution appears. It's amazing."

"I heard only one side of that, but it sounded like our boys might be going sailing."

"I just hope the brass at CID will go along. I'm not sure Jack wants to leave Katie right now, either. It would be better if she finished her senior year without a distraction. Maybe it'll give the two time to mature and think over their marriage."

The phone rang again.

"Hello, Copeland here. Yes, Chief, how could I forget you? You snored all night long. That's true. It could've been any one of you. Yes, Randy and I have discussed the options and think we may have an idea. How would you feel about your witnesses relocating to Florida until they're needed? I don't know anything about the legal conditions. You'd have to take that up with your JAG officer.

"I'm doing everything in my power to get them out of there as soon as possible. I assume you can accomplish the administrative necessities, and we can move forward. Yes, of course. I know there's only one God.

"One thing—correction, two. Could you escort the boys out of the county, and do you have any cash? Great. Discreetly get directions to the home of Nick, a well-known older gentleman who lives in a remote cabin outside Angels Camp. Perfect. I'll look for a call from you. Thanks, Chief."

As he hung up, Rabbit nodded.

"It sounded like that conversation went pretty well," Rabbit said. "I wish we could go to Florida when the ground freezes around here."

"Hell, Randy. It's almost six o'clock. My throat's dry from all this talking, not to mention my brain. I'm going to have a whiskey. How about you?"

Nick called back exactly at 1800 hours.

"Copeland, here. Hello, Nick. Good to hear that. Yes, I have news. An escort will arrive at your house after dark. The car will flash its lights three times. The boys are to accept whatever cash they hand over, follow them across the county line, and not stop driving until they're out of California. They can't do anything that might get them pulled over. They should call me from the first pay phone they find in Nevada. Have you got all that?"

"Let's see. The escort car will blink its lights three times, the boys get some money and follow the car across the county line. They're to call you as soon as they're in Nevada. Is that about it? Yeah, I know. Not bad for an old man. I will, John Copeland, and you, too.

"When this mess is sorted out, we have to sit down and chew the fat sometime. Sure enough. I might take you up on that. I'll surely send them your love and Godspeed. Good-bye, Sir."

Nick hung up, repeating the instructions to himself, then wrote them down. He hadn't had that much excitement in years. He felt like he was doing something truly important.

Cope's phone rang again.

"Copeland, here. Yes, Chief? That's good news. They'll be waiting for you and will expect you to flash your lights three times. Hand them some cash and guide them out of Calaveras County and aimed toward Nevada.

"That's a real good idea, Chief. I like it. I don't have a way to reach the boys right now. You'll have to convince them that's the new plan. If you tell Jack that you're Running Rabbit's friend, he'll trust you.

"This is terrific and much safer, especially if they've got the state police looking for the boys. Good deal. You must have a really good JAG officer. You have a safe night, too. Oh, yes. Please call me as soon as the boys are on their way."

He hung up with a smile.

"What did Chief Graham say?" Rabbit asked.

"Now I know why you're good friends with that man. He rented a bobtail truck with ramps. They'll load the Land Cruiser and the boys to take them across the county line. They'll give them $1,000 and instructions to check in when they reach a phone.

"If everything goes as planned, we'll hear from them when they're in Nevada. All we can do now is wait for the next phone call. Neil will call back soon.

"What do you think, Bear? Did we do all right?"

Bear barked twice, nearly knocking Cope over with a head butt to his chest and a big lick that started at his neck and ended at one ear. Cope grabbed the dog's big head in both hands and shook it playfully side-to-side. Bear let his skull roll in the loose skin, playfully nipping at Cope's hands.

"You know something, Buddy, I met a little yellow Labrador retriever named Clara. She might be just what you want in a girlfriend. I always loved the smell of puppies."

"I know what you mean, Cope," Rabbit said. "It's like the smell of fresh bread out of the oven or chocolate chip cookies and of course, we can't forget cordite."

"You're such a hopeless romantic."

When the phone rang again, it was Neil. Cope wanted to establish a rendezvous between Neil and his sons without giving away too much on the phone.

"I'll have the boys go to that place you told us about when we met," Cope said. "Could you coordinate with your folks and leave instructions for a rendezvous?"

"I understand. This line isn't secure. Enough said. I'll call back in a few days to see what's developed."

14. Killers Come and They Go

Nick, thanking his young friend for letting him use his phone, walked toward his old Volvo. He wasn't a suspicious man, but he was observant. In general, he listened to the little voice in his head that told him something wasn't quite right.

A white van crossed Nick's path at the end of the driveway. The fact that he'd never seen it before didn't arouse his suspicion, but the ladder on a rack on top made his hair stand on end. Nick feared his conversation with Cope was compromised. What if the ladder was used to access and tap the phone line he just used? He needed a plan fast.

Luckily, he made plans for such an emergency. When he got to his house, he found the boys talking on the porch. He had a lot to tell them.

"Boys, I've got news, but let's go inside to discuss it." Nick preceded them into the house with a sense of urgency. The boys, noticing his odd demeanor, looked at each other quizzically, as they followed him into the rustic cabin.

"Otter, Jack, we have a problem. Your father arranged for an escort to come here after dark. The escort was to give you cash and escort you out of state. Unfortunately, I have the feeling the call was tapped. I don't have any hard evidence, but I saw a suspicious vehicle with a ladder, and it made me think.

"Let's assume the worst, that the sheriff or those he works for, which could be worse, are coming. They won't be here to discuss anything or take anyone to jail. You could cause them big trouble. We need to get you two out of here as fast as we can. Grab whatever gear you brought to the house, and let's head to the barn."

The Cuban missile crisis and the movie *Seven Days in May* weighed heavily on Nick's survival instincts. It made sense to him to prepare for a nuclear holocaust, so he had plenty of supplies on hand.

They filled the Land Cruiser's fuel tank and three five-gallon jerry cans from the ranch tank, along with ten gallons of water from Nick's cistern. He told the boys to wait near the Land Cruiser while he went to his hidden bunker under the barn.

He also had a few surprises for them. He knew they had a .45 and shotgun, but neither had the range for the open country they had to travel through to reach Nevada.

He handed Jack a new M1 Garand rifle, an ammo can from the Springfield Arsenal with 1,000 rounds of .30 caliber ammunition, and a case of C rations. Otter received an Army map case complete with maps and Lensatic compass. Nick had already highlighted an escape route through the Sierra Mountains for emergency evacuation.

Jack held the rifle with an awed expression.

"You look like a pig trying to read a wristwatch," Nick said. "Haven't you ever seen a rifle like that?"

"Yes, Sir. This is a U.S. rifle, thirty-caliber M1. It's a clip-fed, gas-operated, air-cooled, semiautomatic shoulder weapon, the first semiautomatic rifle produced by any country and the only semiautomatic rifle in World War Two. According to historians, it gave U.S. forces a huge advantage over the Axis forces."

Snapping to attention, he took the rifle to order arms. Otter repeated the orders for manual arms he learned from his father with his M1 when they were barely big enough to lift the weapons.

"Present arms. Inspection arms. Order arms. Right shoulder arms. Present arms. Order arms."

Jack stood at attention with the fore stock in his right hand and the butt against his right foot. Otter smiled in pride at his brother's performance—and the fact that he remembered the orders.

"I'm proud that John C. Garand's contribution to the modern world is appreciated by another generation of Americans," Nick said. "Hallelujah! We need to keep moving. There's a box of twelve-gauge buckshot and fifty rounds of .45 ammo, too. The course on the map starts at the back of the barn and goes through the hills to the east. It's been a while since I took it, so you'll have to be careful. Go slow and always scout water crossings before you try to ford. You'll need every bit of your four-wheel-drive that Toyota can give you."

Otter laid the map on the Land Cruiser's hood, oriented it with the compass, and studied their path. Jack slid under the Land Cruiser to see if anything was amiss, checking all the fluid levels and the air pressure in the spare tire. They would have to be completely self-sufficient. There was no help where they were going.

Rough terrain wasn't new to the Copelands. They'd been

on many high-country expeditions with their father in the Willys utility wagon. The fuel and water cans were tied down between the rear wheel wells. The rifle and shotgun were sandwiched in the folded jump seats on either side of the back. A wooden footlocker behind the fuel cans contained a toolbox, come along, entrenching tool, bow saw, hatchet, logging chain, and a twenty-foot tow-strap. Elliott's backpack lay across the top of the footlocker, with Jack's small day pack beside it.

"I wish I was forty years younger," Nick said. "I'd go with you. Try to go slow enough that you don't kick up a bunch of dust. It looks like you have everything you need, so you'd better get going before we have company. I hope you boys realize how serious the threat is. If they send men after you, it won't be to talk or take you to jail. They'll want you to become permanently quiet. The trail out of here is dangerous, but it's also your friend. Be wise and treat it with respect. You don't want to end up like the Donner party."

"How can we ever repay you?" Otter extended his hand.

Nick grabbed the boys in successive bear hugs. "Tell you what you can do. Get across the Sierra Nevadas and call your dad. I'll let him know the plans have changed. Remember, loose lips sink ships. Don't give away your location or plans by phone. There are plenty of powerful people here, with plenty of assets and capabilities. Don't underestimate what they are willing and capable of doing. There's too much money at stake. Now get that damn Japanese contraption over the mountains before it's too late."

They got into the Land Cruiser and started the engine. Elliott would be navigator while Jack drove. They'd gone only ten minutes and were over the first foothill out of sight of Nick's place when Jack stopped and looked at his brother.

"We can't leave Nick there alone."

"I know," Otter said. "If they're as dangerous as he says, he's in real danger. Any harm that came to him would be our fault. Besides, this is our fight, not his."

Jack opened the driver door, went to the rear of the Land Cruiser, and swung the spare tire aside to open the cargo doors. He unlatched the ammo can and handed Otter a bandolier with ten eight-round clips for the M1, then he loaded his pockets with as many shotgun shells as he could carry. Unzipping his backpack, he took out the shoulder holster with his .22 pistol.

Otter adjusted the sling on the M1, opened the breech, and loaded eight rounds of .30-06 military ball ammunition. Jack could get only one more round in the twelve-gauge pump without putting one in the chamber.

With his binoculars around his neck, Otter turned toward Nick's place. The house and barn were in a draw between two hills, a flat the size of two football fields. The driveway was a mile long, off a rural gravel county road. It stopped at the front porch, with the barn at the base of the hill on the other side of the flat.

Jack and Otter approached to twenty-five yards of the barn under a large live oak, where they were protected by a pile of fieldstone.

Nick was in the hay loft of the barn with a model 70 Winchester .30-06. He lay comfortably, watching the approach to the house through a 3 x 9 Leopold scope. It reminded him of lying on the beach at Iwo Jima, though he wished his eyes were still as good as they were then, so he could use his M1 instead of the Winchester.

The white van he saw earlier stopped short of the house in the driveway, a Chevy crew cab pickup following. Four men got out of the pickup carrying long guns and walked to the back of the Chevy. One man remained in the driver's seat, and one emerged from the passenger seat.

Two more men with long guns emerged from the side door. The six men spread out across the front of the house, while the man from the passenger seat approached Nick's porch.

Otter watched, as the man apparently yelled something. He knocked on the door, then he went to the Volvo, raised the hood and jerked out a wire between the distributor and coil. He gave a hand signal to the others, and they opened fire on the house with automatic weapons.

Nick's first shot went through the grill and radiator of the white van, shattering the water pump. The second shot went through the Chevy's grill and radiator.

The leader of the group, seeing the muzzle flash from the barn, pointed, signaling the men where to fire. Nick's third shot went through the sternum of the nearest approaching rifleman. The bullet entered the man's body and exited through the spinal column, killing him instantly.

Otter's first round landed short, so he raised the rear aperture six clicks, aimed at the center of mass, gut-shooting him between the hips, leaving him paralyzed. Jack ran down the hill and took a position behind the barn with his shotgun.

Nick moved to a secondary firing position on the other side of the loft and reloaded the Winchester. The approaching men took cover on the edge of the field among the oak trees. Nick waited patiently.

One of the men peeked from behind a tree. Like squirrel hunting, Nick took a deep breath and exhaled slowly before gently squeezing the trigger. The bullet entered the man's head in front of his left ear and exited like a softball, leaving the tree covered in blood and brains.

There were three down and five to go. The leader and his two remaining riflemen retreated to the back of the van. Encouraged by the leader's Uzi in his face, the driver got behind the wheel and drove directly toward the barn.

The fourth round Nick fired was the last experience the driver had. The van continued rolling until it struck the rock wall 20 feet in front of the barn.

Jack went to the far corner and Elliott to the other. The two brothers covered both sides and the rear of the barn.

The leader and one rifleman entered through the double doors in the front, while two other men ran around the sides. It took Otter four shots to hit the running man. Jack's first round of buckshot picked his target off the ground and threw him back five feet. The second round was fired by instinct.

Upon entering the doors, Carol and the other assassin riddled the loft with automatic fire from below. Fortunately, Nick had moved again, to the corner of the loft, abandoning his Winchester for his twelve-gauge double-barreled shotgun. He waited for a head to appear at the top of the ladder to the loft.

Major Carol and the other gunner were looking up when Jack entered through the side door. There was a millisecond between the men hearing Jack burst through the door and seeing the muzzle blast of his twelve gauge. Jack had always been good at jump-shooting quail.

Elliott abandoned his overwatch position and entered behind his brother with both hands on the pistol grip of Major Carol's .45, the hammer back.

"You Copelands aren't very damn good at following instructions, are you?" Nick asked.

Elliott looked at his brother, then at Nick.

Carol was hit from fifteen feet by a load of buckshot. Elliott barely turned away his head before he threw up violently. Jack, affected by his brother's reaction, felt himself salivating heavily when Nick reached the bottom of the ladder, his face white.

Elliott ran from the barn with Jack at his heels, while Nick checked the would-be assassins to make sure they were dead, though a shotgun blast left little doubt. He picked up the Uzi and the M-16 before joining the boys outside.

"The first time I saw a body torn apart by bullets, I was about you boys' age," Nick said. "We were trained for it, expected it, yet there was no holding back the natural human response to violent, bloody death. Though I didn't think much about it then, there was about as much vomit on the beach of Iwo Jima as there was blood. There's nothing for you to be ashamed of. It means you're still human. There's a hydrant at the front of the barn if you want to rinse your mouths."

Jack wondered why he puked then and not on the river when he killed Spider and Johnson. He had to think on that later. It was still time for action, though he wasn't sure what that should be.

It was clear that the men had come as assassins. He and his

brother were the targets. Nick's gut feelings were right, but it wasn't the sheriff or his men who tapped the phone and came to kill them. Government contracts meant union contractors, and the Mafia was deeply embedded in the unions.

"We have to take care of this mess as fast as we can," Nick said. "You two stirred up a hell of a hornet's nest."

Nick started the tractor and moved it to the front of the barn before he lowered the bucket. He searched each man, then Jack and Elliott tossed the bodies into the bucket. They moved across the field, collecting bodies as they went.

They loaded the bodies into the van. Nick knew of a 2,000-foot ravine less than two miles away where the truck and van would go undiscovered for years. After he recovered his distributor wire, he led the way.

The truck and van rolled down the ravine out of sight. They all got in the Volvo and returned to the barn. Nick gave Elliott an undetermined amount of cash he recovered from Major Carol in an envelope for their trip. The boys insisted Nick go to the Copeland Ranch in Junction City.

Ten miles down the road, Nick nearly had a head-on collision with a truck on a tight curve. Chief Warrant Officer Graham spilled his coffee avoiding the collision. Nick kept driving, hoping the boys were long gone if that truck held more bad guys.

Jack and Elliott brushed away their tracks up the trail to the Land Cruiser with Manzanita branches, then they saw headlights coming up the drive. The truck stopped and flashed its lights three times. The brothers worked in silence until they reached the Land Cruiser.

Graham and his sergeant waited for a few minutes in the cab before drawing their weapons and approaching Nick's house.

"Hello?" he called. "Jack, we're friends sent by your dad and Running Rabbit."

The staff sergeant walked around back with his flashlight on, while the chief approached the front door.

"Lots of bullet holes, Chief."

"Same here. I'm going in."

"Coming in the back."

Much to Graham's relief, there were no bodies inside. He found glasses and dishes in the sink, but no signs of blood anywhere.

They went outside and spread out, proceeding cautiously across the narrow field toward the barn. The chief shone his flashlight on an outdoor furnace and made a mental note to investigate the source of smoke.

Once in the barn, they saw signs of a battle, though someone had attempted cleaning. The two men were an effective team, silently and thoughtfully examining everything they saw. Even if they had hours, Nick and the brothers couldn't have hidden all the evidence of a firefight.

The chief opened the door to the outdoor furnace with a shovel. Digging around in the hot coals, he extracted two Italian loafers and a dress belt. They weren't the clothing of an eccentric philosopher or the young outdoorsmen. He tossed them back in and shut the door.

"What do you think happened, Chief?"

"I think their location was compromised. I know at least Jack and Elliott were armed. Information I received says the old man was a highly decorated Marine in World War Two. I'd guess that's who we passed on the way out. Hopefully, the stuff in the furnace belonged to the bad guys. My gut says the Copeland boys survived and are on the run, as is our Marine Jackson. We'll have to burn the house and barn, Sergeant."

"Are you kidding me, Chief? Do you mean that?"

"I'm not kidding one bit. Our witnesses can't be implicated in whatever happened here. Take five gallons of gas up to the house and douse it. I'll do the same with the barn and light it. We'll meet back at the truck. We need to be gone before anyone else shows up. I'll call the Copeland Ranch as soon as I can."

Jack and Elliott, seeing the fire's glow, tried to make sense of it, as they crawled in low gear over the foothills. They drove without headlights, while Elliott used the red lens on the flashlight to navigate.

Keeping track of the distance with the odometer, he tried to guess how long it would take them to reach Nevada. Their route to Topaz Lake was slow and arduous over logging and forest service roads through the Stanislaus National Forest.

They climbed steadily after leaving Nick's place. At 5,000 feet, the Land Cruiser was running too rich and started to sputter for lack of oxygen. The two were exhausted. It was four o'clock in the morning, and they needed a pit stop.

"She's running way too rich," Jack said. "I'll lean out the carburetor before we leave. This trail is killing me."

After getting out, he stretched his arms overhead and arched his back. Elliott didn't speak until both were taking a leak.

"You're lucky you've got the steering wheel to hold onto. If it wasn't for the panic bar, I'd be rolling all over the place. What do you say we eat while we're stopped?"

"No kidding. I forgot about food. How long has it been since we ate? I haven't eaten since lunch yesterday when I met Nick at that restaurant. That seems like a hundred years ago."

"Yesterday was the last time I ate, too, on the river. I'll dig out a couple boxes of C rations."

Elliott opened the back of the rig, while Jack checked the hubs for excessive heat. He opened the hood for a visual inspection and let the engine cool before adjusting the carburetor. Elliott handed Jack a C ration box and opened his, making short work of opening the largest can with his Swiss Army knife.

"All right! I got my favorite—spaghetti and meatballs. I swear I didn't go through the boxes, either, Jack. I picked blind."

"I don't know if I can trust you, Big Brother. You always had a way of ending up with spaghetti when we were kids. Those were some good times, sitting on the riverbank by a fire, heating C rations in a pail of water. Remember how Dad always told Mom that he would do the dishes when we ate C rations from cans?"

"Of course. Those were good times. That's when he had all those good C rations from the war. Mom caught you and me trying to smoke those twenty-year-old Lucky Strikes. She was a lot madder than Dad was. How about a trade? I'll give you my pound cake for your peaches."

"How could I forget that? She chased us for ten minutes

with that switch. I believe that was your idea, by the way. You said we had to smoke like real soldiers. Dad got a kick out of her chasing us. That was the only time she would've laid a hand on us. I was scared to death. I'll keep my peaches. They sound good right now."

"Do you think the law will be waiting for us when we get on the highway? It's only a few miles to Ebbets Pass and paved road."

"I'm not sure. It didn't seem like those people at Nick's were any kind of law enforcement. We didn't find any badges or official ID. The only thing that linked them to a government agency was the M-16 rifles, and that doesn't mean anything. I think they were Mafia hit men working under Major Carol. I don't think law enforcement will be a problem. The Mafia doesn't have the resources to cover every back road in Nevada. We won't have anything to worry about unless we do something stupid and get pulled over and searched. We need to be careful and not draw attention to ourselves."

"I think you're right. That makes sense. We don't need to be riding with our guns in the open for anyone to see. A ranger or game warden might suspect us of poaching. We'll have to hide them somewhere, then check our taillights and brake lights before we get on the highway."

After eating their C rations, they went to the rear of the Cruiser where they emptied all the gear from the foot locker, removed the fake bottom, and hid the long guns. Jack started the engine while Elliott held the small trouble light that plugged into the firewall. Jack adjusted the fuel mixture screws on the four-barrel carburetor until the 300hp engine idled smoothly again.

They checked their running lights, added fuel from the jerry cans, unlocked the hubs, and drove over the pass on Highway 4.

Nick didn't stop driving until Sacramento. He used a pay phone at a truck stop where he bought fuel. The closest thing he had to living family was the two boys who risked their lives to make sure he was OK. His only call was to Cope.

"Hello, Copeland here."

"This is Nick. There's been a little trouble down here. Your boys are OK. They suggested I come see you for a little vacation."

"Of course. Whatever you need. Are you OK?"

"I'd say yes, but there are plenty of people who would disagree." He managed a soft laugh. "Your boys gave me directions. I could be there in as little as four hours."

"I'll have something to eat for you when you get here. Call me from Weaverville, and I'll meet you on Highway 299 and guide you. I'll be driving a Willys wagon."

"That's mighty kind. I'll call from Weaverville." Nick hung up, used the restroom, bought a large black coffee, and drove north on I-5.

Cope was troubled. That was the most-disturbing call he received so far. How could the plans have changed? Were his boys in more danger?

He was closer than ever before to discovering the gold he devoted most of his life to finding. He lost his wife to the river and gave the river the best years of his own life. The huge boulder he discovered held more promise than any other he found. It took many months to move the rocks that filled in around and covered the boulder for untold years. Season after season of toil and hard work brought him to the verge of success, so why did all the trouble have to come at that time?

He knew gold was there, and so did the boys. He wished there hadn't been any trouble and his boys were with him to start work in the morning. Fall would come soon, bringing winter rain, snow, spring thaws, flooding, and thousands of tons of overburden moving downriver toward the ocean. Every year, the river moved from the mountains to the sea, ever-changing. Their window of opportunity was slowly closing. If Jack and Elliott couldn't come home now, he might be forced to wait until the following year to move the giant boulder.

In his heart, he knew that gold wasn't the most-important thing. His sons were the most-important. He sighed. He'd never been a brooding man, and he didn't intend to start then.

"It looks like I won't get much sleep tonight," he told Rabbit. "I'll make a big pot of venison stew."

The two men moved into the kitchen.

Cooking always calmed Cope. He enjoyed the process of preparing food as much as he did eating. It would also help kill some time before Nick arrived.

Cope never used a recipe for his stew. He boiled vegetables until they were soft, then added canned meat. That night's version was similar to most—garlic, onions, carrots, potatoes, a little celery, venison, bay leaves, and salt and pepper. When it was cold out, he made it with hot peppers and cooked biscuits.

The two men began slicing vegetables and sipping sour-mash whiskey until there was nothing left to do but wait for the pot to simmer and for Nick's next call.

"You don't need to stay," Cope told his friend.

"I'm not leaving," Rabbit replied.

They played chess to pass the time until Nick finally called from Weaverville.

The Volvo wagon had to stay in second gear to climb the steep grade over Oregon Summit on the west side of Weaverville. Nick was amazed by the barren landscape left by the monitors. They washed off all the soil and loose rock from the steep hillsides in the 1800s with powerful water cannons. The runoff was forced into wooden sluice boxes that separated the gold and sent the rest downriver. Nothing would ever grow again on those hillsides—a 200-year-old monument to the permanence of short-term gain.

Nick heard about it, but he'd never seen it firsthand. According to accounts at the time, the Trinity River ran brown with silt for the full 100 miles to the Pacific Ocean. The sluice boxes were designed to allow the gold to settle through holes and behind wooden riffles, which worked for all but the biggest nuggets. Those large ones returned to the river to continue their sojourn toward lower ground.

That was why John Copeland settled on the Trinity River and staked his claim there. It was a place where he wasn't merely following behind the Chinese. The mountainsides and creeks were lined with carefully stacked rock, a testimony to their labors.

At the bottom of the Oregon Mountain grade, Nick saw a Willys utility wagon with its lights on. He followed the vehicle south across the bridge along the gravel road to the driveway up to the ranch and parked beside Cope when he stopped. Bear sniffed the new car's tires and left his mark, gave Nick a soft woof, and sniffed his pant leg.

15. Trouble Follows Trouble

"I guess if this dog was a biter, I'd know by now," Nick said. "Good evening. What a beautiful place you have here."

"Welcome, Nick Jackson. I'm Cope, and this is Randy. It's a pleasure to meet you. Let's go to the house."

Shaking hands, they walked toward the porch, with Bear leading the way, bounding up the six steps. He waited for them to reach eye level to remind Cope how much he loved venison stew. The smell had been driving him crazy for hours.

Cope showed Nick the bathroom, set out four bowls of stew, and added bread and butter, along with whiskey and glasses.

They sat at the table. There was plenty to tell, and Nick was a good storyteller. Thankful to be there, he enjoyed the sour-mash whiskey as much as the many generations of Tennessee Jacksons before him.

He started with meeting Elliott hitchhiking to Columbia, then how he met Jack looking for his brother. He told the story of the boys' arrival at his house and the donnybrook at the takeout place.

Cope knew all the phone calls, so Nick skipped to the

return to his house and the arrival of the white van with ladder. Cope and Randy were grateful to Nick for his keen intuition and proud of the way Jack and Elliott returned to help Nick as a matter of honor. Nick mentioned his thanks for that. Seeing the boys had been raised so well made him more comfortable going to Cope's ranch.

"If you were to guess," Cope asked, "how long do you think it'll take them to reach a phone in Nevada?"

"I'd say they'll be looking for a phone near the border sometime around dawn. It's not far, but it's a fair bit of driving."

Bear lay on the floor beside the table, his head on his paws and a puddle of drool on either side. Cope placed his finger in the fourth bowl of stew to make sure it was cool enough, then he set the bowl on the floor. Bear raised his head, waiting for the command.

"OK, Boy."

Bear ate without bothering to stand.

The three combat veterans continued their conversation, enjoying each other's company. When the phone finally rang, Cope answered in a calm voice, though his heart pounded.

"Hello, Dad. It's me, Elliott."

"Great to hear from you, Son. We'll have to keep this conversation short. Travel smart and make no mistakes. I have some instructions only your brother will understand. Can you put him on?"

"Sure, Dad. I wanted you to know I'm sorry about leaving school and all. I love you."

"I love you, too. We'll have time to discuss that later. Watch over your little brother. Keep each other safe."

Elliott passed the receiver to Jack.

"Hello, Dad? We made it to a phone. Did Nick make it there?"

"Yes. He told me everything. Do you remember Clara Bell?"

"Of course."

"Do you remember the contact information?"

"Yes. The island."

"Go there now. Instructions will be waiting for you. Call every twenty-four hours."

Jack hung up and looked at his brother. "We've got a long trip ahead—all the way across the country to Dauphin Island, Alabama. When Dad came down to Fort Rucker for graduation, we went camping at St. George's Island, and we met Neil and his dog, Clara Bell. He was ex-Special Forces just back from 'Nam and was traveling the Gulf of Mexico in an open catamaran. He was a really cool guy, salt of the earth. He told us if we ever wanted to reach him, his uncle would know exactly where he was. He owns a shrimping boat and sells shrimp at Dauphin Island.

"That's where we're going. Can you believe we're driving cross country together, like we talked about when we were kids?"

They pulled into a campground at Topaz Lake. The fee was two dollars a day on the honor system. New arrivals registered themselves and placed two dollars cash in an envelope inside a metal box. The Ranger came around every morning to collect the money and check the campground.

When the ranger arrived, the Land Cruiser was the only vehicle. Checking the box, he saw no registration inside, so he drove around the campsite and found the two young men at a picnic table, studying maps. The registration envelope and two dollar bills were on the table.

"Morning, Gentlemen. How are you this beautiful day?"

"We're doing great, Sir," Otter said. "We just pulled in this morning. I got the form filled out and was ready to take it to the box when I got distracted."

"No problem. I'll take it, since I'm here. How long will you stay?"

"Probably just a day for exploring."

The Ranger took the envelope, said good-bye, and left.

The boys passed their first encounter with law enforcement. They studied the map, deciding to sleep before going farther. Fatigue could cause many mistakes, which they couldn't afford.

Jack put his head on his day pack, his hat over his face, and was quickly sound asleep. Elliott's mind raced. He thought of his mom, how white she looked when they pulled her from the river, and the faces of the dead men in the barn flashed through his mind like a psychedelic light show. He tried not to think about what happened and to focus on what needed to be done next.

He knew the assassins were animals who needed to die if he and his brother were to survive. He and Jack were on the right side, but nonetheless, the lyrics to a John Prine song came to mind.

Jesus don't like killing
No matter what the reason for
And your flag decal won't get you
Into heaven anymore
It's already overcrowded
From your dirty little war

He thought about Spider and Johnson, who beat and robbed him, and how his brother killed them to save their father. Thinking about how brave and capable Jack was made his eyes fill with tears, and his throat hurt. He cried silently, praying to God and his mother and Jesus and whoever else might hear him. Finally, peace and sleep came.

They slept soundly until the sun was high, bringing midday heat. The lake water was cold and refreshing for their swim. Both washed off with a bar of soap, and the cool water helped clear the fog in their minds.

They studied the map in earnest. They would drive through the mountains to Las Vegas, pick up Highway 40 to Dallas, and work south from there to New Orleans and across the Mississippi to Dauphin Island, just south of Mobile.

The route to Vegas was slow, and their first stop was in Wellington, a roadside restaurant. Jack wanted breakfast, but it was too late, so they settled for steak, potato, and salad. They sat where they could see the Land Cruiser and anyone who came and went in the restaurant.

The owner and his wife, accustomed to tourists, thought nothing of the two young men. Elliott never carried as much money as he had. Feeling grateful for the good meal, he left a five-dollar tip.

"That's a mistake," Jack said. "It'll make us more memorable."

Elliott laughed and smiled. "Hell, look at us. We're so handsome, we're already memorable."

Laughing, they drove south, winding through rugged terrain and sharp curves. According to Elliott, their trip would take 2,400 miles. They agreed to drive sixteen hours a day. If they could average fifty miles an hour, they'd reach Dauphin Island in three days. They would switch drivers every four hours, which made Elliott happy that he wouldn't just be riding.

Jack was nervous about letting his brother drive his baby. The distance to Vegas was 439 miles, so it would be after dark when they arrived.

A black Lincoln pulled up to the rafting company parking lot, and two men in suits walked into the office, closing and locking the door behind them. Ferguson stood behind the counter.

"Are you the owner of this business?" one asked.

"Yes, I am. Can I help you with something?"

"My partner and I are with the FBI. We need information about a man who works for you. He was involved in an altercation with a federal officer. Tell us everything you know about him, or we'll shut you down and send you to prison for obstructing justice."

"Of course. His name's Otter. I met him in Burnt Ranch on a rafting trip. He started working for me about a month ago."

"I need his full name, permanent address, and contact information. If you don't cooperate immediately, we'll arrest you for hindering our investigation."

The second man went behind the counter to the only desk and opened a file drawer. In seconds, he located the file labeled *Employee Information.*

"His job application says his last name is Copeland, but there's no address, just a PO Box in Junction City. There's a phone number here, too."

"What about the man who traveled with him? Do you know anything about him? What kind of vehicle did they leave with?"

"All I know is that he was his brother, just out of the service. He showed up here in some kind of Jeep."

"If what you've told us pans out, you're in no trouble. You're required to keep this meeting confidential. If we find out otherwise, we'll be back to arrest you."

The two men walked out as quickly as they came. Ferg wasn't sure if they were really FBI agents, but that didn't matter. He immediately dialed the number on Otter's job application. Cope answered on the second ring.

"Mr. Copeland, my name is Ferguson. I own a rafting company in Angels Camp where your son worked. Two suits just came to my office saying they were FBI agents and wanting information about your sons. Unfortunately, they found his job application, which had your contact info on it. There was nothing I could do to stop them. They went through my files and threatened to arrest me. It happened really fast. One other thing—when they left, I looked at their license plates, and they weren't government plates."

"Thank you, Mr. Ferguson. I appreciate the call. I doubt they were FBI agents. I sure hope they don't give you any more trouble. I doubt it, since they got what they wanted."

"One other thing. Your sons are good men. I wish you and them all the luck in the world."

"We may need it before this is over. The best to you, too. Thanks again for the heads up."

Spending time as a POW had given Cope ample time to plan in detail how he would build his home if he survived. He often considered how to defend it, but he never thought it would come like this. He didn't know if they would scout first or attempt a frontal assault with overwhelming force. If they did, that would be a big mistake on their part.

Tactically, he was prepared for a small arms battle. He designed multiple firing positions with reinforced concrete protection and retreat routes. He just never thought he'd be up against Mafia assassins.

Nick and Randy woke when the phone rang, so Cope told them the news. They figured they had six hours before anyone arrived. It stood to reason that after what happened to the first group, the second would be more careful.

The key to success in any combat operation is thorough planning, which requires anticipating the enemy's actions. All three combat vets at the table had survived by doing exactly that. They assumed the enemy would be more careful in the second attempt to kill Nick, Elliott, and Jack. Cope expected the assassins would attempt a reconnaissance to assess the situation before conducting the full attack.

The three men decided there was no future in hiding. They would lure in the assassins and eliminate them. The probe was most likely to come during daylight, and it wasn't likely that a team could be dispatched to arrive earlier.

Nick enjoyed his stew as much as anyone, managing to spill only small pieces in his ample white beard, reading glasses, and flannel shirt. That gave Cope a good idea he would share the following morning.

"I suppose you ancient warriors won't mind if I take a nap," Cope said. "We might be facing a busy day. A couple hours' sleep would do us all good."

Randy went to the barn where he parked his Land Cruiser and returned with his AR 15 and an ammo can. He strapped on his model 29 Smith and Wesson .44 Magnum revolver in a shoulder holster, then went to the bedroom that was once Elliott's and snapped a thirty-round magazine into his rifle before leaning it against the wall beside the bed. He lay down, instantly falling asleep, a skill he developed in Vietnam when the flight schedule demanded that air crews sleep at all hours to be mission ready.

Cope gave Nick a double-barreled twenty-inch 12 gauge to sleep with in his bed in Jack's room. Even though they didn't expect anyone to arrive until daylight, Cope took first watch. Bear would hear anyone approaching in a vehicle or on foot.

Randy woke at six o'clock in the morning, before dawn, to relieve Cope. They spent a few minutes discussing their plan, then Cope went to catch a few hours' sleep.

At two o'clock that afternoon, a white utility bed truck with aluminum ladders and the emblem of Pacific Gas and Electric appeared at the base of the driveway.

Cope and Nick sat on the porch in rocking chairs, a half-gallon whiskey bottle half-full of tea and two tumblers on the table beside them. Nick wore a soiled white shirt and deliberately had food crumbs in his beard. Cope's pant legs were tucked into his socks, his shirt unevenly buttoned, his chin unshaved, and his hair disheveled. Randy was hidden behind the door with Bear and his AR 15, taking the over watch position.

Two men drove up to the house and exited with little apprehension. They were medium built, wearing hard hats, industrial work shirts, jeans, and new boots. The man who came out the passenger door carried a clipboard and spoke first.

"There's been a report of power outages around here," he said. "Everything OK?"

"The only problem is we've got half a bottle of whiskey left, and the company's poor," Nick said.

Cope gave a slurred guffaw and slapped his leg before taking a long pull from his glass of tea.

"How about you boys join a couple old-timers in a drink of whiskey?"

"No, Sir. Thank you. We're on duty. We have to find the power outage."

Cope stood and staggered, nearly falling down the steps toward the men with his hand extended. "I'll shake the hand of the man who won't have a drink with a drunk on duty today."

The two men shook Cope's hand, turned and went to the truck. They stopped at the phone pole a quarter mile away, where Cope's driveway began, got down a ladder, and installed a wire tap, as they were directed. They identified Nick by his vehicle and description.

They drove back to Junction City. The passenger left the truck and climbed into a black Lincoln town car waiting nearby. The heavyset man in the back seat was anxious to hear the news. The failure of the previous assassins hadn't just been embarrassing. It cost him the lives of some of his best men. They were a family. He didn't care about the reasons behind the hit. Family honor and security were at risk.

He spoke in a deep voice and a distinct New York accent. "Here's the plan. Take my two guys with you in the back of the truck, drive to the house, and kill the old Copeland guy. Don't hurt the one with the beard. I want to make him talk myself.

"I'll find out where the other two are. Hurry back here and get me as soon as you can, and don't fuck it up."

Bear barked once when he heard a truck on the gravel drive. Nick had the coach gun beside his right leg with a blanket draped over the arms of his rocker.

Cope had his Ruger .22 pistol under his leg, held in his right hand, with a drink in his left. Randy was in a concealed fire position on the roof.

Bear growled when two men left the truck. They were approximately ten feet from the top step of the porch when the driver pulled a pistol from behind his back. His hand barely reached waist level when a three-inch Magnum 00 buckshot round drove the fabric of his shirt and his name tag through his heart and out the back of his rib cage.

As the gunshot sounded, Bear leaped from the porch and

struck the other man's chest with his paws, his jaw closing on the man's face. The revolver flew from his hand, as he landed on his back and frantically tried to pull Bear off.

The other two assassins left the back of the utility bed in full view of Randy. By the time the farthest bodyguard realized there was a third man on the roof, his partner had six .223 hollow points in his chest cavity. The remaining man was trapped on the far side of the truck by Cope and Nick on the porch and Randy on the roof.

Cope called Bear off the man on the ground and stood over him with the .22 against his face. His cheeks were punctured and torn, and his nose was barely attached. Cope shot him in the head twice at point-blank range.

"I suggest you throw down your weapon and come out from behind the truck," Cope said. "I'll give you to the count of three."

The man threw out his weapon and came out with his hands in the air, staring at his three dead comrades.

"On your knees," Cope snapped. "Your life depends on how you answer my questions. If you make a mistake, it'll be your last. Do I make myself clear?"

"Perfectly."

"Why did you four come here?"

"We were supposed to kill you, capture the bearded one, and go back for the boss. He would make the bearded man tell us where your sons are."

Cope turned his back to the man on his knees. The man reached for a concealed gun in an ankle holster. The second barrel of the twelve-gauge left him unrecognizable to his own mother.

The smell of gunpowder and blood spread across the ground, triggering memories that Cope tried to forget for years.

Bear walked up to the nearly headless man and pissed on his body. Cope glanced at Nick and nodded his thanks.

"How'd you know he was going for a pistol?" Cope asked.

Nick cracked open the gun, ejected the expended shells, and reloaded. "I figured he knew his killing days were over. If we didn't shoot him, his boss would. He didn't have anything to lose. Assassins and cops usually have a backup piece."

"Nick wasn't the only one," Randy called from the roof. "If the twelve-gauge hadn't ruined his face, you would've seen a neat little 223 hollow point entered the side of his skull before his hand touched his ankle."

"My thanks to you both. Let's go get the boss and driver. Come down, Randy. Help me load these thugs into the back of the truck. We've got work to do."

The four murderers were loaded into the back of the utility truck and covered with a tarp. Randy and Cope donned the hard hats and assumed the roles of PG&E repairmen.

They drove to the rear of the boss' car and simultaneously got out. Randy entered the passenger front seat and put his .44 Magnum against the driver's temple. Cope got into the back seat and stuck the silencer on his pistol against the boss' fleshy ribs.

Nick arrived in his Volvo wagon, parked it, and got behind the wheel of the truck.

"Follow the truck," Randy told the driver.

Cope, Nick, and Randy knew the mob would never leave them alone if they knew their identities. They had to find out if anyone else knew, as well as discover who they were fighting. They would interrogate these men, because the boys' lives depended on it. To Cope, that was all that mattered.

Once the two mobsters were gagged and tied to fence posts behind the barn, they were ready to begin. Cope removed the gag from the driver's mouth.

"Why'd you come to my ranch?" Cope asked.

"I just drive the car. The boss tells me where to go. All I do is drive. I don't know nothing about nothing."

"A man in your trusted position knows almost everything. How'd you find us back here?"

"The two guys in the back of the truck found out. The boss got a call from them last night, so we came here to take care of business."

Cope replaced the gag and moved to the boss, removing his gag. "What do they call you in San Francisco?"

"Don't you fucking worry about it. When I watch you take your last breath, I'll tell you my name. As a matter of fact, I'll carve it into the flesh of everyone you ever loved. I'll make your daughter whimper my name when my family fucks her to death. How do you like that?"

He tried to spit at Cope, but Cope moved back to the driver and removed his gag. "What do you call your boss in San Francisco?"

"You don't know who you're messing with, do you?" the driver asked.

The little .22 hollow point entered the man's skull and bounced around inside without enough force to exit, scattering his memories throughout the universe as he died.

"Apparently, neither do you," Cope commented. He turned and shot the boss' right knee.

He screamed in pain. "My knee! My fucking knee! You shot my fucking knee!"

"Here's the deal, Tough Guy. You tell me who sent you, who knows where you are, and who you're after, and I let you live. Otherwise, I'll keep shooting you with this little .22 until I get bored."

"OK, OK! I got a call. Some of our people never came back to Frisco from a hit on a couple kids who were causing trouble for a big project. You know—a big union job. A couple of my guys went up there to check it out. He calls me and says the targets might be here. We come here to take care of business. That's all. Nothing personal. I got a job to do."

"I've got good news and bad news. I appreciate your honesty, but I don't care for murderers who come to kill me and threaten my family. The good news is I won't keep shooting you in the joints with this .22. the bad news is, I'll shoot you in the head. Nothing personal. If you want a second to make peace, go ahead."

Cope shot him between the eyes at point-blank range. A few minutes later, they had six bodies in the back of the truck.

Nick shook his head. "I feel like I've gotten into the undertaking business. Ain't that the damnedest thing at my age?"

16. Southern Exposure

The Toyota Land Cruiser was suited for loose gravel, boulders, mud, sand, and water crossings. It wasn't suited for long-distance travel at high speed. Every vehicle has a sweet spot, a harmony of engine, transmission differential, and overall drivability. For the FJ40, that was fifty-five miles per hour. At sixty, the tire noise, engine noise, and vibration were too great to endure. Driving two hours each helped break the monotony and fatigue.

The brothers had grown apart while Elliott was in college. Their lives diverged, then suddenly, they were together just like when they were kids. The difference was, the stakes were life and death. They knew what their dad meant when he said to go carefully. They didn't break any traffic laws and watched each other's backs. They didn't want to draw any attention or contact with the law.

They stopped for fuel, food, and driver changes. It was fun to think of going to New Orleans, as they pressed on toward Tinner's Shrimp and Seafood on Dauphin Island.

Live oaks towered like ancient giants draped in Spanish moss that floated as gracefully as any garland on a Christmas tree. The air had the pungent smell of magnolias and sea breeze. Crossing the drawbridge to Dauphin Island, they saw the sign for the seafood company, a forty-foot, single-story structure with a rusty, corrugated metal roof. A covered porch ten feet deep stretched across the front, with an assortment of rocking chairs, benches, and a porch swing in the shade. Various signs hung on the weathered board-and-bat Cyprus walls, while a double door stood in the center.

It was a waterfront seafood house with loading docks, commercial boat slips, an ice house, fuel dock, and bait and beer. A boat ramp on the right, and a large shell-based parking lot. A tree line stood on the left side, strewn with abandoned vessels, vehicles, and assorted indistinguishable rusting metal objects.

Elliott and Jack parked in front of the double doors. Seeing a chest-type soda dispenser, Jack got a cream soda, while Elliott got grape. A sign on the door said the place was closed, so they sat on the swing to drink their sodas. It was nice to be out of their vehicle. All they had to do was wait for someone to return.

The first arrival came in the form of a '69 Z28 Camaro, yellow with black stripe over the hood. A redhead in an Alabama baseball cap backed up in front of the double doors and got out. The first thing they noticed were her long legs, then her supple hips and voluminous breasts trying to escape her bikini top. She opened the trunk and put warm beer bottles into a steel Coleman ice chest. Without turning, she spoke to the boys.

"I used to teach school. I have eyes in the back of my head, and I can see you looking at my butt. You should be ashamed of yourselves."

Turning around, she laughed and smiled. "Now which one of you wants to give me a hand with a bucket of ice?"

They jumped to their feet simultaneously, sending the swing flying backward and nearly knocking them over when it came back and hit their legs. The woman covered her mouth to keep from laughing out loud.

"My name's Catalina, but my friends call me Cat. I assume you're from California?"

"I'm Elliott, and this is my brother, Jack. We're friends of Neil's."

"I won't hold that against you. Would you kindly help me get some ice on this warm beer, so I can welcome you properly to Dauphin Island, and the Redneck Riviera? I've been expecting you."

She unlocked and opened the doors. The boys followed her inside where the smell of seafood was strong without being foul. Cat grabbed a shovel to fill a five-gallon bucket with ice. Elliott took it before Jack could and they went outside to fill the cooler.

"Do you know when Neil's uncle will be back?" Elliott asked, carrying the ice.

"Normally, he tries to make it in by sunset. We always get a radio call when he's coming in. We've been expecting y'all any day. I'm Neil's little sister. There's some kind of secret plan in place. I don't know what kind of trouble y'all are in, but I'm supposed to have you park your rig in the barn beside Neil's. Then we'll take a tour of the island in my car. Are you hungry? We supply all the shrimp to the restaurants on the island and the good ones in Mobile. Y'all just follow me to the house in your Jeep."

"It's not a Jeep. It's a Chevota, a Toyota Land Cruiser with a Chevy power train."

Cat's ponytails flashed crimson in the bright sun as she turned her head while climbing into her Z-28. "Try to keep up in your Chevota." It was no ordinary Camaro.

Jack and Elliott ran to the Toyota, jumped in, and started the engine, and the chase was on. Cat spun her tires across the parking lot, leaving the Toyota in a cloud of dust as she disappeared over the bridge.

When the dust cleared, they saw the Camaro's brake lights where she stopped 100 yards away and waited for them. Elliott pulled up alongside.

The two vehicles sat side-by-side on the empty island road just north of the bridge, both drivers revving their engines. Cat gave them a nod and popped the clutch, and Elliott did the same. The four-barrel carburetors opened wide, exhausts roared, tires screeched, and rubber burned on the asphalt.

The Land Cruiser jumped ahead for a split second, then the Camaro left them behind like they were sitting still, once Cat hit second gear. Elliott let his foot off the gas and pulled into the correct lane on the two-way road. They followed Cat north a mile to where she sat at the entrance to a shell driveway lined with giant live oaks. They followed her to a pole barn sitting on the right side of the drive.

Cat got out of her Camaro and slid open a corrugated metal door, revealing an empty place to park.

"Y'all can park your Chevota here, beside Neil's Green Hornet."

Elliott looked at Jack. "That's one magnificent Cat."

"Yeah, and she's not a bad driver, either. I wonder what she has under the hood."

They pulled into the pole barn, taking the last bay nearest the house, beside a Forest Service green '64 Suburban. It was a four-wheel drive with three-inch body lift, just enough to allow clearance for the thirty-three-inch tires without making it unstable when side-hilling or cornering. It had a black tubular push guard across the front grill with an 8,000-pound winch. The roof was equipped with a full-length black roof rack and auxiliary lights front and back. A large sunroof over the front seat allowed access to the roof rack from inside the vehicle, as well as a convenient shooting platform.

Jack was immediately drawn to the vehicle. Cat followed the Land Cruiser into the barn and watched Jack's reaction.

"How do you like Neil's little toy?" she asked.

"Toy? That's a beast. What a rig! How long's it been sitting here?"

"The only time he didn't drive it was when he was in 'Nam. He parked it again when he took off on the catamaran. It's completely ready to go when we are."

Elliott gave Jack a quizzical look. "We don't know much about what we're supposed to do now. Our dad told us to come here, saying instructions would be waiting."

"I know. I kind of let the cat out of the bag. Your dad, Neil, and my uncle have a plan. I guess you guys have a handler now." She laughed while shaking out her ponytails.

Normally, Jack would've taken offense at someone organizing his life, but when Cat flashed her brilliant blue eyes, and her red hair swung around to cover, then reveal, a smile that could launch a fleet of ships, his only reaction was to smile and say, "Great."

"I don't have specific instructions for you now, though. I'm supposed to show you around the island and get you some Gulf shrimp or whatever you want from the local restaurant. Uncle Rick said you should leave your rig parked here and let me be your tour guide. The water's still pretty warm. I was thinking we should hit the beach with some cold beers. Do you like the water?"

"My brother and I grew up on a river," Elliott said. 'We've been swimming since we were old enough to walk, except in Jack's case. He crawled into the water to swim before he could walk, so Dad nicknamed him Tadpole. For some reason, he doesn't like the name very much. When he won the state wrestling championship at 165 pounds, he thought he deserved to be called Bull Frog."

"All right, then. Are you two ready to try some Southern cuisine? I'm starving." Cat slid the garage door shut as they left.

"Shotgun!" Jack said, walking to the Camaro.

"Damn it, when will you ever grow up?" Elliott asked.

"When they can put three bucket seats in the front of sports cars, and I can ride in the middle with two beautiful girls like Cat."

She put one hand on her hip. "Aren't you the sweet one? You'd better strap on that seat belt." She wore a devilish grin.

"By the way, what the hell is under the hood?"

"Just a little 302 Chevy."

"Yeah? It winds up to 8,000 RPM. No wonder you blew my doors off. That was the hottest small block ever built."

"Come on, now. You don't have to try to scare me to death. My little brother has already done that going through mountains and streams where goats won't go."

"I'll behave," Cat said. "My uncle said we can't get in any trouble with the local sheriff. I'm not supposed to let y'all get any attention. He said somethin' about bein' low key, but of course, I don't know the meaning of that."

She laughed again. She loved being in control of men. Her dad and uncle were very protective of her. Given the opportunity, she would run roughshod over any man who let her. It was her way of weeding out the weak ones. She enjoyed having two muscular, handsome young men to play with, especially when she hadn't grown up with them on the island.

They drove to her favorite restaurant, a one-story building directly across from the beachfront city park. It had a mansard roof with weathered shake shingles and dark blue tinted glass to ward off the intense summer sun. The temperature was already in the mid-80s, but the restaurant was a cool seventy degrees inside.

Jack opened the door for Cat and Elliott, then they took a table for four. A couple of men were drinking at the bar, and a family was just finishing their meal nearby. The midday lunch crowd was already gone. A waitress in her twenties brought ice water and menus to the table once they were seated.

"Hey, Cat, how y'all doin'? I'll take your drink orders. The lunch specials are on the chalkboard."

"Hey, Bonnie. How you doin' today?"

"I'm all right. I closed last night, then went surf-casting till sunrise. I had to come in to prep this morning, so I'm ready to get out of this apron and these shoes."

"I'll bet you're ready for a cold one. When do you get off?"

"That depends on how fast I can get you fed and out the door." She laughed.

"All right. I'll order for all three of us. Bring us a pitcher of draft beer, three glasses, three dozen oysters on the half shell, and five pounds of shrimp to go. We'll eat the oysters here and take the shrimp to the park for a picnic.

"Oh, I'm sorry. Where are my manners today? Bonnie, this is Elliott, and this is Jack. They're Neil's Army buddies."

The men stood and took turns shaking the beautiful blonde's hand. She had an exquisite tan on her athletic body, and her Southern drawl could melt frozen butter.

"Why don't you join us across the street?" Cat asked. "We've got a cooler full of beer. We'll be at one of the covered picnic tables. We can all go swimming. It'll be fun."

"Are you sure you don't want to keep these boys to yourself? You were never much on sharing." Bonnie smiled and walked to the bar to place the order and draw a pitcher of beer.

Bonnie bused tables and finished her tour while Cat instructed the brothers on the nuances of eating raw oysters. Elliott had a hard time taking his eyes off Bonnie when she reached and leaned across tables, revealing her ample cleavage and muscular thighs. She wore cut-off denim overalls, and if it hadn't been for the yellow string, he would've thought she wore nothing else.

Cat observed his attentiveness to Bonnie's every move. For a second time, she placed her hand on Jack's thigh under the table and squeezed.

"I declare, Jack," Cat said. "I think those oysters have

already had an affect on your brother. If I didn't know better, I'd say he was smitten by Cousin Bonnie."

Elliott smiled like the cat that swallowed a canary. "I don't know what you mean. What did I do?" He raised his palms upward and shrugged. "What's in this cocktail sauce that makes it so good?" he asked, trying to deflect the question.

"Don't try to change the subject, Goldilocks," Cat said. "I've seen you staring at Bonnie since we got here."

Jack came to his brother's rescue. "To tell the truth, I've been hard pressed to take my eyes off either of you. You and your cousin are the best-looking girls we've seen across the whole country."

He raised his glass, and Elliott touched it with his. Bonnie returned to the table with a bucket of fresh, steamed shrimp ready to go. She removed her apron and was ready to go to the beach.

Elliott asked for the check, but Cat said, "You'll do nothing of the sort. Your money's no good on the island when you're our guest."

"I can at least leave a tip." He set a twenty-dollar bill on the table. Bonnie folded it in her hand and raised it as if preparing to tuck it in her cleavage, but she tucked it into the top pocket of her bib. Then she walked around the back of Elliott's chair and put her hands on his forearms and her chest against his back to hug him.

"Cousin, I hope this one isn't yours. I might just like him. Have you ever seen such adorable locks on a hunk of a man?"

She moved her hands up his arms to his shoulders and then to his hair. Elliott felt blood rushing up his neck and into his groin.

"Now, Bonnie, don't go embarrassing our guest like that," Cat said. "These boys aren't used to forward women. You've made him blush." She picked up the bucket of shrimp, paper plates, and cocktail sauce, and the four walked out hand-in-hand.

Elliott thought about the times he and Jack double-dated in the old Willys wagon when they were in high school. Bonnie and Elliott sat in the back seat, and there was no arguing about which one rode shotgun.

They drove the short distance to the picnic area at the park across the street. Cat opened the trunk and Elliott and Jack carried the green cooler to the covered picnic table at the top of the sand dune that separated the beach from the parking places just off the road. Everyone was hungry. The shrimp were large, warm, and seasoned with homemade Cajun mix that was better than anything the boys had on the California coast. They were sweet and spicy, and dipped in cocktail sauce, there was nothing better.

The Gulf of Mexico rolled gently only forty yards away across white sand. The warm, blue-green water beckoned them for a swim. Bonnie stood and slipped the shoulder straps aside, unbuttoned the hips, and wiggled out of her overalls, revealing an hourglass figure in a yellow bikini. Elliott felt another warm flash that required a long pull from his twelve-ounce beer bottle.

They left their shirts and shoes behind, as they raced to the Gulf. The September water was almost as warm as the air. They played like school kids, splashing, swimming, floating, flirting, and having chicken fights.

To say that Elliott and Jack were competitive was a massive

understatement, but the girls had it, too. With Cat on Jack's shoulders and Bonnie on Elliott's, they pushed, pulled, and shoved until someone fell. They agreed to a best-of-five match. When the score was 2-2, they were interrupted by a pod of dolphins.

"Shark!" Jack shouted when he saw the first dorsal fin. He threw Cat into the air and caught her with his arms under her thighs and rib cage.

Elliott copied him, then the boys ran like hell for shore. Bonnie and Cat laughed and squealed like little girls, trying to inspire their valiant steeds. By the time they were in waist-deep water, Cat composed herself enough to tell Jack to stop.

"Stop!" she called. "They're just dolphins!"

Jack turned and saw the pod working on a school of mullet. Jack and Cat submerged together. When they came up, she had her arms around his neck and her body pressed tightly against his. Jack started to say something, but she put her finger against his lips and kissed him firmly. Jack returned her kiss. Watching the dolphins, they slowly moved back to deeper water, her arms still around his neck, and her legs locked around his waist.

Jack thought how he'd never do something like that in the cold Trinity River or the Pacific Ocean. The Gulf was hotter than he imagined. The only lovemaking he ever experienced was with his childhood sweetheart. When Cat put her hand on his erection, it caught him off guard, and he drew back his hips, but she held on. He never met a mature, playful woman.

"Whoa, Cowboy. Where do you think you're going? Come back here." She lowered herself slowly onto him. "Don't move."

She embraced him tightly with arms and legs, enjoying the fullness of him inside her.

Time stood still for Jack. His head spun, and he had an out-of-body experience when he nearly drowned while having an orgasm.

They sat at the picnic table, drinking cold beer, when Elliott and Bonnie returned from an extended walk down the beach that included a trip into the relative privacy of sand dunes. Elliott went to the cooler for two beers.

"Where'd y'all go?" Cat asked, her eyebrows raised.

"Wouldn't you like to know?" Bonnie responded with a smile. "Not so far we couldn't see y'all floating around all close and cuddly."

"Bonnie, let's take Jack and Elliott to the fort for sunset. Have y'all ever seen the green flash?"

"I thought I saw it earlier," Jack said.

Cat pinched his leg under the table.

"We're the tourists," Elliott said. "When in Rome, do as the Romans do. Obviously, Jack and I will do whatever you girls want."

They sat at the top of abandoned gun turrets watching the sunset. Bonnie hoped she wouldn't see her dad's shrimp boat coming in, so she could have a full night without his supervision. She wanted to wake up in Elliott's arms in the morning.

Jack and Elliott had been on a whirlwind adventure, or misadventure when they considered the carnage. The days' events were in striking contrast to the reality of the emotions that lay under the surface. Laughing gulls performed acrobatics, and pelicans made huge splashes when they dove on pods of baitfish. The horizon looked like an orange cream sickle with a ball of fire in the middle.

They watched until the last crescent of the sun descended into the water, but they didn't see the green flash. In response to their skepticism, the girls swore it was real. Cat finished her beer and stood, pulling Jack by the hand.

"The no-see-ums and mosquitoes will carry us away if we stay here much longer," Cat said. "If we haven't seen Uncle Rick's boat yet, I don't guess he'll be coming home tonight. Oh, crap! I completely forgot the envelope I was supposed to give y'all. I have it in case you got here before he was back from his trip."

Bonnie took Elliott's hand and pulled him off the rock wall. "Come on. Let's shower and get dressed. There's a great band playing down at Lulu's in Fairhope. You boys probably never heard any Alabama redneck beach music. It's kind of country, Southern rock, reggae, bluegrass, and Calypso all in one. Lulu's brother is near famous. You guys will love the place. They have a pirate ship stage, great food, and it's a kick-ass good time. You California boys won't have seen anything like it."

"That's a great idea, Bonnie," Cat said. "Why not? I was told to entertain them and keep them out of trouble. Just you keep from getting arrested for smoking those left-hand cigarettes in the parking lot."

"OK, Cousin. I remember a little redhead who was wild in high school, too."

They laughed at their semiprivate joke.

Loading up in the Camaro, they drove back with the top down. It ran like a scalded cat, forcing them back in their seats when Cat accelerated.

When they were at the house, Cat produced the letter from Uncle Rick, handwritten in a sealed envelope. The girls were very curious about the situation and wondered what kind of trouble the brothers were in. Years of living around the waterfront and fishermen taught them not to ask too many questions. They knew the importance of discretion. The coming and going of boats and quiet cargo was a reality of the smuggling trade enjoyed by coastal watermen throughout time. Many shrimpers from Houston to Key West had new trucks that rarely went to the fish house to unload seafood.

The foursome gathered around the breakfast bar, while Jack opened the letter and read it quietly to himself. Uncle Rick was a man of few words.

> *1) Neil is anchored downstream from the Myakka River Bridge in El Jobean, Florida, waiting for you. It's probably a twelve-hour drive across the Panhandle and down the Peninsula on Florida's West Coast.*
>
> *2) You can see his boat from the bridge. If the dinghy is there, he's on the boat. If not, it'll be on the beach on the east side of the bridge, within walking distance to a watering hole called Tolliver's on the main road. Look for him there.*
>
> *3) Neil wants you to leave your vehicle here and ride in his Suburban. His sister will accompany you and drive the Suburban back.*

4) Call your dad from a pay phone between six and seven Pacific Time at the Diggins.

5) Bring the two large green trunks from the shop. Very important! Cat knows which ones.

6) Checklist is in the glove box. Use it.

Jack handed the letter to Elliott, who read it aloud.

"I guess we're headed for El Jobean," Elliott said. "We need to call Dad at six Western time. You must've made a good impression on Neil for him to trust you with his truck and his sister."

"If you knew my brother and I well, you'd know that he would be more worried about y'all with me than me with y'all." Wrapping her arms around Jack, she pulled him close.

"I guess we'll spend a few more days together," Jack said.

Bonnie looked hurt, then a look of determination came to her face, followed by a big smile. "That just won't do at all. I won't have my cousin driving with two strange men on an overnight trip and then drive home alone. That ain't happening. I'll be loading up in that Suburban, too."

Jack, looking at his watch, did some calculations. It was nine o'clock local time, so they could call their father.

"Come on, Elliott," Jack said. "Let's get our packs out of the Yo. I could stand a shave and shower."

After Elliott untangled himself from Bonnie's intoxicating touch, they went to the pole barn.

"Damn, Jack," he said. "I can't believe what's happening to us. Five days ago, we were in hell, fighting our way out. Now we're in heaven—warm water, cold beer, and beautiful women, and it ain't over yet. When we were driving all night through the

Sierras, I was certain our lives were destroyed. Now we're in a situation I couldn't have dreamed up in my wildest imagination.

"All I can think of is a Beach Boys lyric going through my mind. 'And the Southern girls, and the way they talk, they knock me out when I'm down there.' Bonnie's killing me. I think I might be in love."

"I don't know what to say. There was no way in hell I would have ever thought of cheating on Katie. I feel bad when I think of that, but I couldn't help myself, nor did I really want to. I guess I'm just a dog, damn it."

"I know what you're saying after the past few days and everything that's happened. I plan to enjoy it while it lasts. Who knows what will happen to us? We might end up in prison or hunted by the Mafia to the ends of the earth. Before you beat yourself up, just remember, as Randy used to say, that a hard dick has no conscience. Try to keep things in perspective.

"Have a good time. These girls are terrific, and they like us. Don't do a bummer on yourself. Do you remember the story about the two woodpeckers that flew from North Carolina to California? One went into a giant redwood and came out the other side. His buddy asked how he did it, and he said, 'You never know how hard your pecker will get until you're 3,000 miles from home.'"

"Yeah, I get it. These girls are terrific, and we've had a hell of a terrible three days. I plan to have a good time. Let's remember to get a hundred dollars each to take with us tonight. We'll treat the girls and buy gas. I'm anxious to talk to Dad. I hope everything's all right back there."

"Me, too. You haven't said much about Neil. If he's at all like his sister, we're in for a treat."

"I met him for only a day and a half. He's really cool, Special Forces. He's probably in his mid to late twenties. We met him when he was cruising the Gulf of Mexico in an open catamaran, beach camping with a yellow Lab. We drank beer, fished, and spent time around a fire on the beach. He said he was trying to find the part of him that was taken by the war. Their dad disappeared while he was gone, and he's looking for answers.

"He appreciated Dad's perspective from his World War Two experiences. He's trustworthy and rock-solid dependable. Someone I definitely wouldn't want to get sideways with. He's lean, agile, strong, and trained."

"How do you feel about leaving the Land Cruiser?"

"I'm not too worried about it. I just want to hear what Dad has planned. I'm curious what happened after we left. Let's get back to the house."

"I can't wait to take a shower, especially if I don't have to do it alone."

"I hope you weren't talking about me. I know we're brothers, but we're a little too old to shower together."

"Glad to see you haven't lost your sense of humor. I was thinking more about Bonnie, though."

Bonnie and Cat sat in the kitchen discussing the trip. Bonnie wasn't sure her dad would approve of her going, but he couldn't argue with a note that was left behind. Both girls decided it would be a kick to have a road trip. They'd take the coast route around Mobile Bay, have fun at Lulu's, and finish up the night at the Flora-Bama Club and sleep under the stars on the beach. All they needed was a cooler and beach blankets.

Bonnie called the restaurant to say there was a family emergency, and she'd be out of town for a few days. The cousins were as excited as little kids on the night before a family vacation to Disney World.

When Elliott and Jack returned, the mood was contagious, and they were quickly caught up in the excitement of the trip. The idea of Lulu's, Flora-Bama, and moonlight and romance on the beach triggered a bouillabaisse of hormones and emotions.

It was the best of seasons—the water was warm, and the air was cool at night. The summer crowd was gone. Flannel shirts and blue jeans, Alabama tags on a jacked-up, hot rod four-wheel drive made them look like ordinary Redneck Riviera kids on a night at the beach, except for their looks, which were anything but ordinary. They were strikingly beautiful women with handsome, athletic men.

Jack and Elliott carefully went through the checklist in the glove box. They checked fluid levels, belts, tire pressure, including the spare, jacks, shovel, tow strap, toolbox, gas and water in Jerry cans, and emergency rations. The truck was ready for a safari or anything else. Neil had even installed a snorkel to enable the Green Hornet to go through deep standing water.

They transferred the footlocker from the Land Cruiser, Neil's two boxes, and a cooler from the house, their backpacks, and an overnight bag Bonnie and Cat shared.

Jack started to feel like it was a vacation, but inside, he felt as if trouble might strike at any moment. He watched for an enemy behind every tree. When Bonnie startled him walking from the garage to the house, he nearly took her down. They laughed, but she made a mental note about Jack's edginess, wondering even more what the brothers were running from. She also wondered what the real relationship was between her cousin and the brothers.

When Neil returned to Dauphin Island, he'd been secretive and quiet. Everyone knew his father's disappearance weighed heavily on him. The two had always been close. Many people speculated about the mysterious disappearance of the man and his boat. Some attributed it to a rogue wave or maybe drug dealers. Some said the DEA was involved.

The sea was a selfish keeper of secrets. Neil was doing more than looking for himself. He was certain he'd find his dad or evidence of the boat's demise. He would search the entire coast of the Gulf of Mexico and the Caribbean if he had to, but he would find the truth. No matter where it was, if someone else was responsible, he would make sure that person would be held accountable.

He spent only three weeks in-country before he left. Bonnie, more like a sister to Cat after her dad disappeared, was excited to see her brother and hoped he was home to stay. The house was lonely without him and her dad. She loved having it full again and wished Neil was back for good. Uncle Rick even offered Neil a boat to captain whenever he was ready. Neil knew the business as well as anyone.

17. Redneck Riviera

A fresh tank of gas, cool night air, the smell of the sea, and a woman's freshly washed hair; Jack rode shotgun beside Cat. Clearing the lights of Mobile, they drove east, taking Highway 98, skirting Mobile Bay, and heading south. A blinking marquee boasting fresh oysters, shrimp poor boys, and fifty-cent draft beer, brought the Spanish moss to life as it drifted in the breeze from a 100-foot live oak.

At Jack's request, Cat pulled into the parking lot where they saw an assortment of rusted pickups, a Volkswagen Thing, and a blue Rambler station wagon with laundry baskets in the back full of freshly washed clothes for the upcoming workweek. A pay phone sat empty in the corner of the lot under the oak, the perfect place to park and call the Diggins.

Jack and Elliott closed the phone booth door, as Patsy Cline crooned in the distance about walking the highway after midnight. Elliott dialed.

Randy, Nick and Cope were sitting at the bar near the pay

phone having a red beer and a microwave burrito when the staccato ring of the phone brought Cope to his feet.

He lifted the receiver and said, "It's your dime."

"Dad, it's Elliott. We're in the place we were supposed to call from on our way to see the yellow Lab."

"That's great news. Is everything else OK?"

"Fantastic. Better than I could've imagined. Did your guest arrive?"

"Yeah. I got who I was expecting, followed twelve hours later by six more who weren't welcome."

"Dad?" Jack asked. "I've got my ear to the phone, too. What happened?"

"Jack, it's good to hear your voice, too. We got a call from Elliott's boss alerting us to the fact that company was coming. We were prepared for their arrival and departure. Nick told me everything that happened. I'm real proud of you boys. You made good time, too. Do you have everything you need?"

"What should we do now, Dad. I mean, I know where we're going. Have you seen Katie and told her anything?"

"Jack, I don't have good news, but it's probably for the best right now. She came by to drop off the engagement ring. She said she wasn't ready and didn't think you were, either. Honestly, Jack, you kids need some time. I know it doesn't make it any easier.

"The first part of your question isn't much easier, either. We're working with Rabbit's old buddy to get things cleared up. You can plan on spending the winter with that yellow dog and company. Continue calling me here. I'll expect to hear from you after the next leg. I love you boys. Elliott, take care of your little brother, and Jack, watch out for Elliott."

"I love you, Dad," both boys said in unison.

Elliott, hanging up, saw tears in Jack's eyes. They hugged each other in the phone booth.

Bonnie and Cat knew something must've happened. They were watching from the car but didn't have time to talk about it before a jacked-up El Camino fishtailed into the parking lot and slid to a stop near the phone booth. A huge, burly man got out and saw Jack and Elliot embracing.

"What the fuck's going on here? Goddamn faggots are everywhere. Get the fuck out of the phone booth!"

He grabbed the phone booth door and almost jerked it off its hinges. He took the brothers in a headlock, with one on either arm, and started yelling to his buddy, "I caught us some faggots!"

The brothers each grabbed a leg and flipped the man almost as fast as he grabbed their heads. Jack put his foot on the back of his head and shoved him hard into the dirt.

"Listen here, Asshole. We aren't butt buddies. We're brothers who happen to love each other. I'm in no fucking mood to be messed with. We'll let you up, and we expect an apology, or you'll be back on the ground again, but it won't be half as nice. You got it, Asshole?"

They released his legs, and he fell onto his stomach. He got up to his hands and knees and charged Jack like a nose guard. His 300-pound body propelled Jack backward. Jack shoved his head down with all his strength, hooked the guy's right arm, and used his momentum to shove his head through the bonnet on the grill of the El Camino, knocking him out cold.

The second man, much smaller, jumped out of the car. "Holy crap! You got any idea what you just did? Man, you just started a war. Do you know who that is on the ground?" His eyes widened, and he ran for the bar, shouting, "They killed Big Daddy!"

"Get in the car!" Cat shouted, starting the overbuilt 454 engine.

Seconds later, the bar emptied into the parking lot to the sound of straight pipes in the distance and vanishing taillights. They carried Big Daddy into the bar and wrapped his lacerated head. With the help of smelling salts from the first-aid kit, Big Daddy woke up but couldn't remember what happened. Of course, his buddy spun a different story.

"It happened really fast. Big Daddy was going toward the phone when two guys jumped him out of nowhere from behind a tree and started beating on him. I think they sprayed him with something, so he couldn't see, then they shoved his head into the grill." The Chevrolet bonnet made a perfect outline on his shaved head.

"When I jumped out with a tire iron, they ran toward a big, jacked-up Suburban. It had big tires, a push guard, a winch, and even a snorkel for deep water. I think it was green. There was two girls in it, and one was driving."

Bonnie and Cat watched the fight, which lasted only twenty seconds. They'd been around long enough to know their troubles were far from over.

Cat quickly covered the twenty miles to Lulu's. They felt they had time for a quick beer before putting enough miles between them and Big Daddy to be safe.

Bonnie and Cat knew all about Big Daddy. He was a

legend. He played football for the University of Alabama before he was kicked out of school for drinking, fighting, and partying. Following his football debacle, he tried professional wrestling and soon had a following of jackasses he ran around with, causing trouble at the local bars from Mobile to Pascagoula. He wasn't allowed in Florida anymore after he and his friends tore up Panama City during spring break one year.

Cat pulled into a full parking lot at Lulu's. They parked the Suburban and waded through the crowd to the tiki bar for beer. A local band was playing *Free Bird* and people seemed to be having a good time.

Lulu got onto the stage and introduced her brother, who just produced his second album.

"I want y'all to give a warm welcome to Jimmy, just back from recording his latest album, *A White Sport Coat and a Pink Crustacean.* He'll play a couple songs for us now."

As Jimmy took the mike, the crowd went crazy. "I'm looking around here on a Sunday night, and it looks to me like there's a lot of people who don't give a damn about going to work Monday morning. Friday on Sunday. I love it."

He sang *Grapefruit Juicy Fruit* and was in the middle of *Why Don't We Get Drunk and Screw* when the sound of motorcycles grew louder than the music.

The musicians stopped, and the crowd opened to let Big Daddy ride his cycle up to the pirate stage. He took the mike from Jimmy and addressed the crowd.

"I want you all to look at my head and know that here among you are two men who violently, for no reason at all, attacked me. I want you to look around and see if there's someone you don't know who don't belong here. They're here. They came in a Suburban parked over there. Me and my friends are going to come in and take this place apart and everything in it until we find those cowards."

Jack didn't know why he was so angry, but he was. He calmly handed his beer to Cat and headed toward the stage, gaining momentum as he went. He clotheslined Big Daddy with a flying tackle, wrapping his neck like a boa constrictor in his powerful arms. The bike went one way, and Big Daddy writhed helplessly on the ground, clutching at Jack's grip until the blood flow to his carotid was cut off, and he passed out.

Jack stood, picking up the dropped mike. "I'm really sorry about this. This man is an absolute liar. He attacked me twice this evening after he saw me hugging my brother. He called me some kind of queer. When he wakes up, you can assure him I'm no coward or a queer, so he doesn't have to feel ashamed. Sorry for the interruption, Mr. Buffet. I think we have to go now."

Jack handed Jimmy Buffet the mike, and the crowd cheered. Bonnie and Cat were already in the Green Hornet with the engine running, the four-wheel-drive hubs locked in, and the transfer case in low. Elliott had the 1911 .45 ready in case of an attack. Cat handed Jack his unfinished beer when he got in the front seat. It was still cold.

"What took you so long, Little Brother?" Elliott asked.

"I had to put Big Daddy to sleep, then I made a speech." He looked at Cat. "Can you get us out of here without a riot?"

Cat punched the gas pedal, and the four-barrel opened up. The Green Hornet jumped like a tarantula through the creek, over the sand dunes, and down the beach. They were gone within seconds.

The crowd picked up Big Daddy and his bike, then Jimmy resumed singing, and the party grew with the addition of Big Daddy and his entourage. Not wanting to be upstaged, Big Daddy offered an apology.

"I hope everyone here enjoyed the show by Big Daddy Productions and event security of LA." He raised his arms and shook his fists from the bow of the pirate ship, looking much the part with his bandaged head, dew rag, and loop earrings.

The crowd cheered, and Big Daddy felt better in front of his adoring fans. His fame spread when a clip of Jack clotheslining him appeared on a local news channel, putting Big Daddy back in the spotlight again. The Flora-Bama Club called him the next morning to work a beach party the following day.

Cat didn't see any headlights behind them, so there was no need to hurry. She downshifted, letting the vehicle crawl toward Fort Morgan, at the entrance to Mobile Bay to the east and Fort Gaines on Dauphin Island on the west. In the Civil War, the Union Navy paid a heavy price passing between those two forts when it attempted to take Mobile. Neither the forts nor Mobile fell, though the port was lost to blockade runners.

Growing up in California, Jack and Elliott knew very little about that war, so they enjoyed their tour of Fort Gaines. Soon, they were approaching Fort Morgan on the other side of the bay's mouth. It was horrifying to think what it must have been like during the battle, filled with smoke and the deafening sound of cannon fire as incoming shells exploded against the fort's brick walls.

Suddenly, Cat slammed on the brakes. Jack caught himself

on the dashboard, while Bonnie and Elliott nearly flew over the front seat. A clutch of emerging loggerhead turtles were frantically crawling down the beach, while two coyotes enjoyed the chance at easy prey.

"Shoot those damn things!" Bonnie told Elliott. "Shoot 'em before they get any more turtles. I hate coyotes."

Elliott fired a couple of ineffective shots into the sand, scaring off the coyotes.

"So much for quietly easing down the beach," Jack said.

That was the first time the brothers saw a clutch of turtles moving toward the sea. They were delighted. They also saw heron, crabs, and sandpipers, though there were no more turtles.

The fort, illuminated by the moon, loomed formidable against the dark sea and sky. A set of headlights up ahead appeared momentarily before going out, causing them some concern, until they saw a lantern being lit to reveal a fisherman setting out surf rods.

Cat knew the way through the trails and sand dunes to the fort parking lot from years of fishing with her brother and his friends. The fort was one of Neil's favorite places. The fisherman on the beach was the only other soul around.

They got out and opened the steel gate to the fort, walking hand-in-hand through the brick arches up to the parapet overlooking the Gulf of Mexico and Mobile Bay. The brick was worn smooth, wet and cool to the touch in the night air. Waves crashed against the point, and the call of sea birds was mesmerizing.

They stood together, leaning against the parapet while looking seaward. Jack thought about Cat's dad and how she must feel not knowing what happened to him.

"Do you think about your dad a lot?" he asked. "It must be hell not knowing."

"I do, but I think he's OK, and I think Neil will find him. I know that in my heart. He's being held somewhere against his will, or he'd be here. I'd know if he was dead."

"I feel the same way about Uncle Jim," Bonnie added. "As long as we're asking serious questions, I have one for you. Are you absolutely fucking nuts? I can't imagine anyone doing what you did, except maybe Bruce Lee or Chuck Norris. I thought I saw everything when you rammed Big Daddy into the grill of that Camaro. When you flew over his motorcycle at a full run and jerked him off that bike, well.... I never saw anybody do anything like that, except for stunt men in a movie."

"Bonnie, sometimes I wonder—not if I'm nuts—but why crap like this keeps happening. We aren't looking for trouble, but it seems there's always someone trying to hurt me or the people I care about. I snap. There was no plan or calculation. I acted instinctively. That's how Elliott and I grew up.

"Don't be confused about my big brother. He was always the better athlete. He's taller and faster."

Jack wrapped his arms around Cat, breathing deeply from the side of her neck and through her hair, drifting on the night breeze. She realized how safe and warm she felt with his arms around her waist, and she overlapped her arms on his, squeezing back firmly. Jack felt her breasts against his arms, and the desire to make love was like a rising tide on the full moon.

"Elliott, did you know what Jack was planning back there?" Bonnie asked, squeezing Elliott's hands and pulling on his arms.

"I didn't know what he was going to do, but when he

handed off his beer, I knew he was planning something. He really hates being called names. Like he said, you never know exactly what you're going to do, you just do it. When faced with overwhelming odds, you have to be unpredictable.

"Take the crowd back at Lulu's, the ones who came with Big Daddy. They expected a big beat down spectacle from their fearless leader. They thought we'd be afraid and would run. Instead, Little Brother did the unexpected. He attacked in the face of danger, cutting the head off the snake. It's like that in football. If it's third and one, the defense expects a run, so throw the long ball."

Cat turned her head to regard Elliott. "What position did you play?"

"Elliott was the best quarterback in the history of Trinity High," Jack said. "He broke every record and was most-valuable player in the state championship game, which we won. He's probably one of the best athletes you'll ever meet." He raised his right arm, giving a high five to his big brother.

"I believe the most-valuable player of that game should have been my little brother," Elliott said. "He was middle linebacker and led the defense in tackles, interceptions, and even a fumble recovery in the championship game."

They shared another high five. The football talk helped cool Jack's rising temperature, and hunger began to set in.

"What kind of food is in the cooler?" Jack asked.

"We have sandwich stuff," Cat said. "But let's go to the Pink Pony. I love that place. It's right on the beach at Gulf Shores, not far from here. It's been there forever and survived every hurricane with only minor damage. They've got oysters, shrimp, cheeseburgers—you know, beach food—and cold beer."

She pulled his hand, leading the way back to the truck. The heavy steel doors creaked a mournful good-bye, as Jack and Elliott closed them. The ghosts could resume their haunt with the rats and nesting birds.

They drove down a lightly traveled road toward the lights of Gulf Shores, passing only one other car. They found a few cars in the parking lot and a couple of people drinking beer at the bar. Sunday nights were slow in the off season.

"What will you kids have?" the waitress asked.

"We were hoping we could get something to eat," Elliott said, sitting at a round table.

"You'd better order fast. It's a slow night, and the cook's ready to go home."

"I can understand that," Bonnie said. "I work in a restaurant. How about four dozen raw oysters, a pitcher of draft, four fry baskets, with shrimp, scallops, oysters, hush puppies, and coleslaw for sides?" She looked around the table and received nods of approval.

The waitress put away her pad with a smile. "I sure like it when people know what they want. Johnny," she called to the cook, "I need four dozen oysters shucked and four baskets with scallops, oysters, shrimp, and hush puppies." She turned to the table. "I'll be right back with your beer."

The mugs arrived frosted, the beer was cold, and the oysters were fresh and plump. Soon, four steaming baskets of fried seafood arrived. The group dipped them in tartar sauce and ate hungrily.

Elliott paid the bill and left another twenty as a tip, with an additional ten for the cook. As they discussed where to spend the night, the local evening news showed a clip from Lulu's.

The narration touted local heroes Big Daddy and Jimmy Buffet collaborating at an area club. The video showed Jack's flying tackle and Big Daddy's monologue from the bow of the pirate ship stage. It was a great piece of advertising, which the boys didn't want.

"Oh, shit," Jack said. "I hope the wrong people don't see that."

"Who are they?" Cat asked.

"We'll have plenty of time to talk later. Let's find a room."

They found a beachfront motel two miles down the strip with first-floor adjoining rooms that opened onto the beach. Jack and Elliott knew the girls were curious about their situation. Even though they trusted them, they had to stonewall for a while. There was no need to expose them to the ugly truth of their situation. The two fair-haired boys were actually killers on the run.

They needed a cover story, though, a partial truth they could tell with a straight face. They decided to use the simple truth with a few omissions.

"I guess from all the secrecy," Elliott said, "you figured we're on the run. My brother and I were attacked by people who work for some important people. You can probably imagine that people were hurt. Then their people got mad and sent more people after us, but they got hurt instead. They still want to hurt us. In order not to have to hurt any more of them, we decided to leave town for a while. I know that's a little vague, but that's the long and short of it."

He smiled, glad he was able to tell the truth, even if it was highly edited.

The two couples went to their rooms and acted like honeymooners.

The maid woke them at ten o'clock the following morning by knocking on the door. After they checked out, they drove east along the fifty-mile stretch of Alabama coast to the Flora-Bama Club.

The club started as a roadside liquor store on the state line. Half was in Florida, the other half in Alabama. Its popularity grew with each addition. It was famous for Southern rock, volleyball, live concerts on the beach, excessive alcohol consumption, and beautiful women in bikinis.

It was the crown jewel of the Redneck Riviera. The boys agreed it wasn't too far out of the way, and they could afford to stop to see it, but they needed to reach El Jobean before they were on any more news channels.

The parking lots were full of cars and motorcycles. A box truck of speakers and amps was being unloaded, and a stage set up at the back of the club faced the beach. Excitement filled the air.

They entered the front door of the original liquor store, stopped at the first bar, and bought beer. The bartender told them Jimmy Buffet would give a free concert that night. Suddenly Big Daddy's 300-pound body filled the doorway to the open-air tiki bar. He recognized the brothers immediately and wished he knew Cat and Bonnie.

"Hey, Boys," he said. "I guess you weren't so light in your loafers after all."

Jack felt adrenalin race through his body like electricity. He jumped to his feet, followed by Elliott, both ready for a brawl.

"Wait a minute!" Big Daddy said. "I had you two wrong from the start. I started the trouble in the parking lot for no good reason. I was doing what I do best, showing off and acting up. I was real sore about what happened, then I saw it was for the best.

"Our little scuffle got me on TV again, and that's how I got the job for today. Whatever your names are, you did me a favor. I'm even gonna have a cool scar that's the shape of my Chevrolet grill at the top of my skull. I'll keep my head shaved, so everybody can see it. It's better than a tattoo."

Elliott looked quizzically at Jack, then turned back to Big Daddy. "So you're not mad at us? You don't want to fight any more?"

"No. Not just no, but hell no. I learned my lesson. I got a busted head and wounded pride, but most important, I'm a changed man. I'm through messing with people. You know, to each his own. What do you say I buy you men and these beautiful women a drink? I'm getting reinvented as we speak. I'll provide security and master-of-ceremony services from New Orleans to Key West. It's Big Daddy Productions and Security of LA. That's Lower Alabama to you, if you aren't familiar with the Riviera. Bartender, set up five shots of Patron for my good friends and me. Put it on Jimmy Buffet's tab."

"I'm real glad we could help in your personal development," Elliott said. "When we first met, you were way out of line. Like you say, it's all behind us now, right?"

"Damn right. To show I'm sincere, I want to hire you boys to work the show today. What do you say to $500 for the whole bunch. You girls can be bikini dancers on stage, and you guys can provide personal security for Jimmy. That means keeping people off the stage and away from his trailer. Food and drinks will be free. You can even use the trailer to sleep in after the show. What do you say?"

Bonnie and Cat's faces lit up like Roman candles, and they started dancing to Marshall Tucker playing in the background.

"Man, that's such a cool offer," Elliott said. "Under different circumstances, you wouldn't be able to get rid of us."

"Sorry, Big Daddy," Jack said. "We can't do it this trip. We have important family business to attend to, but I'd sure like a rain check."

The pouting women made sour faces at him.

"I understand. Y'all got to do what y'all got to do. Big Daddy will always have a job for you if you ever get back here. Take my card."

They downed their shots together and shook hands with Big Daddy, except for the girls. He kissed their hands instead.

"You know, you two look awful familiar to me," Big Daddy said.

"The last time you saw me," Cat said, "I was with my brother, and I was about fourteen. You remember Neil Tinner from Dauphin Island?"

"The hell you say! You're his little sister? I knew I saw that green Suburban somewhere before. Hell, it's been ten years or so since I have seen him. How's he doing? I heard he went to Vietnam."

"Yeah. He made it back in one piece. I'll tell him I saw you."

"Give him my regards. I'm sincerely sorry about being a jackass, but I'm a changed man now."

They left through the meandering walkways of picnic tables and boardwalks, past the stage to the beach. The bright sun reflected off the snow white powdery sand. Blue-green water from the Gulf rolled gently between a sandbar offshore and the beach.

"If we can't get paid to dance, drink for free, and hang out with Jimmy Buffet," Cat said, "at least we can swim. Come on, Bonnie."

The girls removed their flannel shirts and blue jeans, leaving them in a pile on their flip flops.

"It reminds me of the *Wizard of Oz*," Elliott said, staring at the pile of clothes, "when they threw water on the Wicked Witch, and she melted."

"Oh, well. What's a couple minutes in the big picture?" Jack stripped down to his boxers and ran into the water with the girls.

They swam together like a pod of dolphins in the gentle trough, enjoying the refreshing warm water. They swam on their backs, their sides, did the breaststroke, or treaded water, talking about their twelve-hour drive and the approximate arrival times.

The girls wanted to meander the barrier island paradise of the Panhandle, the string of beautiful white beaches with Caribbean blue water. They agreed it would be best to spend the night somewhere en route and arrive during daylight to meet Neil. Cat and Bonnie wanted to go to Juana's Pagodas on Navarre Beach for lunch. They would drive somewhere south of Tampa and find a room off the interstate that evening.

The day warmed nicely. By noon, it was eighty degrees, which wasn't bad for October. Jack and Elliott traded their wet boxers for dry shorts and T-shirts in the relative privacy of the Suburban. The girls put on dry clothes in the back seat and agreed to let Elliott and Jack drive to Navarre Beach.

They drove down the beach road, past the big lagoon around Pensacola, and back down to Highway 98. Their trip stopped at the drawbridge to Santa Rosa Island to allow a sailboat to pass. Cat identified it as a classic Alden, a graceful black sleek boat with lots of wood. A woman with a Mona Lisa gaze stood at the bow with a man at the helm, probably heading south before the cold weather arrived.

A pair of dolphins escorted the sailboat through the bridge opening. The name on the stern read *Essay.* Elliott fantasized about living on a sailboat as they waited.

Once across the bridge, they planned to turn right and go to Fort Pickens, but they chose to eat first. Elliott was confused by the name of Juana's Pagodas. He knew pagodas were Buddhist temples, but Juana sounded Mexican.

It was a great surprise when they got there and saw the structures didn't resemble pagodas at all. Juana, who had red hair and freckles, was anything but Mexican. Nonetheless, they were starving, and instead of Buddhist burritos, they had half-pound cheddar cheeseburgers with bacon, avocado, jalapenos, tomatoes, mustard, and ketchup. On their way out, they stocked up at the bakery and deli.

Interstate 10 was the fastest route but not the most pleasurable. The girls convinced them to take the coastal road by going to Navarre. They were committed to Highway 98 at least to Panama City, and they hoped to convince the boys to stay on 98 all the way to 75. They would have minor slow spots, but there were also huge live oaks and Victorian and Antebellum mansions surrounded by magnificent magnolias.

The Florida State parks read like a litany of saints—Santa Rosa, St. Joseph, San Blas, St. Andrews, St. Vincent, St.

George, St. Mark's, and San Mateo. It was called the Forgotten Coast, largely because it was uninhabited and undeveloped, a land where the trees were valued more for their shade than feared for the damage they might cause during a storm.

When they saw the signs for St. George's Island, Elliott remembered that was where Jack and his father went camping and met Neil right before the accident.

"How far were you from St. George's Island when you had the accident?" he asked.

"I didn't know you'd been here before," Cat said. "Of course, there's very little I know about you actually, except my brother trusts you. That, of course, will have to change now that you defrocked his little sister."

Jack wondered how Neil would receive news of their relationship. He would have to tiptoe around that. Trusting a person was one thing, but sleeping with his sister was quite another.

"I hope it doesn't come up," Jack said. "There's no reason to publicize our private relationship. I wouldn't want him sore at me, or anyone else, for that matter."

Bonnie and Cat laughed hysterically in the back seat. Elliott looked at Jack.

"I don't think it would be funny if your brother decided to kick Jack's ass for messing with his sister," Elliott said.

"Neil's like a brother to me," Bonnie said. "He's just as protective of me as he is of Cat."

The brothers played along with the joke.

"Seriously, though," Bonnie asked, "what kind of accident were you in?"

"I was in a car accident right after graduating from flight

school. My dad picked me and another Warrant Officer up at Fort Rucker. We spent a weekend at St. George's Island fishing and camping. That's where we met Neil and Clara, they spent two days with us on the beach.

"It was a great time. Neil said he was traveling the Gulf hoping to find the part of himself he lost in Vietnam. He spent a lot of time talking with my dad, who's also a combat veteran and a prisoner of war survivor from World War Two. I'd be in Vietnam right now, except for the accident when we were heading back to Fort Rucker on Highway 231."

"I'm sorry you were in the accident," Cat said, "but I'm glad you didn't have to go to Vietnam. How bad were all of you hurt?" She leaned forward from the back seat and put her hands on his chest, kissing his neck, whispering, "I'm real glad you didn't go."

"Yeah, well, some of the situations we've been in since I left the Army make me wonder which would've been more dangerous."

"No kidding," Elliott said. "We've encountered a lot of really violent situations and assholes I don't want to remember."

"To answer your question," Jack said, "my buddy, Dennis, wasn't hurt at all. Dad was banged up a little and I ended up in the Naval Hospital in Pensacola in a coma. I walked away from the Army with a steel plate in my head."

"The stuff Neil told you about finding himself was more like he's trying to find our dad," Cat said.

"What do you mean? Why would he mischaracterize himself like that?"

"I'm sure there was truth to what he said, but he suspects foul play. The drug cartels have been using shrimping boats and fishing boats to smuggle cocaine. If Dad's boat was lost at sea, there would've been flotsam, like an oil slick, coolers, or floating debris. He would've made a Mayday call. He had a life raft that automatically deploys.

"Neil is certain there was foul play, maybe smugglers or drug dealers. Trust me. He's not looking to find himself. If he finds the one or ones he thinks did something to Dad, well.... You think you've seen trouble, but you haven't seen Neil when he's angry. It ain't pretty."

Cat looked at Bonnie, who said, "I was there when he fought a whole bar full of men after someone tried to welch on a hundred-dollar bet. He never quit until there was no one left standing. He sent several to the hospital. That's when he was given two choices. He could join the Army or go to state prison."

"I can't imagine how we'd feel if our dad went missing without a trace," Elliott said. "I guarantee we'd be looking for answers, too."

Jack realized their next journey wasn't a pleasure trip. They would join Neil on his quest. It was an honorable thing to be part of. He knew there would likely be more trouble, but that didn't matter. Whether fate, destiny, random coincidence, or divine intervention brought them to that juncture didn't matter. The Copelands were joining a mission.

Cat understood that, too, and she was happy with it, as well as being happy with Jack.

18. El Jobean

Despite the Spanish-sounding name, the town wasn't founded by conquistadors or Portuguese explorers. Nothing of historical significance happened there, unless one considered the filming of the first Tarzan movies a few miles upstream significant.

The Myakka River narrowed a bit, making it an optimal place for cars and trains to cross. In its glory days, there was a waterfront hotel, and the circus came every winter with elephants and tigers, but that was a long time in the past. The train no longer brought the circus to town, and the trestle became a fishing pier.

The only business in El Jobean was the fishery and a small retirement community that found its way off the beaten path. The old train depot sold burgers, bait, and beer, but visitors had to go somewhere else to get their mail. The fixed bridge stopped vessels with masts of any height from venturing any farther upriver.

It was a perfect place for a seedy waterfront dive like Tolliver's. The planked wood floor warped and sagged to the ground. Dock crabs scavenged with impunity. The bar listed fifteen degrees. A hole in the wall between the men's and women's bathrooms negated even the most-liberal concept of privacy.

Tolliver's had some redeeming qualities, like a pool table, pay phone, parking, and walking distance to the trestle for fishing. It was a favorite haunt of commercial and recreational fishermen. No one cared if someone came in wearing rubber boots and smelling like crab bait. Neil could beach his dinghy less than 100 yards away, drink a beer, and keep an eye on his boat. It was a perfect place for him to get information about Charlotte Harbor from the locals. That night, however, he met with Fred to get a file of maintenance records on the *Sally Jo.* Clara sat beside him on the floor when Fred arrived.

"Hello, Fred," Neil said. "How are you this fine October evening?"

"Just fine, just fine. Hello, Clara." Fred held her head in his hands, rubbing her ears before kissing the top of her head. She rose, put her paws on his chest, and licked his nose. Laughing, he sat down with an armful of papers in a manila envelope.

"I've got all the records here," he said, "every piece of paper I ever got for anything we did or bought for the boat."

"Thanks, Fred. I really appreciate that. I'm sure it'll be a big help."

Fred, looking around apprehensively, lowered his voice. "I really need to talk to you someplace private. There are some things you need to know about the *Sally Jo,* Betty, and me."

Neil finished his beer. "What do you say we walk over to the trestle and see how the snook fishermen are doing?"

They walked away.

"Neil, this is a little hard to explain," Fred said, "but I hope you don't judge me or think less of me. It's a long story, so just let me tell you.

"Betty and I went to the Exumas, a place called Fishmonger Cay. Unbeknownst to me, the most-prolific drug cartel in the world took over the island. We went to the anchorage described in the cruising guide called the Pond. It was hard to reach, but once we were there, it was idyllic and serene. The water was crystal clear and protected all around. We thought we died and went to heaven when we dropped the plow.

"We were having sundowners in the cockpit when two skiffs approached from either side. Armed men said we were invited to supper on the island. They explained it wasn't an option if we wanted to live."

Fred stopped halfway down the old trestle, to avoid the fishermen at the end.

"We were taken in one of the skiffs by an armed man and a driver. The other skiff stayed behind. I saw the other two men board our boat, as we motored toward a large dock where several other boats were tied. A truck waited, and we were ferried to a beautiful oceanfront home overlooking the Atlantic.

"We were told we'd be dining with El Hefei and some other gringos who were his guests. We were also told to be silent and only speak when spoken to if we knew what was good for us. No one who offended Felipe, El Hefei, survived.

"We were terribly frightened, given only two choices. We could take cocaine back to El Jobean or die in the Pond and be fed to the sharks. The two men who were on our boat brought back all the leverage they needed. They had our address book and mail from the kids. El Hefei said if we did anything to double-cross him or notify the authorities, they knew where our grandchildren lived and would kill them all after raping and torturing them. They had us over a barrel."

Fred took a deep breath, staring out over the Myakka River. "That crap about our being too old to sail was a lie. That bastard stole our lives."

"I don't know what to say," Neil said. "There's no way in hell I would've imagined you and Betty to be drug traffickers."

"That's what everyone else thought, too. That's how we got away with it for so long. We weren't the only ones victimized. The whole island is under their control. The homeowners' property was stolen, and they were evicted from the island at gunpoint. They kept several Americans prisoner who they threatened to kill unless they worked for them. These people are ruthless. There's no telling how many they've killed. They bring tons of cocaine from Columbia and ship it to America in all kinds of vessels.

Neil's heart pounded. Something told him he was closer to finding his father. "Is that why you sold me the boat so cheap?"

"The drug dealers used fear, but they also paid well. We paid for that boat after three trips. I can't say I'm proud of it, but we had little choice. There's no way in hell the police could protect our kids and grandkids. I didn't tell you this so you could judge me but to warn you that there might be some danger in owning that boat. I wanted to give you the option to change your mind.

"You should know that the water tanks under the salon sale were modified for smuggling. Their capacity is less than twenty gallons, which can be a real problem. The only reason they let us out of the game was because of our age and for a lie I made up.

"I told Felipe that Betty had cancer and had only six months to live. We thought he might kill us anyway and take our boat, but he hasn't killed us yet. We unloaded our last shipment right before we met you at Boca Grande. Betty and I felt strongly, and still do, that you were destined to have our boat."

"I suppose El Hefei probably feels strongly about it, too." Neil's mind raced with the possibilities.

Fred stared out at the water. "I don't think anything happens randomly. We were supposed to meet. Our destinies were wound together long before that day. The first night at Fishmonger Cay, I prayed for an avenger, someone who could avenge the wrong these people are doing. We don't know why, but Betty and I feel you're the one. No, not felt. We knew it in our heart of hearts."

Tears flowed from his eyes, and he embraced Neil in a bear hug. They held onto each other hard for a moment, then Fred bent over to hug Clara before walking away.

Fred and Betty never saw Neil again. They left in the middle of the night for an unknown destination deep in the Ozark hills and hollows of Missouri.

When Filipe's men arrived to cut Fred and Betty's throats, the house was empty. The second part of their instructions were to sail the boat back to Fishmonger Cay, but it wasn't there, either. All they could do was wait until morning and try to locate the sailboat.

Neil returned to Tolliver's, ordered a beer, and sat down. A commercial fisherman and regular customer saw Neil coming and going from his boat and admired Clara.

"Hey," he said, "my name's John. How are you doing?"

"Fine. How are you?" Neil stood to shake hands, surprised by the man's Wisconsin accent. He looked like a local with a wide-brimmed straw hat, red bandanna around his neck, a long-sleeved tie-dyed T-shirt, khaki pants, and white boots, but he talked funny.

"I'm pretty good. When I first saw the boat anchored out there, I thought it might be Fred and Betty waiting on the tide to get in to the canal. Then I saw you coming and going for a few days and figured it out."

"You're partly right. She used to be theirs. Now she's mine. I got the rest of the paperwork today."

"I can't believe they sold her. That was a really good boat for them. They go back and forth to the Bahamas all the time."

Neil, highly suspicious of John, gave no indication. He believed in keeping his enemies close and never giving away what he knew or didn't know. The two men sat and drank beer, talking about fishing, the local area, and where a fellow might provision a boat conveniently.

Neil said he was going to the Dry Tortugas. John said he could come up the canal and dock at his house, even use his truck to get whatever he needed. Neil liked that idea and agreed to move the boat up the canal as soon as his crew arrived. The two men took the short walk to John's house.

He showed Neil where to tie up. "I don't know my own schedule, so just come in at high tide and act like you own the place. My boat's in the yard getting a bottom job, so there's plenty of room."

Neil went back to his dinghy, starting the little Johnson engine on the first pull. Clara rode the bow like a maidenhead, ears flopping the whole way. When they reached the *Sally Jo,* she leaped over the toe rail.

Sleep came hard for Neil that night. He had a lot to plan. He wondered if Jack and his brother, whom he never met, would be willing crewmates for what might be a very dangerous trip. Though he liked and trusted Jack, he refused to become complacent in such a potentially deadly game with the cartel. He wasn't sure how much he should tell them when they arrived.

By 7:30 AM, the Green Hornet was driving down Highway 75 with Cat at the wheel and Jack riding shotgun. They took River Road off the interstate to El Jobean Road. As they crossed the Myakka River bridge, they saw what they suspected was Neil's boat. A dinghy trailed from the stern with the outgoing tide, so they parked on the far side and walked back to the middle of the bridge.

Neil was loading the dinghy when he saw them waving. He was heading in for a cheeseburger at the Bean Depot. They watched from the bridge to see where he was heading, and then they followed. Their paths intersected between the mangroves and Tolliver's.

Neil grabbed his little sister in a short embrace. "How's my Green Hornet?"

Cat slapped him playfully. "Is that all you care about, your precious truck? She ran great, but we had to go through some saltwater. I did a little evasive maneuver through the creek at

Lulu's and down the beach to Fort Morgan. Jack had a confrontation with your old pal Big Daddy. It lasted twenty seconds, and we made a hasty departure."

"That's nothing to be ashamed of. He probably outweighs Jack by 150 pounds. How are you, Jack? You don't look too bad for going twenty seconds with that animal."

"Brother," Cat said, "when Jack walked away, your old pal was out for the count. We left, because he brought about fifty bikes with him."

"Unbelievable. I won't ask why. Did you bring my green footlockers, tackle boxes, and all?"

"I haven't seen or heard from you in months, and all you care about is your stuff."

"You're right. We have plenty of time for that. It's great to see all of you—Sis, Cousin, Jack, and you must be brother Elliott. I was just on my way for a cheeseburger at the Bean Depot. Let's go. This is the coolest spot. The train used to come across the river, and it was a real depot, with a post office and even a jail. A guy who dove a hundred feet through fire into a tub of water used to own it. They named the bacon cheeseburger in his honor. It's a Suicide Simon Burger."

"With a name like El Jobean," Bonnie said, "I was expecting Spanish architecture and burritos."

"Sort of like Juana's Pagodas," Elliot said. "What's the story with that?"

"It's a funny one. The guy who incorporated this town was named Joel Bean. Rearrange the letters, and you get El Jobean. He must've had a great sense of humor."

They sat around a picnic table at the Bean Depot.

"You can't imagine how happy I am to see family and

friends again," Neil said. "I can't wait to show you the *Sally Jo.* We have a lot to do to prepare for our maiden voyage, plus a little more since you took the Hornet swimming. The doing part starts right after lunch. We'll begin with a thorough washing of the Green Hornet to get the salt off the undercarriage and make sure there's no water in the gearboxes and differentials.

"Then, when the tide's coming in good this afternoon, we'll take a little boat ride up into the canals and tie up for a few days while we provision. We leave for the Bahamas as soon as we're ready."

As Neil spoke, he conveyed a sense of both calm and urgency, as well as the confidence of a seasoned combat warrior.

"Neil," Jack said, "you know my brother and I have never sailed, right?"

"Not to worry. If you can fly a chopper or paddle a kayak, you can crew on a sailboat. It's hours of pure boredom with an occasional moment of terror. The most-important thing to remember is that there's only one captain, and that's me."

Neil raised his mug like a triumphant emperor who just conquered the continent. They raised their mugs and laughed, except for Bonnie, who took the moment to interject her own thoughts.

"You're all laughing now," she said, "but you've never been on a boat with him. There's nowhere to run or hide from the ever-overbearing Captain Ahab."

They laughed, though they soon found out just how serious Neil was about being prepared, which included complete maintenance and inspection of all systems on the boat, as well as the specialized tools for their mission.

After lunch, they found the local car wash and jacked up the Suburban, removed each wheel and brake drum, and washed salt off the brake shoe assemblies, cylinders, and backing plates. Neil had installed hoses over both differential vents to protect them from water contamination, and the ninety-weight lubricant was still the color of maple syrup. The same was true for the transfer case and transmission. If there was water present, the oil would have been milky and in need of changing.

Jack took a grease gun and hit the zerk fitting on each universal joint in the driveshaft, as well as the front end. While the weight was off, Neil inspected the front wheel bearings for excessive play. Bonnie and Cat vacuumed the interior and cleaned the windows. The whole process took two hours with all working together.

The tide had already turned when they arrived at John's house in the Green Hornet. Neil walked to his dinghy and returned to pick up his crew at John's dock, a wooden structure fifty feet long with pilings every ten feet. The roof was made of sagging rafters and rusted corrugated metal. It wasn't rated for snow load, but it would block the sun and rain.

The dock was set up for a commercial fisherman. It had a small boat ramp at one end, a fish-cleaning station at the other, mangrove bushes on either side, and teemed with crabs and lizards of all kinds.

The nine-foot Avon inflatable sat low in the water with five adults and Clara as they headed toward the *Sally Jo.* The reliable six-horsepower Johnson engine pushed them to the side of the boat where the ladder waited. Jack adeptly climbed up to the toe rail and steadied the little raft while the others came up.

There was a lot to see, feel, and touch, as the four took Neil's guided tour. A wide beam provided plenty of room below for the separate fore and aft staterooms with individual heads, a large salon, and a generous galley. Cat and Bonnie were very happy for Neil. He always wanted a sailboat big enough to cross the ocean.

Sally Jo was perfect. She was forty-two-feet long, thirteen feet wide, with a four-foot draft, a ketch rig with center cockpit. She was designed and built by Ted Irwin for the shallow waters of Florida and the Bahamas. Equipped for extensive cruising and shorthanded sailing, she was in better shape than the day she was bought, except for the diminished water capacity.

The secret stowage would serve Neil's purposes on the trip more than the extra water. He found the hull to be clean and unblistered when he dove to inspect it. Studying the old maintenance records, he saw the preventive maintenance schedule had been documented and regimented by the hours of engine operation recorded by the Hobbs meter on the three-cylinder Yanmar diesel engine. She was hauled regularly, and the fiberglass hull was nearly bulletproof.

The jib was a Genoa on a roller furling, with plenty of life left in it. The rest of the sails were fresh and crinkly, too. Ground tackle included a good plow and large Danforth anchor, both with 100 feet of chain in the bow locker.

The cockpit was equipped with a smaller anchor that could be deployed in an emergency. A manual windlass enabled Betty to pull the heavy anchor. Overbuilt davits extended four feet beyond the stern, strong enough for the inflatable tender and engine. A folding swim platform provided comfort and safety for swimmers.

Neil, starting the diesel engine, demonstrated the windlass' efficiency at raising anchor. Engaging the engine from the pedestal controls in the cockpit, they began the short trip to the dock. Elliott and Jack took places at bow and stern for docking.

It was a high-energy trip with an enthusiastic crew. Afternoon clouds threatened daily showers that abated the otherwise intolerable heat of the Florida sun. Neil had been handling boats since he was a child. Negotiating the narrow channels into John's dock went flawlessly.

A slight thrust of the prop in reverse killed their forward momentum, and the *Sally Jo* landed. Dock lines were attached fore and aft, and spring lines and fenders were secured just as the wind picked up ahead of the thunderstorm.

"I guess we'll have a meeting at some point and discuss what we're doing," Captain Neil said. "A rain shower is a perfect time."

"Jack," Elliott said, "we're supposed to call Dad as soon as we got here. In the excitement, I almost forgot."

Neil tossed him the keys. "Take the Hornet. There's a pay phone at the convenience store by the public boat ramp."

John's house was directly behind the dock with a small lane between the two for loading and unloading vehicles. The house, thirty by forty, sat ten feet off the ground on pilings. It was graced with a waterfront rusted-metal roof and weathered Cyprus board and bat exterior. A covered porch wrapped around two sides with staircases at either end, commanding waterfront views of the Myakka River and Charlotte Harbor to the south.

John appeared at the screen door upstairs. "I see you made

it in with your boat. Did I hear someone say he needed to use a phone? There's one under the house you can use."

"Thanks, but it's long distance," Jack said.

"Welcome to the waterfront garage and lodge," John said in a tone that made them all feel welcome, as if they were long-lost friends.

Neil introduced Bonnie, Cat, Elliott, and Jack, and all received warm handshakes. It seemed as if John was happy for the company, or maybe it was the addition of two beautiful young women. The brothers left in the Hornet to call their father.

"I should show you all the amenities," John said. "My boat's getting ready for the mullet season, so you don't have to be in a big hurry. I've got potable water, electricity, and even an ice machine. You can swim in the canal if you know how to wrestle alligators." Laughing, he slapped his leg.

"We'll leave alligator wrestling to the locals," Neil said, "but everything else sounds great. If you're serious about letting us tie up here for a while, I'd gladly pay you what I would pay someone else. It would be a great convenience for us. I don't need a month and maybe not even a week. We just have to get the boat ready and buy provisions. She's in good shape. I just need to change fluids and inspect some systems."

"I know Betty and Fred are squared-away sailors," John said. "The mechanic I occasionally use when I'm stumped worked on that boat. They didn't spare any cost or leave anything to chance. He had carte blanch when it came to maintenance and repairs. I'll bet you find everything is shipshape."

"Everything I've seen so far has been good. I definitely want to take a sample from the bottom of the fuel tanks, though."

John nodded. In the diesel engine business, clean fuel and filters are critical. Water at the bottom of a fuel tank can remain undetected until the seas are rough, and that is when an engine is most needed, only to suddenly fall silent.

Bonnie and Cat explored the boat while Neil and John attached shore power and water. John reluctantly agreed to accept $25 a day as a docking fee. Neil insisted and paid for one week in advance.

The two watermen had a lot in common—commercial fishing in the Gulf as well as sport fishing. Neil felt his instincts were right about John, but he knew that gaining trust was the hallmark of an effective operator.

Both knew how to throw a net for bait or set a gill net to catch a school of mullet. They talked about the similarities and differences between Mobile Bay and Charlotte Harbor. Snook live in Charlotte harbor. It is arguably not only the best eating fish in the Gulf, but it was one of the hardest to catch. Due to their aggressive nature, they were fairly easy to hook, but they were incredibly strong. Their razor-sharp gill plates were effective in cutting off lines and leaders. A snook would strike like a freight train, but once feeling the hook, it would run toward the mangroves and cut the line on oysters and barnacles.

"I have an idea," John said. "After the thunderstorms pass, we can take my skiff out to the trestle and see if we can catch some snook for supper. If you don't think it's the best fish you ever ate, I'll be surprised. Don't get me wrong. Flounder, cobia, hogfish, triple tail, redfish, mullet, snapper, sheepshead, whiting, and the tourist favorite of grouper are all good, but snook is the best. Fry up some snook in peanut oil, and you'll think your mouth is having an orgasm."

Jack and Elliott crammed themselves into the phone booth at the convenience store with a roll of quarters and dimes. Following several coin insertions, the old phone at the rear of the Diggins Bar rang on the other side of the country. It rang a few times before a passerby answered.

"There's a phone call for Mr. Copeland!" he shouted.

"Be right there." Cope's long legs brought him to the pay phone quickly. "Hello? Cope, here."

"Hi, Dad," Elliott said. "We're here as planned. Everything is OK, but we're not sure what to do next. Are you OK?"

"That's good. Everything here is under control. I sent something general delivery to the post office nearest your location. You two get lost for a few months. Enjoy the warm winter and stay in contact. Write to Rabbit's, not here."

Jack took the receiver. "Dad, it's Jack. Have you seen Katie?"

"No, Son. She's focused on her schoolwork. I sent you the letter she left here in the care package addressed to you at general delivery. It should arrive in a day or two. You need to have your wits about you. The situation could be a lot more dangerous than we know. Sometimes, things aren't what they seem. Trust your intuition."

Elliott took the receiver back. "Do you think there are people still after us?"

"I can tell you they tracked you to here. They've got long arms and ears in lots of places. I'm not trying to worry you unnecessarily, but you need to be vigilant. All right. I love you boys. Godspeed. Enjoy your vacation. I look forward to the three of us down on the river after the spring floods. We've got work to do."

"Good-bye, Dad. We love you."

Elliott hung up and looked at Jack. "I guess we're sailing to the Bahamas."

"I wonder what Neil has up his sleeve. You remember what Bonnie and Cat said about his real purpose. Looks like we're on a quest."

"Oh, well. We never minded mixing work with pleasure, did we?"

"When we have our meeting with Neil, we'll find out more about his plans. I've gotten used to spending time with Cat. I'll hate to see her go. Do you like Bonnie?"

"Of course I do. I'm having fun, but I'm not looking for a forever lover or a lifetime commitment. We're both in the moment. If something more develops, I'm not against it. I'm just not looking for it. You, however, are in the throes of a rebound. Like they say down under, it's boomerang love. Take it slow, Little Brother. That foxy redhead could eat you up and spit you out. Did you ever consider that you might be a sport fuck? Maybe she just wants to get her hooks into you so you'll help her brother look for her dad."

"I hear what you're saying, and you could be right, but I really like the girl and don't want her to go back to Alabama. How cool would it be if they came with us?"

"Jack, you're thinking with the wrong head. Can you imagine what would happen if big brother took a notion to get mad about you with his little sister? There won't be anywhere on the boat you can run."

"For once, Elliott, you're making sense. You've always been the impulsive one. I thought I was the pragmatic one. Maybe the past week has affected my judgment."

As they drove back to John's stilt house, Jack was reflective and quiet, his thoughts of Cat and how he wanted to be with her. The Spanish moss on the oak trees and the palm fronds flew horizontally, as the sky darkened, lightning flashed, and thunder vibrated.

Neil, John, Bonnie, and Cat were under the protection of the stilt house on folding chairs, enjoying the storm, when Jack backed the truck to the dock to unload their gear. Jack and Elliott ran to join the others out of the rain in what John called his saltwater garage.

John and Neil were debating the merits and dependability of outboard motors, which was like a Chevy guy talking with a Ford guy. They would never agree. John loved Mercury engines, and Neil was certain a Johnson was the best motor anyone could buy for the money. However, they agreed that if a person wanted an able, seaworthy tender, there was nothing better than a Zodiac Grand Raid. That was definitely on the to-buy list, as well as a brand-new motor of at least twenty-five horsepower. The little Avon with its six horsepower wasn't enough for their expedition.

Finally, the rain let up, and the sky cleared, as the storm passed.

"I guess we can unload our gear into the boat," Jack said. "You have a plan for where you want us?"

"Yeah, Jack," Neil said. "Why don't you and your brother set up in the aft cabin. I assume you can share a bed. We can work that out later. There's plenty of room, but for now, stow your gear back there."

Jack saluted and walked to the Suburban for his gear. Cat waited a few minutes, then announced she was going to the truck for her possessions.

"You and Bonnie can set up in the V berth in the bow," Neil told her.

A minute later, Jack and Cat stood side-by-side with the cargo doors open.

"Cat, I can't stand this," he complained. "I want to wrap my arms around you, hold you, kiss you, and make love to you. I don't want you to leave."

"I can't believe you said that. I feel the same way. As soon as my brother goes fishing with John, we'll have some time together. My brother isn't as protective as Bonnie and I said. He knows I'm a big girl. He's protective but not stupid. We're all grown-ups here."

She slid her hand up his baggy shorts and gave him a reassuring squeeze. Jack felt lightheaded again.

As they busied themselves with the unloading of the Suburban, Neil and John went snook fishing.

The couples went to opposite ends of the boat for private time.

Neil and John stood side-by-side in the center console of the skiff. The plan was simple. Diving birds revealed the location of schools of bait fish, so they eased forward to that spot, tossed out a net, put the bait in the live well, and went to catch some fish. They found bait, thread herring, nearly as big as their palms. John used seven-foot spinning rods with 300 Mitchell reels, a number-three hook at the end of an eighteen-inch, twenty-pound leader on fifteen-pound test monofilament. Once securely anchored, he retrieved two rods from the top and handed one to Neil.

"Live lining," he said. "I know you do that up in Mobile Bay. It's no different here. Just remember, you have to turn the snook back away from the trestle immediately. The first thing they'll do when they feel the hook is head for the pilings."

Like their different preferences in outboard motors, they had different ways of hooking a minnow. John liked to bring the hook through the upper lip and out the head. Neil hooked his bait between the dorsal fin and spine. Those two options will be argued as long as there are fishermen on the planet, and neither will be able to convince the other of the benefit of the opposing technique.

John was glad to instruct Neil on the nuances of trestle fishing. "What I've found works best is to cast ninety degrees to the boat and let the current carry the bait to the pilings. Once your bait is close, I start a slow retrieve to present the bait where the snook like to hang out. There's lots of other species out there, like trout, Goliath grouper, cobia, and redfish. You never know what you'll catch. I've been broke off here so many times, you can't imagine. I wouldn't set down my pole, either. I've seen more than one get snapped in half."

The skiff was anchored off the bow and trailed in the current toward the trestle. Neil cast off on the port side, with John on starboard. Neil closed the bail on the Mitchell 300 when he thought the bait was almost at the pilings.

Just as he flipped the bail over, his rod bent in half and almost leaped from his hand. The drag on the reel screamed, then stopped. His heart pounded, and adrenalin raced through his veins, but there was nothing to do but tie on another leader.

John's bait didn't fare any better. No sooner than it was near the trestle, his rod bent violently, and the reel started singing.

He grabbed the spool with his left hand and raised the rod's tip high, backing toward the bow, the trick to turning the snook's head away from the piling.

No other species of fish exhibited the tactic as often as the snook. They were crazy strong, fast, and smart. A three-foot snook with mouth open wide and gills flared broke the surface and shook its head left to right like an angry bull coming out of the chute at a rodeo. There was no need to shout, "Fish on!"

Neil traded his rod for the landing net, as John fought the fish. The huge snook ran, jumped, and dove repeatedly until it finally eased up to the side of the boat and rolled onto its side in exhaustion. Neil, sliding the net under its head, brought it into the boat.

"I've got this," John said. "Get your line in the water."

Avoiding the razor-sharp gill plates, John carefully removed the hook and put the large fish into the live well. Neil baited up and cast again, determined to be ready.

His bait drifted in an arc forty feet abeam of the boat, arriving in front of the trestle pilings. He was taking up the slack when his thread herring did a frenetic dance across the water. Acrobatic but short, the dance was the harbinger of a predator circling for the kill.

Neil grabbed his spool to prevent his line from dragging out and backed up as instructed. The fish ran toward the boat, and Neil reeled frantically, knowing giving a fish like that any slack meant he would lose the battle. The fish jumped, shook, ran, and jumped several more times before finally rolling over with its white side up, waiting for the net.

"Holy King Fish catfish!" Neil said, shaking his head. "I didn't think there's anything that fights harder than a redfish.

My goodness. If they eat as well as they fight, this will be the best fish in the world."

"You're about to find out."

They fished for another hour, releasing several they caught and finally releasing the bait in the live well. The fishing had been intense. It was the only time since Fred told Neil about the drug cartel that he wasn't thinking about his father and the possibility that he and his boat were being held captive at Fishmonger Key.

John started the engine and idled against the current to give Neil slack on the anchor line. Neil pulled up the anchor, and they headed back with two nice snook in the live well. John took out a bottle of Army-issue insect repellent and applied it to his bare legs, arms, and neck.

"The mosquitoes will be hungry when we get back to the dock," John said. "Did you ever try this stuff? I get it at the surplus store."

"I lived on it for a while in the Army. Did you serve?"

"No. I'm 4F. You know—fuck Kennedy, fuck Johnson, fuck Nixon, and fuck the military establishment they work for. In reality, I'm not a pacifist hippie tree hugger, either. I just don't believe in that war. It's too far away to be significant or worthy of one drop of American blood. That's just my opinion. If we have a real enemy, I'd fight to the death to protect our country, but not in Vietnam. Were you there?"

"I had the misfortune of serving two tours. I was proud to serve my country, as were my ancestors before me. I'm not a politician or scholar. I was just a soldier following orders. I didn't have the luxury of deciding the morality of the war. I was trained to kill or be killed. I made it back."

"I sure hope I didn't piss you off. I have the utmost respect for people who served and fought. Most people who went to Vietnam didn't have a choice. It was like the Civil War, when the Irishman stepped off the boat in New York without a penny. The rich and moral fucking industrialist sent the immigrants to fight their pseudo-ideological war against the South. The royals and rich politicians of the world take advantage of the loyal and courageous. It's been that way since civilization began."

"No, you didn't piss me off. My country did that. They sent us to fight a war they didn't have the political will to win. They exposed us to disease and poisoned us with Agent Orange, then spat on us when we came back like it was our fault. I'm getting over it, though. I hadn't thought about it since I bought the *Sally Jo* and saw your military bug repellent. It's funny how certain things, like smells, bring back memories."

They stood side-by-side behind the pedestal, idling up to the deck beside the *Sally Jo.* The brothers and cousins sat in the sailboat cockpit in pairs, tangled up and drinking cold beer.

19. Shootout at the Salt Water Garage and Lodge

Jack and Elliott jumped down to the dock to see their catch. Elliott raised the two snook for viewing, and Bonnie got some good photos with her Cannon AE-1. Neil and John stood side-by-side holding the beautiful fish horizontally, smiling like six-year-old boys.

"We caught 'em, so you have to clean 'em," John said, laying the fish on the stainless-steel cleaning table. "Everything you need is on the table. Just remember to turn off the water when you're done. I could use some help upstairs if one of you girls doesn't mind. I've got some barbecued beans and cabbage to make coleslaw. Does that sound good to everyone?"

"I'd love to help." Bonnie followed John to the kitchen upstairs on the stilt house.

"How do you want the fish cleaned?" Jack called.

John stuck his head out the screen door. "Just filet them and cut into two-inch pieces. I want to fry the backbones, too, so keep them. Make sure you poke the eyeballs, or the heads float in the canal and stink. Here's a tub for the fish."

John tossed down a rubber tub. Elliott was touching up the filet knife on the sharpening stone when Crosby, Stills, Nash, and Young came over the stereo. It was their live album called "*4 Way Street*".

Neil found himself alone with his sister. The pairing of the couples hadn't gone unnoticed. The music masked their conversation, but they went below for more privacy.

"How was your trip?" Neil asked. "What do you think of my crew?"

"The trip was fine. The Hornet ran great. We had a little fun, too. They didn't act guilty like criminals or anything."

"Did they say anything about what kind of trouble they're in?"

"Not exactly. I know they had at least one pistol with them, and both of them are badasses. Jack used your 300-pound pal like a rag doll twice. I can't think of anyone I'd want to be in a tough situation with more, except you."

"Did you tell them what I'm doing?"

"I mentioned I thought you were doing more than just trying to find yourself. It was more like finding our dad. The only thing they said was that they ran into some trouble. They called it ugly people or something like that."

"OK. Great. I'll share the plan tonight. We'll have two or three days of prepping. I need to get a long-range weather forecast for the tropics. Tomorrow we're taking a road trip to Tampa to get a new tender and outboard. I'm glad you brought Bonnie with you, so you won't have to drive home alone."

"We were hoping to go with you for a while, maybe down to Key West."

"Was that before or after you started sleeping with them?"

"That's a little uncalled for."

"You're a big girl, and I don't care how you get your kicks. I just don't like it when it interferes with my plans or relationships with friends. This isn't a love boat cruise. When we find dad and his boat, we'll probably have to fight to get them back. He wouldn't want you involved in that. This could get ugly really fast. These are violent, bad people. I don't think this is a good time for distractions. God knows how bad you've turned their heads already."

He hugged his sister. "I love you even if you're a little on the slutty side."

She punched his stomach with just enough force to remind him he taught her how to fight.

Bonnie was in the kitchen, making coleslaw and cheese grits. John appeared with egg wash and seasoned flour. She added oil to the skillet and lit the fire. A kitchen match lying in the peanut oil ignited when the oil was hot enough for cooking.

Elliott helped Bonnie carry down paper plates, coleslaw, and grits. They sat at the picnic table when the last fish came off the skillet. John called them Twinkies, because of the golden crust and pure white meat inside. Clara lay on the ground beside Neil, content with the knowledge that she would eat fish, too.

They held hands, and Neil offered a lighthearted prayer that was very sincere. "Dear Lord, thank You for family, fish, friends, and our safety on Your waters."

They raised their beer bottles in a toast. Soon, they agreed it was the best snook they ever tasted. The secret to the cheese grits, according to John, was the Wisconsin cheese from his native county. The coleslaw had the right amount of vinegar and sweet taste.

They ate beyond full. Bonnie and Cat went upstairs to work in the kitchen with John, while Jack and Elliott joined Neil in the salon, where he laid out some charts.

"I don't know what kind of trouble you two are in," Neil began, "or if I need to know. What can you tell me? Is there anything I need to know about?"

The brothers looked at each other, then Jack said, "I guess the easiest way to explain is that we ended up in a firefight with what we assume were Mafia hit men. We survived, and they didn't. Apparently, they tried Dad next, with no better success. Dad said we were supposed to crew for you, stay out of harm's way, and come home in the spring."

"I'd be proud to have both of you as my crew. The harm's way part is a problem. I got this boat from some people who'd been forced into drug trafficking. We've always suspected that our dad and his boat were taken by the drug cartel operating out of the Exumas. Sources I know have confirmed that the location of their operations is Fishmonger Cay. I plan to go there and liberate any hostages and prisoners, as well as disrupt and destroy their operations. This is a personal mission, not sanctioned by anyone or any organization, though I've gotten some information from unofficial sources."

Neil waited for their reaction.

"I believe if the shoe was on the other foot," Elliott said, "you'd help us find our dad."

Jack nodded. "We've got at least three or four months before we have to be anywhere."

"I knew y'all were quality people when we met at St. George Island. I just never expected we'd be here together," Neil said. "I just remember hoping and praying that you and Dennis returned from Vietnam. Helicopter pilots don't live very long."

"The way things have been going," Jack said, "things haven't been very safe here, either."

"We have a lot to do tomorrow," Neil said. "The first thing is to get a Zodiac, outboard motor, and any other gear we need. The boat is well provisioned with canned food, but we'll need fresh stuff, too. I'll get fuel delivered here, so we don't have to go to a marina."

Neil was an excellent captain. Neither Elliott nor Jack knew sailing or were skilled in tactics, but they had great water skills, common sense, courage, and athleticism. They went to bed excited about the prospect of a new adventure.

Frank and Tito were told to kill the old man and woman, steal their money, and bring the *Sally Jo* to Fishmonger Cay. Frank expressed slight regret, telling Tito, "I kind of like that old couple."

Luckily, Fred and Betty were gone, and the dock was empty. The two men didn't find any money, either. Knowing they'd probably be shot for incompetence, they decided to snort more of the kilo of cocaine they stole from their boss.

They were driving across the bridge in the throes of despair and panic when their luck changed, and they saw the masts of the *Sally Jo* at John's dock. They whipped a U-turn on the other side of the bridge, drove past the place, and confirmed the sighting.

The boat was only two canals away, and hopefully, they'd find Betty and Fred. Failure with their boss usually meant final termination.

Tito and Frank did lines and drank cognac to celebrate their change in luck. They returned at three o'clock the following morning with bloody purpose and no conscience.

Bonnie and Cat slept in the V berth. The hatch was open with mosquito netting snapped in place. A small fan hummed, stirring the sultry night air.

Jack and Elliott were in the aft cabin, while Neil occupied the long settee in the salon. The only sound louder than the fans was the Cuban tree frogs.

Clara lay flat on the holly and teak sole when a new noise struck her ear, bringing her awake. She sat up, her nose twitching for a scent. She placed her nose near Neil's head and growled softly.

Neil woke instantly, feeling the boat rocking as someone moved on the deck. He saw legs through one of the portholes. Just when his feet hit the deck, Tito appeared in the companionway with a .38 aimed at him. Frank stood behind him on the dock with a pistol in his hand, too.

"Hey!" Tito called. "It's not the old man and woman." His eyes bulged in surprise, and he looked like he just ate twelve powdered doughnuts.

Clara launched herself five feet through the air and bit into Tito's gun arm just above the wrist. Neil quickly grabbed and slashed a razor-sharp, nine-inch kitchen blade across his neck as the pistol discharged harmlessly through the plywood sole into the bilge.

John burst through the screen door of the stilt house like Steve McQueen playing Josh Randall, buck naked with a twelve-gauge pump shotgun in his hand.

"If you so much as flinch," John said, "I'll splatter you like a tomato and feed you to the sharks."

Jack had his Mark 2 Ruger with silencer aimed at Frank, too. Frank's final act was to spin and fire. Jack shot him in the head with the .22, and John knocked him five feet from where had been standing with a magnum load of double-ought buckshot.

Then the night was dead silent. The gunshots made Bonnie and Cat sit up violently and bang their heads on the low ceiling.

"Is everyone OK?" Neil asked quietly.

John remained in overwatch position from the deck above. Jack cautiously went outside to see if there were any more threats.

"Bonnie and Cat," Neil said, "stay where you are. We've got a big mess to clean up."

Elliott and Neil moved Tito's body to the cockpit and hung his nearly severed head over the deck to let the blood drain overboard and minimize the mess. John pulled on a pair of shorts and came down to the dock.

"I guess I showed him," John said. "Never fuck with a man with a twelve-gauge pointed at you. I've always wondered what one would do to a man at fifteen feet. It's a hell of a mess."

John pulled on white rubber boots and bibs. Jack returned from his scouting to report a car parked down the street. Inside he found a large bag of cocaine, a lot of cash, a roll of thick plastic, duct tape, and two cinderblocks. It was clear Frank and Tito hadn't come for a friendly visit. They were looking for Fred and Betty.

"Yeah, pretty messy," Neil said, "but effective. Do you know who these men are? They must've been looking for the previous owners."

"I know who they are," John said. "They work for Felipe, the same man Betty and Frank worked for. Didn't you ever wonder why the waterline was so high on your boat? I don't think Felipe approved of their retirement plan. Once you get tied up with a man like that, you can't get away. I hope they make it. They were nice people. Let's get rid of the mess."

They lifted Frank by his hands and feet and lowered him into the skiff. Neil and John walked the skiff to the cockpit, so Elliott and Jack could lower Tito on his buddy. They covered both with a tarp and a cast net.

"Is everyone OK?" Cat whispered. "Can we come out now?"

"Come out through the hatch," Neil said. "There was an accident in the salon. John and I need to take a boat ride. If anyone has stomach for it, there's bleach and cleaning supplies under the sink."

The skiff disappeared into the night to a place where wild pigs and gators could be trusted to keep secrets.

Jack and Cat worked quietly to clean up. Elliott and Bonnie went back to the would-be assassins' car to secure the duffel bag of money from the trunk, and the remainder of the kilo of coke.

Jack and Cat worked with quiet efficiency. Rinsing blood from the dock, salon, and cockpit, they thoroughly bleached the areas. The smell almost made Jack puke.

"Did people die here tonight?" Bonnie asked Elliott.

"Bonnie, I don't want to talk about what happened. The only thing you have to know is we're all safe. What you don't know can't hurt you." He held her close. "Those bastards came here to kill someone. They were paid assassins and don't deserve a moment of thought."

She felt the .45 tucked into his belt and felt safe.

Everyone was waiting for the sunrise when they finally heard the skiff return. The group gathered in the small room in the middle of John's garage. The cocaine was easy to get rid of. Jack emptied the bag into the canal, rinsed it, and tossed it into the trash.

The guns and personal possessions ended up at the bottom of the river. The $60,000 in cash was split half and half between the *Sally Jo* and the garage and lodge.

Neil followed John's truck to discard Tito's Monte Carlo, which they drove into a quarry lake near Cape Haze. On the way back, they talked.

"I guess you know now, if you didn't before, that you inherited more than a little trouble when you bought the *Sally Jo*," John said.

"Yeah. I figured as much, but I didn't think they'd be so brazen. I thought they'd approach us on the water, maybe with a feigned distress signal, then try to hijack us. I'm really sorry for the trouble tonight."

John laughed. "Hell, I'd shoot 'em all day for thirty grand. Those two worthless bastards should've been shot a long time ago. I don't have a problem with it. Felipe will be looking for his goons to return with the boat, though. Their bodies will never be found. The few people who live around here at this time of year are used to nighttime thunder.

"The only real problem I can see is the boat. Felipe believes it belongs to him. His network of smugglers will never stop looking for you."

"You're probably right. We'll need to rechristen her. There must be hundreds of boats that look the same."

"Except the black masts make the boat very distinctive even at great distance. I could always identify it when it came into the harbor. When you paint over the name, make sure you paint the masts."

"That's a damn good idea. I think we'd better leave as soon as possible, too, just in case more of Felipe's goons are around. I'll try to get out of here today. I don't want to make any more trouble for you."

"That's a good plan for you, too. What will you do with your rig?"

"My sister and cousin will drive it back home once we get back from Tampa." Neil caught himself before he accidentally said, "Dauphin Island."

With Felipe's money, Neil bought a new red-and-black Zodiac inflatable and a thirty-horsepower motor. Their next stop was a dive shop, where Neil bought tanks, regulators, fins, masks, and spears. Next was the tackle shop, where he purchased two big pen rods and reels, a five-foot gaff, spoons, and skirts.

At the marine supply house, they loaded up on white and black paint, two bosun's chairs, a throwable life ring, fuel and oil filters, impellers, propellers, and extra belts. It was a good thing Jack was the only one with Neil. By the time they loaded up the spare five-gallon fuel and water cans, the Hornet was full. Their last stop was a sporting goods store for ammunition. When they returned, fuel had already been delivered to the boat.

Bonnie and Cat were hauled up the masts in the bosun's chairs to apply two coats of white paint on both. The name *Sally Jo* on the stern was scraped off with a razor blade, with the shavings saved for a christening ceremony.

John volunteered to carefully paint on the name *Tipsy Gypsy* in its place. Neil returned from the grocery and liquor store with their final provisions. Clara Bell, unsettled the whole time Neil was away, watched for his return from her vantage point on the deck. Recent events left her on edge. She nearly knocked him down when he stepped out of the truck. He went to one knee, wrapped his arms around her, and hugged her like a long-lost lover.

"You saved our lives last night," he told her.

The new Zodiac was inflated, the engine mounted and started, then it was raised on the davits. The spare parts, dive gear, tackle, ammunition, and food were carefully stored. Neil systematically removed all references to the name *Sally Jo*.

All of them gathered while Neil invoked Poseidon to strike the previous name. He scattered the paint scrapings overboard and said, "Bless the *Tipsy Gypsy.*"

After he broke a bottle of champagne over the bowsprit, he opened a second bottle for the crew and witnesses.

"You can never be too careful in matters of tradition," he told them.

Neil and Cat agreed it was too late to start out for Dauphin

Island that evening. They would all take the *Tipsy Gypsy* out into the bay and spend the night anchored far enough from civilization to avoid being seen.

They turned her forty-foot length in the canal with dock lines and boat hooks. John gave them a final shove as they cast off and told them about a secluded place to anchor.

They turned east out of the canals and were safely tucked in Tippecanoe Bay when the sun set. The evening sea breeze kept no-see-ums and mosquitoes in the mangroves. A scattering of clouds created scoops of orange sherbet in the sky. Dolphin and manatee performed water ballet, while osprey and pelican gave an air show.

John arrived just before dark with two gallons of cooked stone crabs. "I didn't know if you ever ate these before. They're still hot."

"This is a wonderful surprise," Cat said. "Dad brought us back some of these from one of his trips. They were delicious. It's been a few years. I'll make garlic butter. I think there are some mallets in the galley."

She untangled herself from Jack and descended the companionway into the galley. Jack wrapped John's bowline on the cleat and grabbed the bucket of crab claws. Neil turned on the propane for Cat and came into the cockpit.

"Hey, John. Long time no see. Stone crab claws? My favorite."

He handed John a cold Heineken. Bonnie and Elliott migrated back to the cockpit from the bow, where they watched the luscious sunset. Cat returned with mallets and forks for breaking into claws and butter or vinegar for dipping the rich, dense sweet crab. There was no discussion of the previous twenty-four hours. All were content to gorge on crab and cold beer.

John gave them advice about the local waters and prevailing winds. He went down to the salon and marked good anchorages and hurricane holes from Marco Island to Georgetown, Exumas. Neil never revealed his destination other than the Dry Tortugas and an itinerary of loose cruising and gunk holing.

John noticed the many wooden footlockers of military origin and had some suspicions about his new friends, though that was merely about intent, not distrust. Neil shared information on a need-to-know basis. They agreed no watch was necessary, so they could have their last full night of sleep before starting a watch schedule.

The boy-girl separation was violated soon after dark. Elliott went forward to spend quality time with Bonnie, and Cat slipped down the rear companionway to join Jack. Both couples heard John and Neil laughing above the sound of the stereo, well beyond midnight.

Jack, waking before sunrise, enjoyed an enthusiastic lovemaking session with Cat.

"I want to go with you," she said, "but my brother says it's too dangerous. You may not know this, but I can shoot as good as any man and probably beat ninety percent of them in a fight. I have as much right to go as he does. He's my father, too."

She spoke softly, as if hoping Jack could change Neil's mind.

"I understand Neil's position. If we have problems with bad

people, I don't want to be worrying about you. I'd rather know you were safe and sound on Dauphin Island. Did I mention having you watch over my Land Cruiser?" He held her tightly.

"What if you don't make it back? What if this is the last time I see you?"

"Don't think like that. I'll see you before you know it. Let's make breakfast for everyone." He watched Cat's exquisitely toned body as she slipped into her cutoff shorts and bikini top.

She had the finest body he could imagine, with beautiful freckles, tanned skin, milky-white breasts with pink puppy-nose nipples. He wanted to spend the whole day in bed with her, but duty called. Together, they made coffee and rattled pans.

John said good-bye after breakfast and left for the boatyard in his skiff. It was clear he'd become a good friend.

The Zodiac was lowered on its davits to take the girls to the Salt Water Garage and Lodge, then to the Green Hornet for their drive home. Neil, hugging them both, kissed their cheeks.

"There's an envelope for both of you in the springs of the back bench seat for when you get home." He gave them the keys and $400 for traveling money, then he stayed aboard and studied the charts as the two couples left.

The thirty-horsepower Johnson made the raft jump onto plane as they left. Elliott remembered the package his father said would arrive soon, so they went to the post office before the girls headed back. After warm kisses, the two young men watched the Green Hornet disappear into the distance.

Elliott carried the box from their dad. They took the Zodiac back to the *Tipsy Gypsy.* Some people have trouble steering a raft with a tiller motor, especially one with so much power. Too much throttle without weight in the front could flip it over, but Jack and Elliott were highly skilled.

Jack flew into the anchorage and did a figure eight just for fun before bringing the tender abeam the ship to be unloaded. He pulled the dinghy to the davits hand over hand along the toe rail, snapped the davit lines to the lifting points, and boarded the ship from the swim platform. He and Elliott raised the dinghy and secured it bow and stern to prevent it from swinging.

"I see you got your package," Neil said. "What's in it?"

Elliott opened his Swiss Army knife and carefully removed the tape seal. The box weighed at least ten pounds.

"We're about to find out." He handed Jack an envelope addressed to him on the top of the box. The familiar handwriting brought a wave of pain behind Jack's eyes and in his throat. Hitherto, Cat had kept him from thinking about Katie. Jack kept the letter in one hand as Elliott investigated the remainder of the box.

He found a watch box containing his Rolex that Randy bought from Spider and returned to Cope. A note in the box said the watch had been professionally cleaned and serviced. It should still be waterproof. His dad warned him not to lose it again.

Next, he found a larger box that contained a Ruger .22 semiautomatic pistol and silencer, just like Jack's. There were two nylon shoulder holsters, extra magazines, and a brick of .22 caliber long rifle hollow points.

There was also a note.

Dear Sons,

I hope you're well and the only thing you have to shoot are targets. Enjoy your vacation and adventure. We might have to join you when it gets too cold up here. Maybe you could arrange a meeting between Ernest and me in Key West. Try some of his books when you get bored. My favorite, of course, is The Old Man in the Sea. Second favorite is Island in the Stream.

Speaking of action, we think we have things cleaned up around here. Hopefully, we won't see any more unwanted company. Nick, Bear, and I are enjoying the cool weather.

I look forward to a call from you when you get the chance. One thing—the best watermen in the world are also the best weather forecasters. Remember what happened to the Spanish Armada? Let the weather make your schedule. Nothing else is important.

Another fact you might want to consider is that most men who drown do so with their zipper down—i.e., they fall off the boat while taking a piss and go unnoticed at night or when on watch alone.

Before I close, there's one more principle to keep in mind. If you think you might have to reef, don't delay. Reef immediately. You can always take out the reef if it's not needed.

There's also an envelope of cash, so you won't be a burden to Neil. Give him my regards and know that I love you. Randy said he's jealous, if you can imagine that. He also said something about Southern girls that I won't repeat.

Love,
Dad

Elliott took out four loaded magazines, screwed on the silencer, and with Neil's blessing, shot forty rounds at a floating coconut. He put on his watch, an old friend he never went without before it was stolen.

Jack caught Cat's lingering scent, as he placed the letter under his pillow. He was able to compartmentalize his emotions, a critical survival skill when under duress. That day, they would go sailing on the ocean. He would have plenty of time to read later.

20. The Headless Helmsman

Once the engine started, Jack and Elliott used the windlass to pull the anchor. Neil had the mainsail uncovered, clipped to the halyard, and turned *Gypsy* into the light breeze. Following Neil's instruction, Jack raised the sail up the mast hand by hand until it was too hard to pull. He then wrapped the halyard around the winch, cranking the handle until the sail was completely up the mast before cleating the halyard.

Neil turned south, and the sail filled. They unfurled the jib over the starboard side, and it, too, filled with wind. Lastly, they raised the mizzen sail at the stern.

The wind was out of the east, putting them on a comfortable beam reach for their first sail. Neil ran the engine to charge the batteries for the first three hours. They sailed west once they cleared the Cape Haze shoals toward Boca Grande Pass and into the Gulf. Soon, they ran with the wind behind them.

The tide was on its way out, which increased their speed through the narrow pass. The water color changed from root beer in Tippecanoe Bay to green in Charlotte Harbor, then blue once they were in the Gulf of Mexico. Five hours later, the sea breeze came up, and an onshore breeze took control.

Cumulus clouds built vertically, increasing the likelihood of afternoon thunderstorms. Neil was used to that. He hoped the sea breeze pushed the storms inland. He used a plastic sailboat as an instructional aid to demonstrate the relationship between the boat and the wind.

They took turns at the wheel, getting a feel for the helm, sails, and how to steer a course. When they weren't at the helm, they studied chart symbols and navigational aids. They practiced man-overboard drill and discussed the many possible emergencies.

Coastal sailing and dead reckoning were easy in daylight. It was a pleasant sail down the coast as the thunderstorms moved inland, and the seas were light. The only excitement was the welcome sound of the Penn reels screeching when one of the many Spanish mackerel struck. The fish, fighting like crazy, were a challenge to net. By the time they lowered sail, they had six fillets on ice. They anchored off Marco Island in eight feet of water with a light breeze and calm conditions.

"Captain, let's break out those new snorkels and masks," Jack said. "I could use a swim."

"That's a great idea. We can take a look at the anchor to make sure it's hooked. We don't want to drag if we get a big thunderstorm."

They lowered the ladder off the side, and Neil was the first into the water. After a little coaxing, Clara jumped off the bow. Together, they swam around the boat, followed the anchor chain, and studied the flukes of the Danforth anchor to ensure they were embedded in the sand.

Swimming for almost an hour wasn't just a great workout, it was also fun. The Copeland boys enjoyed the warm, buoyant

Gulf waters. They left the water as the sun set, feeling refreshed and invigorated.

Neil was happy. The visual inspection of the hull, driveshaft, prop, and anchor, was good. He also liked his crew's exceptional swimming and diving skills. That gave him more tactical options.

Dinner that night was simple—sliced tomatoes, avocados, sautéed mackerel, and bread. Clara ate only fish. Elliott cleaned their few dishes.

It was the perfect opportunity to discuss their course. Neil turned the VHF radio to the local NOAA weather forecast. Nothing of a severe tropical nature was predicted, just typical thunderstorms. Wind would continue from the east at 10-15 knots. After hearing a good forecast, they had time to plan and talk, so he turned the radio back to channel sixteen.

"We should make the Shark River tomorrow evening," Neil said, "then Marathon the next day. We'll refuel there and cross the straits. We'll have to wait for a weather window. It's only sixty miles or so to the Bahamas, but it can be treacherous. The Gulf Stream flows north between the Bahamas and Florida in the Atlantic. If the wind blows anywhere north of east and west, it opposes the strong, northerly flow of the water and kicks up humongous waves. Did you ever wonder why there are so many ships on the bottom of the sea off the Florida coast? It's a fool who doesn't respect that current.

"I won't chance it. I like to cross when the winds are out of the south and forecast to stay that way. We may have to wait awhile for a good forecast."

"You're the captain," Elliott said. "You know best. We've got plenty of time. I don't care if we wait a month. Besides, from what I've heard, there's plenty to do in the Keys. We can hunt for lobster, sunken treasure, go spear fishing, and enjoy the crystal-clear water and beautiful reefs." He smiled at the idea.

"Cape Sable will be a good place for us to spend a day," Neil continued. "It's got miles and miles of deserted beach at the very southernmost tip of the Florida Peninsula. It's surrounded by the Everglades and guarded by the most-ferocious flying parasites you'll ever see. I doubt we'll see any other human beings there.

"We'll go through all the tactical gear we have on board, service and test fire all our weapons, and I'll bring a shotgun to the cockpit for tonight's watches. We know Felipe has people watching for this boat. I don't think he has any way of knowing what happened to his goons. When they don't check in after a week, though, the search will be intense.

"We're probably fine right now, but I don't want to risk complacency. It's better to be vigilant all the time, especially at night. We have to treat any boat that approaches us at night as a threat. Pirates don't give second chances. That shotgun should be on hand at all times. The whole crew, if alerted by the watch, should be armed and prepared to repel boarders."

In a moment of levity in an otherwise serious mood, Neil added, "And don't shoot a hole in the boat."

They chuckled.

"Neil, if I'm in the V berth and Jack's in the aft berth, both with our fans on, you'll need the air horn to wake us up," Elliott said.

"Good point. I was getting to that." He rapped the Fiberglas where he sat, and the sound resonated throughout the hull.

"That's the best way to signal on the boat. Three raps from the watchman brings all hands to battle stations. The forward firing position is the V berth hatch. From the salon, you'd come up the companionway to the cockpit. Aft berth is the same, coming up to the cockpit. I'll sleep in the salon. I like being near the food."

They smiled.

"When we're sailing, we need two men on hand at all times. We need only one person for anchor watch. We can each do three hours tonight. Elliott, you've got nine to midnight. Jack has twelve to three, and I'll take three to six. We'll start at sunrise. I know I don't have to say it, but no drinking on watch. We'll use the red lights in the salon and red lenses on our flashlights to protect our night vision."

Elliott prepared for the first watch. Jack went to the aft cabin, and Neil lay down in the salon. The moon slowly slid up the eastern sky, bringing shimmering light to the glass-calm Gulf. Clara lay on a cushion in the cockpit with Elliott.

She reminded him of Bear. She raised her head whenever she heard a passing bird or disturbance in the water. The predators were busy, and occasionally, Elliott heard schools of baitfish showering, as they tried to escape. The acrobatics of a leopard ray brought him to his feet when it slapped the surface.

He shone his flashlight into the water when a manatee surfaced and gave him the fright of his life. He'd heard of them before, but not at night with a red light. It was somewhere between an alien and the creature of the Black Lagoon.

Only a few boats came and went from Capri Pass during his watch. They never came close, but he couldn't tell how far they were, either.

When Jack came to the cockpit just before midnight, the two brothers sat together for a few minutes in awe of the sea and night sky. Jack passed the hours watching the horizon and listening. At three o'clock, he stuck his head into the companionway and was surprised to see Neil coming up for his watch.

"Nothing to report, Captain, except a manatee that almost made Elliott soil his pants."

"I guess no news is good news. Are you sleepy?"

"Not too bad, but I won't have any trouble falling asleep, either."

Neil patted his back, as he descended the companionway toward the V berth. "Sleep as long as you want until six o'clock."

Clara got up and greeted him as if she hadn't seen him in weeks. They walked to the bow together, inspecting the anchor. Clara's nose was busy while Neil took a minute to look around. She squatted and urinated on the deck. Neil praised her, retrieved a bucket of water, and rinsed off the deck.

The moon was two days past full and high in the sky, providing excellent visibility.

Clara was the first one to come alert. Her ears went up, then she lifted her head and looked toward the sound. Neil looked in that direction and saw a green and red bow light approaching fast from the north right at them.

He rapped on the cockpit floor with the winch handle. Powerful engines neared. He lay on the cockpit floor with his twelve gauge pump out of sight.

Elliott popped out of the hatch in the V berth with his pistol in hand and lowered the hatch gently as he hugged the deck. Jack saw Neil's stay-down signal and held his 1911 .45 in his hands.

The sound of the outboards died down, as the power boat came alongside.

"Tito?" someone called. "Frank? You guys sleep like old ladies. What if we were pirates? We could kill you in your sleep. Tito?"

"There's no Tito here," Neil said. "You have the wrong boat."

"I think you're wrong. Maybe you're on the wrong boat. Come up so I can see you. I know this boat for many years. It belongs to my boss, Felipe."

"No. You're making a mistake. There are many boats like this. This is the *Tipsy Gypsy.*"

"OK, *Amigo*. This is your boat—maybe. Why don't you come up and talk in person? I like to see who I'm talking to."

The man was Felipe's lieutenant, a cousin he trusted to oversee drug shipments up the Florida coast and bring the cash back to the Bahamas. The two other people on the boat held handguns.

Neil stood, aiming the shotgun at the man's head less than ten feet away. His men immediately raised their pistols.

"My *amigo,* I didn't mean to alarm you. There's no need for violence. Maybe this is a misunderstanding."

"You aren't my friend. There's no Frank or Tito, and this isn't Felipe's boat."

"That's brave talk for a man with two guns aimed at him."

"Just so you understand what will happen here, the two guns might get me, but I guarantee I'll get you and at least one of them, too."

"You have a point. Maybe tonight we call this a Mexican standoff. The next time I come, I'll kill you and take this boat."

Elliott took aim at the nearest shooter. Jack came out of the companionway with his .45 cocked.

The evening quiet was shattered when the shooter on the right accidentally fired on Jack, grazing his head. Jack sent two rounds of 240-grain hollow points into the man's sternum, lifting him from the boat into the water.

Elliot fired ten rounds of .22 hollow points, hitting the other gunman in the head three times and four times in the neck. One round was lost, and the other two hit the lieutenant. That wasn't, however, the cause of his death.

Neil shot him in the face with the twelve gauge, leaving behind a headless body. His torso fell forward over the center console, pushing the throttle to the full open position and throwing the other gunman overboard. The twin engines howled, and the boat took off into the night with a headless driver.

Jack felt something warm running down the side of his neck.

21. Little Marco to Shark River

Neil retrieved his M-5 medical bag and applied a bandage to Jack's head. When the bullet grazed the side, Jack jerked left, striking the edge of the companionway track.

"Our plan has changed," Neil said. "Elliott, pull the anchor and throw your brass overboard. Jack, get rid of your brass."

Neil picked up his expended shotgun shell and threw it overboard before starting the engine.

They motored southwest without lights for an hour. The nearly full moon produced a two-foot tide, hopefully enough to pilot the boat across the shallow shoals of Cape Romano.

Neil stood on the bow with a lensatic compass, directing Elliott at the helm with arm signals. Neil was gambling there would be enough light to see. Cutting across shoals was an old tactic for smugglers, blockade runners, and people avoiding the authorities. *Gypsy's* shadow spooked fish in all directions. The shoals teemed with life at night. Prey came to the shallows to hide, and predators came to feed.

They touched bottom several times but managed to get through. Neil wanted as many miles as possible between them and Little Marco Island. The last thing they needed was to be boarded and searched by the Coast Guard or Marine Patrol.

Once they were across the shoals, they slid south along the uninhabited Ten Thousand Island coast a couple miles offshore. There was minimal risk of contacting anyone. They could only estimate where they were, because the coastline was invisible. It was miles and miles of wilderness. The moon abandoned them eventually, so they navigated by compass until the sun brought light to the eastern horizon. A fiery array of low clouds heralded the triumph of light.

Dawn lifted their spirits, like an unsolicited atonement. Neil went below, and the quiet drone of the diesel was replaced by *Here Comes the Sun* by the Beatles at full volume through the cockpit speakers. He brought up three breakfast beers, and Elliott proposed a toast to the new day.

"May I never have to witness another man shot at close range with a twelve gauge," he said.

Daylight inspection of Jack's scalp revealed a hairless strip down the left side and a two-inch gash for Neil to suture on the right. Once their course was established, Elliott set the autopilot and went below to cook bacon, avocado, cheeseburgers.

The previous night made it perfectly clear that Felipe expected Tito and Frank back in the Bahamas on the *Sally Jo* with his money. It was also clear that Felipe had a network of operators who provided eyes and ears along the coast to protect his trade.

The three men were unanimous that the search for the boat would become more intense with the discovery of the headless boater. The authorities would suspect a drug deal gone bad, or a turf war, but it wouldn't be considered suicide.

Felipe found out about it on the news.

"In breaking news this morning, a fishing charter out of Fort Myers came upon a small pleasure craft performing circles ten miles off the coast. The driver of the boat was slumped over the center console in what witnesses called a gruesome scene. Authorities are investigating the incident as a homicide. Speculations are circulating about the victim's possible connection to illegal drug trafficking."

Felipe went into a rage. Tito and Frank failed to communicate prior to departure, and now his cousin was found dead when he went looking for them? Had Tito and Frank gone rogue?

He doubted they had the balls to steal from him, but if they were using his products, anything was possible. He wondered who had the balls to cross him. Had everyone gone loco? Law enforcement didn't operate like that.

He felt it was a personal attack to challenge the cartel. Someone wanted the boat and his money. He intensified the search for the *Sally Jo,* sending word to Miami to look for a black-masted ketch and offering a $20,000 reward for its return.

Elliott produced burgers from below for the crew, including Clara, and they discussed the situation while eating.

"What kind of weapons do y'all have besides the .22s and .45?" Neil asked. "We need to prepare to engage at a longer distance. The next boat that approaches us might shoot first and ask questions later."

"We have a twelve-gauge pump," Jack said, "but the only long-distance weapon is the M-1 Garand with open sights."

"Good. Get it out and load it. I'll get out binoculars."

"It'll take a few minutes to reassemble it. Had to break it down to fit it into the footlocker."

A few minutes later, Jack returned to the deck with the assembled rifle and a bandolier of loaded clips. Neil handed him the binoculars and disappeared below, only to come back with a .50-caliber sniper rifle with fifty power magnification scope, tripod, and silencer. He also had an array of specialized bullets, including armor piercing, white phosphorus, exploding, and untraceable sabot.

The water behind the boat exploded, as a large tarpon rose into the air. The Penn reel screamed. Neil ran for the rod, pulling it free of its holder and tightening the drag. Elliott, quickly idled the engine and slipped into neutral.

They so intently watched the fish jump and run, they missed seeing the approaching craft. Elliott finally noticed it first and recognized it held wildlife officers. He called out to Neil and Jack.

Neil was amidships, fighting the fish, while Jack was ready with a landing net. The game wardens saw them fighting the fish and stopped fifty yards away. They were fishermen, too, and didn't want to jeopardize the catch. It wasn't everyday yachters who could bring such a fish onboard.

The fish danced on its tail, shaking its head, and the lure flew from its mouth to land harmlessly on the water. The fish vanished below the surface.

"Good afternoon, Gentlemen," the officer called. "How are you doing today? Sorry you lost the fish."

"I was doing great until it spat the lure back at me," Neil said, reeling in the line.

"Have y'all seen any suspicious activity?" the game warden at the wheel asked.

"Not that I can think of. Last night we heard a fast-moving boat real late, but we didn't see any lights."

"Thank you. Keep your eyes open. A man was found dead earlier today on a boat. We think it was related to drug-trafficking, so be careful."

They idled up to the *Gypsy*, holding onto the rail to chat.

"I have some literature here, regulations you need to be aware of when fishing in the Everglades Park."

"You bet, Officer," Neil replied. "Thanks for the warning." He accepted a fishing bulletin. "If we see anything, we'll call on channel sixteen."

Working his way to the stern, he placed the rod back in the holder. The game wardens sped off in their eighteen-foot Boston Whaler, while Neil reeled in the other line, thinking that fishing was too much of a distraction.

"That could've been bad," he commented.

The brothers nodded.

They sailed south, hugging the coast in six feet of water and taking turns watching with binoculars. They reached the Shark River at sunset without seeing another boat. They went upstream to where the river narrowed to less than 100 feet. Live oaks streaming Spanish moss lined the banks, camouflaging their masts. They were safe from everything except biting flies and mosquitoes.

Luckily, the Bimini top was equipped with mosquito screens that snapped around the perimeter. Without those, it would have been impossible to stay in the cockpit.

It reminded Jack of an Alfred Hitchcock movie. The

screens were quickly covered with bloodsucking insects, and the night was alive with the sounds of millions of creatures. Waves of high-pitched insects, amphibians, and what sounded like women screaming while being murdered permeated the air. Occasionally, the water or bushes exploded with thrashing, and Clara growled at the sound of large creatures.

It was eerie, if not downright frightening, for high mountain Californians standing watch at night, surrounded by the Everglades. They knew that not far away were twelve-foot gators, panthers, pigs, venomous snakes, large constrictors, poisonous spiders, quicksand, sharks, and more. Jack felt certain that death from any of them would be better than living with the no-see-ums and mosquitoes.

Daylight provided light at the chart table. Neil drew probable search patterns based on an average speed of five knots. If he were Felipe, he would try to guess where Tito and Frank might go with a stolen boat. They wouldn't stay around Florida or the Bahamas, so where would they try to hide? Maybe Tito would sail to his native Mexico. They could live like kings on $60,000.

The three men gathered at the salon table to study the course headings Fred and Betty used for many years. Neil doubted Felipe would expect the *Sally Jo* to arrive at Fishmonger Cay, but that was where he planned to go. He hoped that would give him the element of surprise. They would definitely be outnumbered, so they needed every advantage they could get.

A member of the Bahamian Defense Force recently infiltrated Felipe's operation and reported that Americans were being held and forced to work. Encoded contact information was passed to Neil by the game warden who stopped them earlier. Neil had a man on the inside and a way to contact him. The man would monitor VHF channel seventeen every night from nine to ten, waiting to hear the word "cobra" three times. He would respond with the word "mongoose" three times to confirm.

They would then rendezvous on a small beach in a cut on the north end of the island thirty minutes after establishing communication. Neil, balling up the fake bulletin, threw it away, then they drew straws to see who would get swarmed by flies when pulling up the anchor.

Clara accompanied Jack out of the protection of the mosquito netting but quickly retreated, bringing plenty of biting flies into the cockpit. Anchor pulled and engine running, they left, with a menacing trail of flying teeth for several miles.

The wind picked up out of the east, filling the sails and enabling them to make 5.5 knots without the engine. Neil went to his locker, brought out a sharp knife and hollowed out perfect rectangles halfway through the center of four cockpit cushions. He sealed them with duct tape and enclosed a Claymore mine in each one. The business side, which would face the enemy, was placed against the uncut fabric on the outside of the cushions. He wrote the words *toward enemy* in very small letters on it.

He connected detonators to each and attached them to the toe rail with the straps on either end. When detonated, they would destroy everything within a sixty-degree cone that extended out fifty yards. The detonator wire ran down the toe rail into the cockpit.

It was a six-hour southerly run to the fuel dock at Marathon Key. The only boats they saw were a sport fisher and a trawler until they reached the Sawyer Bank. Neil retrieved the cushions when they went under the Seven Mile Bridge. He told the brothers it would be best if they stayed below while the boat was docked.

An hour and a half later, they were tied up at the fuel dock at Boot Key Harbor, buying diesel and ice. Unknown to them, they were observed by the drawbridge operator.

Boot Key Harbor had only two ways in. Sisters Creek on the Atlantic side was used primarily by small boats or through the drawbridge. The harbor was often full of vessels waiting favorable weather to cross the Straits of Florida to the Bahamas and beyond. The Seven Mile Bridge was one of the few high enough for sailboats to pass under. The harbor also offered abundant marine services and supplies—an ideal place to have someone watching the water.

The bridge operator dreamed of taking off like the thousands of boaters who passed through each fall on their way to paradise. He came down the Mississippi River in his small sloop from Illinois and was given his first taste of cocaine free. In a three-week period, he spent his entire cruising money on that thrill with his new girlfriends. The girls mysteriously disappeared when his money and cocaine ran out.

This was his third year on a mooring buoy in Boot Key Harbor, perpetually out of money and down on his luck. Locals attributed his condition to Key's disease, a term used in association with vagrants who were content to live a subsistence existence in the tropical warmth of the Florida Keys. Many took up residence in the protection of the harbor on boats that didn't leave until they were towed ashore, abandoned, or sunk.

The $20,000 reward for locating the *Sally Jo* would greatly enhance the man's circumstances. He could quit the monotonous, boring task of assisting the boaters he resented. The only good thing about his job was watching the women on the boats, but that too was ruined by the knowledge that none of them would look twice at him. When there were no boats to open the bridge for, he revised the list of things he wanted to buy for his boat.

He became excited when he saw the *Tipsy Gypsy*. Everything about the boat was right except the color of the masts. His heart pounded, as he stared at the boat through his binoculars. Seeing defects in the fresh white paint over the black masts, he knew it was the right boat.

"Fred, is Joey at the bar?" He was so excited, his voice cracked, as he spoke to the bartender at the Brass Monkey. "I need to talk to him."

"Look, this is a bar, not an answering service for a pharmacist. Try his pager."

"Come on. This is urgent. I got to talk to him."

"Yeah, yeah. It's always urgent when you want Joey. Try his pager." Shaking his head, the bartender hung up and looked at a regular fisherman who came to drink at noon. "These fucking dope heads are driving me crazy. Why can't they just drink like normal people?"

The old waterman had little use for the new breed of smugglers and dope peddlers that descended on the Keys.

Somehow, he didn't see any hypocrisy in the fact that he made a fortune during Prohibition smuggling rum from Cuba. If he were thirty years younger, he might have been running cocaine for Felipe. He and the bartender watched the noon news.

"Following yesterday's gruesome discovery of a headless man ten miles offshore, two more bodies were discovered by fishermen this morning off the coast of Marco Island."

A picture of one man's face flashed across the screen.

"The public is asked for help in identifying the victim of another apparent homicide. Sources close to the investigation suspect it's another case of foul play in association with the growing drug trade off the Florida coast."

Joey sat in the Overseas Bar and Grill watching the same broadcast. He knew trouble was coming if someone was killing Felipe's men. Felipe wouldn't take that. He also wondered why Tito and Frank tried to double-cross Felipe. They must've lost their minds after too much cocaine. No one in his right mind crossed the maniacal kingpin.

The pager in Joey's pocket buzzed. When he saw who it was, he assumed the man wanted an advance until payday and almost didn't return the call, then he remembered the boat Felipe was looking for and called back.

The *Tipsy Gypsy* was in full sail in light winds, motoring past Sombrero Key lighthouse, when Joey made a quick call to Felipe.

Two hours later, a cigar boat with four heavily armed

gunmen left Key West, and a thirty-foot sport fisher left Bimini to join the hunt. Felipe also called Nassau and had an ex-pat pilot launch a Hughes 500 helicopter to locate the sailboat and coordinate its capture with the two boats.

22. Marathon to Saddle Cay

"I can't believe the color of this water," Elliott said. "What would you call it? Blue or purple?"

Neil was rigging an eight-inch silver spoon with a four-foot steel leader, while Jack was below, taking a three-hour nap.

"We're entering the Gulf Stream," Neil replied. "You can always tell when the water color changes. I probably should avoid the distraction of fishing, but I can't stand going through these waters without dragging a hook."

He let out the spoon approximately thirty yards behind the boat.

"Besides," he added, "it makes us look more like sportsmen rather than a threat to anyone."

"I like the way you think. What do you think you'll catch?"

Neil attached a bullet-shaped lead head with a purple and pink rubber skirt to the other rod with a steel leader, too. "If we're lucky, we might get some mahi mahi, the flat-headed fish. If we're really lucky, we might catch a wahoo. They're hard to get on the table, though."

A loggerhead turtle raised its head beside the boat. Neil pointed out several at a distance since leaving Marathon. They looked like floating debris with barnacles to Elliott. That one, however, was close enough to look into its eyes. Elliott loved everything about being on the water except for the armed conflict.

The sound of an approaching helicopter was masked by the boat's diesel engine. The chopper flew twenty feet off the water, and the pilot saw the sailboat and circled closely enough to identify it. He knew the boat well from its many visits to Fishmonger Cay. He also heard the story of Tito and Frank, who were well trusted, so the situation made little sense.

He lowered altitude to get a closer look at the crew.

Elliott, hearing the chopper approaching, rapped three times on the deck to wake Jack. He came up the companionway with the M1 in his hand.

The pilot held the cyclic in his right hand, pointing his left index finger at the men below, mimicking a pistol, to tell them they were dead.

Neil nodded to Jack, who shot the tail rotor three times and shattered the gearbox. The pilot tried to climb by pulling up on the collective, but that exacerbated his uncontrolled spin. Realizing his mistake, he lowered the collective and pushed the cyclic forward to gain air speed in an attempt to force the fuselage to weathervane behind the nose.

That was his last mistake. He descended quickly, and the

front skids, then the rotor, struck the water. The little helicopter was gone as fast as it appeared.

Seconds later, the pilot appeared, blood flowing liberally from his nose and mouth. Elliott put the engine in neutral.

One of the big Penn reels screamed. Neil went for the rod and then the second one screamed. Jack was closest, so he threw his rifle on his bunk in the aft berth and went for the other rod. Two bull dolphins struck almost simultaneously.

The pilot was only thirty feet from their boat. "Hey! I need help! Please come get me!"

"Can't you see we're fishing?" Jack shouted back.

"I'll die if you don't help me! I'm bleeding!"

Neil's fish leaped into the air twice. Elliott killed the engine and walked to the throwable life ring.

"Neil, you want me to throw him a ring?" Elliott asked.

Neil looked at Jack. "I think my fish is bigger than yours."

Jack smiled.

Neil directed his next question to Elliott. "Ask him what he's doing out here and who sent him. If he gives you an honest answer, you can toss him the ring."

"I was just out on a lark," the pilot protested. "You know, just flying around. I was just messing with you guys."

Jack's line went slack, and he reeled in the head of what would have been a very large dolphin.

The pilot swam a few strokes toward the boat.

"Well, Mr. Helicopter Pilot," Neil said, "I suggest that in light of the fact that a fifteen-foot hammerhead just ate a five-foot dolphin only ten feet from here, you'd better rethink your situation real fast, since you're bleeding."

"OK, OK! I'll tell you everything. I fly for Felipe. Please get me out of the water. I don't want to die!"

He begged for his life, while Elliot tied a line to the life ring and threw it at the man. Jack gaffed the remaining huge dolphin for Neil, and they brought it onto the deck, where it flopped repeatedly, swinging blood from one side of the cockpit to the other.

They pulled the pilot to amidships and lowered the ladder. He climbed rapidly despite his injuries.

He was a young man in an Air Force jumpsuit, bleeding from superficial face wounds. Jack, getting out his filet knife for the fish, eyed the man.

"If you stutter, blink excessively, or I have any inclination you're even thinking of lying to me, I'll slice you and drag you behind the boat for the sharks and call you, 'Chum.' I'll drink a beer and laugh at your stupid ass. Now tell me exactly what the fuck you're doing out here?" He casually sharpened the knife on a whetstone.

"Can I at least have a drink of water first?"

Jack walked closer, pointing the knife at him. "I'm losing my patience. In ten seconds, you'll have all the water you want, back with the sharks."

Elliott decided to play good cop while Jack began bleeding the fish. Clara watched the activity intently.

"Come on," Elliott said to Jack. "Can't you see the guy's hurt?" He handed him a towel and whispered, "you'd better start talking. I think he really wants to watch you being eaten by a shark. It's one of his fantasies. You know, it's a sadist thing. He's chumming the sharks right now."

The pilot's demeanor changed, and he began talking. "I was

given your approximate departure time from Marathon and was supposed to locate you and direct two boats to you. One's coming from Bimini, the other from Key West. That's all I know. That's all I was hired to do."

Jack, wiping blood off the knife, looked menacingly at the pilot. Suddenly, he remembered the man. He was an Air Force second lieutenant who washed out of flight school and was kicked out of the Air Force after being caught with marijuana during a health and welfare inspection of the bachelor officer's quarters. Jack hadn't known him well, because he was a warrant officer candidate, but he remembered the smug little asshole who insisted on being saluted in situations where it wasn't warranted. He hadn't liked him then, and he didn't like him now.

Neil was amused by the interrogation so far, but it was time to become professional. He used duct tape to tape the man's wrists behind his back, then his ankles. He searched the flight suit and found call signs for the two boats.

"Did you contact either of these boats?" he demanded. "Your life depends on the answer."

"No, Sir. I saw you just now. I came in close to make sure it was the right boat and see who was onboard before I called. I thought Tito and Frank must've had a change of heart and decided to return the boat."

Jack finished filleting the fish while Elliott scanned the horizon. Jack was putting the meat on ice when they heard the roar of twin engines on the Donzi Cigar boat from Key West.

Neil finished his tape work with a couple wraps around the man's mouth and directed the others to battle positions. He arranged the detonators on either side of the companionway front to back, so he could choose which one to set off. He doubted they would come in shooting until they were certain of the situation.

He heard the engines idle down, as the boat came alongside. A glance showed him four men with machine guns.

"Steady...steady...," Neil muttered. "Good-bye, Assholes."

He squeezed the detonators, and the four men were shredded. The fiberglass hull sank stern first within seconds, leaving an oil slick and a few floating items to mark the men's graves.

He was pleased with the effectiveness of the Claymores. The pilot wasn't.

"One down and one to go," Neil said. "Let's return to our little conversation. What kind of boat are we looking for out of Bimini?"

He pulled duct tape off the man's mouth.

"It's a sport Fisher, about thirty feet, blue hull outriggers. I think it's a Viking."

Elliott went to the helm and started the engine to reestablish their course. Jack stood beside the mast, scanning the horizon to the east with binoculars.

"I think you're lying," Neil said. "That boat out of Key West couldn't' have found us that easily unless you directed it. You have an important choice. Do you want to sink with this boat?"

"They aren't coming to sink it. They're supposed to bring it to Felipe, along with anyone on it."

"One more time—did you or did you not make a radio call to both boats?"

The pilot, seeing Neil becoming angry, gave. "OK, OK. I gave them your heading and approximate latitude and longitude. They said they were two hours out, but the other boat was real close. I gave them a magnetic heading to your location. I'm sorry. I was doing my job. It wasn't like I knew you guys. It's just a job. I do what I'm told and get paid well."

"You aren't sorry. You're worse. You're a traitor to your country. You disgust me. Good men and women have died to preserve our society and way of life, and you, for a handful of gold, would turn against that very society and help poison its kids. You're a traitor and an opportunist."

"I'm no traitor. I'm a veteran. I served my country. I'm a patriot, and my father served in World War Two."

"Then why are you helping destroy it? You might as well be working for the Russians or the Chinese. Comrade Khrushchev promised an entire generation poisoned by dope and fueled by the greed of dealers and assholes like you, who's afraid to make an honest living. The more I think about it, the more I want to throw your ass overboard. I have a better idea, though. You might prove useful yet."

With Jack's help, they dragged the pilot out of the cockpit and lashed him to the mast. Neil went below to rig two more Claymores for the next visitors. Getting out the .50-caliber sniper rifle, he prepared a firing position from the forward berth hatch.

"You'd better keep a vigilant eye out for that Sport Fisher. Your fate is tied to it."

The autopilot maintained a steady easterly course, while Jack made sandwiches and distributed water. He even gave the pilot a drink.

Hours passed without their seeing anything but tankers and two container ships. The monotony of scanning the horizon with binoculars was fatiguing. They took watches at thirty-minute intervals.

Neil selected and loaded an incendiary for his first shot. The white phosphorus would start a fire aboard the boat after passing through the helmsman. He gave Elliott a model-700 Winchester .30-06, and Jack had his M1. Their plan was straightforward. When they saw the boat, they would shoot the people aboard and sink the boat.

They averaged six knots for eight hours. When Jack finally saw diesel smoke on the horizon, the sun was setting behind them to the west, which gave them an advantage.

"Battle stations," Neil said. "Eleven o'clock. Smoke on the horizon. Confirmed blue outriggers, and holy shit! It looks like a minigun on the bow." He paused for a moment. "Target identified. They see us."

The boat pitched slightly nose up, as he squeezed the trigger, making him miss the minigun operator but shattering the windshield behind him and sending burning phosphorus through the cabin.

He loaded the next round, as the minigun barrels spun and flashed. Elliott shot the helmsman on the flying bridge with his first attempt. Shooting without a scope, Jack emptied his first eight-round clip into the boat's center of mass.

Neil's second round struck the minigun operator and exited through the salon. The helmsman held onto the wheel as he collapsed, turning the boat broadside.

Neil recognized the flash of a shoulder-fired rocket and the incoming projectile. Elliott squeezed off another kill shot before the 40mm LAW projectile hit the mast, cutting it and the pilot in half.

The mast crashed over the side, suspended alongside by the stays. The deck and their firing positions were covered by jib, boom, and mainsail.

Jack and Elliott were hit with shrapnel. The second man on the flying bridge regained control, as smoke billowed from the salon, which was burning in earnest.

Jack cleared the sail off himself and fired, hitting the helmsman at the bridge in the shoulder and leg. The man, turning the Sport Fisher directly at the *Gypsy*, opened the throttle.

Diesel fuel escaping from the fuel tank reached the salon. Two men jumped from the burning boat as it raced toward the *Gypsy*. Elliott grabbed the wheel and turned their boat into the path of the oncoming one, giving it full throttle.

The two boats passed so close, they felt the heat from the fire. Fully aflame, the boat burned like a Viking funeral and disappeared amid a trail of black smoke before they saw a final explosion.

Neil got out the bolt cutters and quickly cut the stainless stays, while Elliott and Jack cut the numerous lines entangling the deck. Elliott vomited when they freed the lower half of the pilot's body from the remaining three feet of mast and tossed it overboard.

Night fell, and they were still four hours from the Bahamas Bank. When Elliott attempted to engage the engine, it died. Neil had been afraid of that and assumed one of the lines attached to the sails was wrapped around the prop. He would have to dive before darkness made it impossible to see.

Elliott and Neil jumped from the dive platform together. The halyard was wrapped many times around the propeller and shaft. Elliott held onto the shaft while Neil cut the line, that's when he saw the shark. Shoulder to shoulder, the two men watched it circle closer. Neil poked its nose with the knife and it sped away. Blood from the pilot's torso had attracted the sharks.

The two men surfaced long enough for a deep breath, then dove again.

Relieved to be back on board when the prop was free, they motored east. Lightning crisscrossed between towering cumulus clouds in the distance. The low rumble of thunder echoed the flashes. The brothers alternated between the helm and the salon, so Neil could remove the several pieces of the aluminum mast that were embedded in their skin. Luckily, none were big enough to require stitching.

The sky turned black, and the horizon vanished. A cold breeze sprang up. The seas rose to eight feet as the winds approached thirty miles per hour.

Rain fell in torrents. Neil passed out rain gear and lifejackets as a precaution before taking the helm. Clara wore hers, too. It would be difficult to see the light at Gun Cay with the rain. It was a very narrow passage, barely thirty feet wide, with rocks on either side. There was no room for error.

Neil turned the boat to the west, deciding to wait out the storm in the safety of deeper water. It would be uncomfortable, but it was better than breaking up the ship on the rocks.

After a tumultuous fifteen minutes, the storm passed. They were able to see the light clearly and negotiated the pass between Cat and Gun Cays. They anchored in six feet of water, protected from the ocean swells on the east side of Gun Cay. At least the rain washed the pilot's blood from the deck.

Their adrenalin finally ebbed. Twenty hours after leaving

Shark River, they sunk two boats, a helicopter, and killed at least twelve people. Neil raised the yellow quarantine flag on the mizzen mast, not wanting to violate Bahamian law.

They were easily visible in the moonlight, and it would be foolish to think they were secure. Captain and crew gathered around the salon table, while red lights cast a macabre hue to their faces.

After Neil passed out beers, he proposed a toast. "Here's to the survival of the good guys."

Touching bottles, they drank.

"I've been in plenty of combat situations with a lot of people. I want you two to know I'm proud of you and would go anywhere and fight anyone with y'all. Here's to you."

They touched bottles again.

"This is just the beginning, though. When Felipe realizes he lost two boats and a helicopter, along with at least twelve people, he'll declare war. I guarantee there'll be a big reward for the boat and crew who did it. I'd hate to get caught."

"I feel like a sitting duck," Jack said. "We stick out like a sore thumb."

"I agree completely."

Clara barked, and Neil understood what she wanted. "Of course you want to go ashore. I think we should all go ashore. I can't believe I didn't think of it myself. There must be a reason that dog spelled backward is God.

"Early pirates were able to hide their boats by running them aground and pulling them over by their masts. We draw only four feet. We can heel the boat over with the anchor, and it'll look like a wreck. We'll have to wait for high tide to leave, but we can use a break. We'll take turns sleeping."

Clara barked, jumping in excitement. She loved it when a plan came together.

"You think we'll have company tonight?" Jack asked. "That's a stupid question. Of course, we will. We just have to be prepared."

Neil organized their tasks. They loaded water, C rations, Claymore cushions, detonators, rifles and ammunition, and ferried them to shore in the Zodiac. They donned camouflage jungle fatigues. Clara ran up and down the beach like a six-month-old puppy.

Neil started the engine and ran the boat into the shallows as far as he could, turning it broadside to the beach. He lowered the anchor to Elliott, who secured it in the rocks. Neil captured the anchor line with a snatch block and secured it to the far toe rail, using the big winch in the cockpit to heel the boat onto its side.

He motored out in the dingy to see what it looked like. The blue hull blended into the landscape, looking like an abandoned wreck on its side in the shallows.

As he beached the Zodiac, he raised the outboard and lowered the landing wheels. The three men towed the boat out of sight and secured it.

Neil chose the top of the bluff that separated the Atlantic Ocean from the Bahamas Bank for an overwatch position with the .50-caliber sniper rifle. Jack and Elliott took positions ten yards away, north and south. Neil positioned the six Claymore cushions around their position. Each man controlled two.

It was a tidy defensive position commanding a 360-degree view of any approaching vessel. Making themselves as comfortable as they could, they ate cold C rations before taking one-hour watches.

Elliott lay in the sand wrapped in a poncho. The night was cool. The Atlantic Ocean crashed against rocks thirty feet away. Looking up at the moon, he wondered how he came to be there. His sentiment toward the war and the gruesome images he saw in *Life* magazine made him think he was a pacifist. It didn't make sense that he had become involved in taking human lives. He remembered the childhood Army games he and Jack played, practicing infantry tactics when they were children.

He thought about the commercial on TV against the war, which quoted the Bible verse, *When I was a child, I thought as a child.*

Reaching into his soul, he thought about the pilot, who begged for his life and how he might still be alive if they put him below instead of tying him to the mast. The picture of his body blown in half filled his mind's eye, and his throat constricted. Tears rolled down his face.

Elliott prayed for forgiveness. He never wanted to hurt or kill anyone. Football and wrestling were just games. Out of nowhere, the memory of his mother came to him. Suddenly, he floated above his body, warm and limitless, a comforting peace stilling his mind and soul. He felt God speak to him through his mother.

"Do not grieve, My Son. You have no choice in these things but to follow the path I have prepared for you. Be at peace, for I am with you."

He awoke to the warm caress of Clara's tongue licking away his tears. He had fallen asleep with the dog cradled in his arms.

Neil scanned the horizon in all directions, trying to anticipate what Felipe would do. What would he have done if someone was killing his soldiers and stealing his money? How would he find those people? He also knew Felipe would do exactly what he was doing—trying to anticipate his adversary.

He finally decided that Felipe would expect his adversary to run and assume that the thieves would merely try to escape in the boat with the money. It might give Neil an advantage if Felipe became obsessed with finding him rather than defending against an assault.

The problem was that Felipe wasn't rational. Alcohol, cocaine, and lack of sleep transformed him into a madman. The furies controlled his mind.

He rode around the island in the back of an FJ 45 pickup equipped with a .50-caliber machinegun drinking whiskey and shooting anything that moved. He carried pearl-handled .45s on each hip and wore an Australian bush hat, making him look like Patton in an episode of *Rat Patrol.* No one else on the island was allowed to sleep, either. He posted around-the-clock foot, vehicle, and water patrols. Four armed guards were posted around his house, and his converted cistern that was his secret money and cocaine stash. The Island Beach Club served twenty-four hour food and nonalcoholic drinks to his men.

It was over an hour when Neil woke Jack from a sound sleep. They traded places, and Jack took the overwatch position with the .50 caliber.

Jack saw red and green navigation lights on the bow of a vessel approaching from the south. He acquired it with the powerful scope on the sniper rifle and was relieved to see two Bahamian fishermen. He watched them pass a cigarette back and forth before they turned east across the bank.

Eating C rations brought back memories of childhood on the river with his brother, playing Army. The pound cake and peaches always were his favorite.

A shadow in the water caught his eye. A huge shark swam along the shoreline and around the *Gypsy*. Jack dismissed it as a normal predator behavior. He wasn't superstitious, especially about animals. A hooting owl wasn't a harbinger of death, and a black cat crossing his path didn't bring bad luck.

Elliott slept for two hours before Jack woke him by shaking him gently.

"Elliott?" Jack asked.

Elliott raised up to lean on his elbows, then he sat up completely and rubbed his face. "Yeah, yeah. I'm awake. What time is it?"

"It's three-thirty, Sleepyhead. How'd you sleep?"

"I think I was visited by Mom or the Holy Spirit. It was crazy. I was feeling bad about the pilot and suddenly, I was out of my body. Mom said it was OK, I was doing the right thing. This is our destiny, like it or not. I feel a hell of a lot better. Have you seen Clara?"

"She's been with Neil since you went down."

"I could've sworn she licked my face when I went to sleep, then she cuddled up with me."

"You always were the mystic in the family. You probably just needed a little sleep. That guy was trying to get us killed. He chose his side. Anyway, I saw only one boat. A couple fishermen came out of Cat Key and went east. I'm getting some sleep now. Love you, Bro."

They traded positions. Elliott's watch went without incident. He woke Neil at four-thirty as the moon set in the west.

At five-thirty, when Neil woke Jack for the next watch, the moon was completely down. When the sun rose at six-thirty, Neil and Elliott dragged the inflatable to the water and set the anchor in deep water. By moving the snatch block to the other toe rail, they were able to winch the *Gypsy* upright.

Jack remained in the overwatch position while they ferried the rest of the gear and secured it on deck. Clara exercised herself by chasing birds up and down the beach, stopping occasionally to roll in unknown substances in the seaweed.

Jack whistled, alerting everyone. "We have company coming, a sailboat on the horizon heading our way from the west."

Neil waved him to come down, while Jack carried his rifle and day pack to the beach. Elliott brought the inflatable to shore. Clara rode in the bow on the short trip back to the boat.

Within minutes, they started across the shallow Grand Bahamas Bank, a seventy-mile passage in open water. Using only the motor, they estimated they would reach the Northwest Passage at dark.

Jack covered the grill with mahi mahi twice, cooking the whole fish. Elliott cooked rice in the galley, and they ate a glorious meal of fresh fish, avocado, and tomatoes. Clara ate at least a pound, leaving several pounds for later. Each would get four hours' sleep, with two on watch at all times. The men working for Felipe wouldn't be getting any sleep.

23. The Battle of Fishmonger Cay

Everything on the island depended on generators for electricity. The Beach Club was the biggest draw with walk-in freezers, an ice maker, and coolers. It was the social focal point for the island, and it had been converted into the headquarters for the ongoing security operations.

The man responsible for keeping the generator full of diesel overlooked his task out of fatigue, so Neil's father was sent for to get it running. As he was priming it, the physician came over.

"He's gone stark, raving mad," the doctor said. "He hasn't slept in two days."

"I'm just trying to stay away from him. I heard one of his sergeants say he told them if he catches anyone sleeping, he'll have the person executed."

"I wonder if his fears are justified, or he's just delusional and paranoid? I've been praying for someone to rescue me from this hell in paradise for too long."

"What's he got on you, anyway, Doc?"

"Same as you, most likely. If anything happens to him, he said my wife and kids would be killed. I guess he's afraid I might poison him."

"I hear you. I just worry that if something happens to him, his people in New Orleans will go through with a hit on my daughter. If it wasn't for that, I would've killed the son of a bitch a long time ago."

"Is that all you have, a daughter?"

"No. I have a son, too. Last I heard, he was still in Vietnam. If he was home, I wouldn't have to worry about her." Jim turned on the electric pump, sending diesel through the lines, injectors, and bleeders. "That should do it."

He hit the start button. The generator turned over, and the lights came on in the Beach Club. The doctor stepped closer and whispered, "If he keeps going like he is, we may not have to worry. The problem will take care of itself when he ODs."

A tall black man carrying an M-16 over his shoulder approached. "Hey, you two. Come help. Follow me."

Leading them to a walk-in freezer, he closed the door.

"Look, Mon. My name's Marcus. You going to have to trust me. Something big gonna happen here. I'll come for you. Stay together. Someone come soon to get you off dis island."

"The problem isn't leaving," Doc said. "It's what Felipe said he'd do to our families."

"Don't worry 'bout dat, Mon. I don' think he be in business much longer. Now you better carry dis food in to Cookie."

They carried several frozen grouper, sausage, and bacon to the kitchen.

The Nassau news was on TV. A sport fisher out of Bimini was found by local fishermen burned to the waterline, and a helicopter failed to return to Nassau from a sightseeing trip.

Jim began to think the big Bahamian man knew a lot more than he said. He heard a .50-caliber machine gun firing on the island. Felipe was shooting at a sailboat traveling north several miles offshore. The red tracers falling harmlessly into the ocean mesmerized him. Their only affect was leaving him temporarily deaf.

He told the driver of his Land Cruiser to take them to the top of the island, where he placed a cabin cruiser abandoned by one of the island's former occupants on the highest precipice. Two men stood watch up there, equipped with a military starlight telescope and could see anyone approaching from miles away. It was also Felipe's favorite place to watch the morning sun.

He climbed the ladder at the stern of the cabin cruiser to find the men staring north intently at a vessel. "What's going on?"

When he didn't hear them answer, he assumed they were asleep and shot them, emptying two clips into their bodies. He turned to the driver. "Throw them off my boat."

He didn't hear the driver respond, but he saw the man's mouth moving and realized something was wrong. "I think I'm deaf. Shit! I can't hear a thing. Take me to my house and bring the doctor to me."

He didn't hear the driver say, "Yes, Sir." Deafness made him even more paranoid, so he snorted more cocaine.

Reaching his house, he moved his desk and chair to a corner, so no one could sneak up on him. His bodyguard met the doctor at the entry.

"Doc, I hope you can help him. He's been up for two days. He's all jacked up. I think he blew out his eardrums. He says he can't hear anything."

When the bodyguard opened the bedroom door, Felipe

was ready with a pistol aimed at them. "You'd better have that quack with you."

The doctor came in with his medical bag. Felipe was in bad shape. His bloody eyes bulged in their sockets, and his hair was greasy and matted. The foul odor of a three-day binge exuded from his body, saturating his clothes with nervous perspiration.

The doctor put a stethoscope on Felipe's chest and Felipe grabbed his arm and put a pistol in his face.

"It's not my heart, you fucking idiot! I've gone deaf. There must be something wrong with this coke. I must've gotten some bad shit. Somebody will pay for this."

"OK, Felipe. Take it easy. I'll have a look at your ears, but I never heard of cocaine making anyone deaf."

"What did you say?" Felipe set the gun on the desk and sat in the chair, while the doctor examined his ears.

"I can't see anything obstructing your ears. Are you using hearing protection when you shoot?"

"What? What did you say?"

The doctor wrote a note.

You have what is known as traumatic hearing loss. Your hearing will come back if you rest.

"Do I look like I can rest? There are people trying to kill me, and my own trusted men are falling asleep on duty."

The doctor wrote another note.

Let me give you a shot to help you relax, so your ears will hear again.

"What now? You want to kill me, too?"

It looks like you're doing a pretty good job of that yourself. You keep me here to be your personal physician, so let me do my job. Your blood pressure is dangerously high, you have a fever, and your heart's beating itself out of your chest. Let me help you before it's too late.

Felipe felt his chest pounding, and he was burning up with fever. He slowly nodded.

The doctor administered a dose of benzodiazepine. With the help of the guards, they carried his limp body to a cool tub of water, then to bed. The guards knew what Felipe did to the men on watch, and were relieved that their boss was asleep. Everyone felt safer not having a madman running around the island willy-nilly shooting a machine gun and killing his own people.

The seas were calm, allowing the *Gypsy* to make good time across the flats. They entered the Northwest Passage, bypassed New Providence, and arrived at the northern edge of the Exumas at ten-thirty that night. Neil used the time en route to equip explosives with mechanical timers. He planned to use explosions to confuse and overcome a much-larger force.

With a detailed map and an area reconnaissance photo, Neil gave his team their operations orders. The primary objective was to rescue any hostages on the island, as well as to recover the boat suspected to be his father's. The vessel was tied to a large dock inside the pond, but the picture was too blurred to make positive identification.

Fishmonger Cay was perfect for Felipe's operation. The island, seven miles long north to south, was divided east and west by tidal flats and a well-protected saltwater pond, accessible through a narrow, shallow cut to the Atlantic. The entire island was connected by road and the pond. There was an airstrip on the southern end, a commercial-grade dock, and a protected anchorage. The interior of the island was an impenetrable tangle of mangroves and pepper trees.

The shoreline on the Bahamas Bank side was rock and sandy beach, while on the Atlantic side it was mainly rock bluffs. To the north of the cay was a narrow passage and a small sand beach where Neil would rendezvous with Marcus, a Bahamian national who had infiltrated the Cartel for the DEA.

They anchored the *Gypsy* in the protection of Iguana Cay to the north under cover of darkness.

At 11:30, Jack was concealed across the narrow cut to the north of Fishmonger Cay, watching Marcus on the beach through the scope of the silenced .50-caliber rifle. His purpose was to ensure that the rendezvous hadn't been compromised.

Marcus waited for forty-five minutes before he heard the words, "Cobra, cobra, cobra," spoken softly over his handheld VHF radio.

Jack saw him raise the radio to his mouth and reply, "Mongoose, mongoose, mongoose."

Two minutes later, the Zodiac beached. Elliott moved down the beach to provide additional security.

"Mon, you come at da good time," Marcus said. "Felipe gone crazy. He done shot two of his Bahamian men for no good reason. Nobody had any sleep for two days, maybe tree."

"What about the Americans? Are they OK?"

"Ya, Mon. I talked to dem early. Dat mechanic and doctor s'pose to stick together. Told them somet'ing was going to happen, and they would be leaving. They bot' say Felipe threaten to kill their family if they escape. I tol' him don' worry 'bout him no more after you leave."

"Can you confirm where Felipe is?"

"Ya, Mon. Doctor give him da shot to make him sleep. He's at da house in da middle of da island. Da house has a volcano roof and sits right on da rock bluff. Dats where da doctor is, maybe da other man, too. He got four guards outside and da bodyguard. He prob'ly only one dat care about Felipe. All Bahamians hate him now."

"Are there any Bahamians you can trust?"

"Plenty, Mon, after what he done. They would all leave tonight if they was a way, maybe cut his throat if da could."

"That changes things a bit. Maybe we can help them, too. Where does Felipe keep his dope and money stashed?"

"He made dat cistern behind da house for cocaine and money. No more water."

"How many of his own men, besides the bodyguard, are loyal and will still fight?"

"Maybe two dozen cartel soldiers from U.S. and Columbia." Neil studied his watch, calculating. "Can you have the two Americans at the dock in the pond at two o'clock this morning?"

"Ya, Mon. No problem."

"Get as many Bahamians as you trust to meet us there, too. Anyone else on the island is an enemy combatant. We won't discriminate."

"Ya, Mon. Deese dangerous people. Dey got people walking

wid da mean dog and a fifty-caliber machine gun on dat Toyota Land Cruiser. Up in dat boat on da hill, dey got people watchin'. Most of em, I tink, will be sleepin' in dat big hangar dat's used for barracks. I tink that crazy mon keep everyone awake too long. It's a good time for you to come."

"Does the whole island get its electricity from the generator at the Beach Club."

"Dere is two more, one at volcano house, another at hangar."

"You know anything about the shrimp boat in the pond? Is it seaworthy?"

"Felipe took dat boat from da American for trips to Columbia. He says it ready to go."

"OK. That'll be our ride off the island. Once the island lights up, we'll meet you there as soon as we can. I'll establish radio contact. If you can, secure the dock and that vessel. Scuttle any other boats. We don't want any pursuit."

"Dat won' be no problem. How many men you got."

"There are three of us." Smiling, he shook Marcus' hand.

"Dat's all you got, Mon? You either crazy or crazy brave. No matter which, you still crazy."

The engine noise from the approaching Land Cruiser was masked by the ocean sound. The driver illuminated the beach as he drove, revealing the Zodiac. It was common for small vessels, such as dinghies, to be lost from yachts and wash ashore. He thought it was good luck until he saw a distant flash, followed by a thud, and then the Columbian gunner flew off the back of the vehicle. When the driver turned around, he saw his windshield shatter.

The American from Chicago who sat in the passenger seat

caught Jack's second round in his Adam's apple. The Bahamian driver rolled out of the vehicle only to run into Marcus and Neil. He was quick to offer help.

"No, Mon. I help you. Dat Felipe kill two good men, one my wife's cousin and a man I crayfish wid before we get dis bad job. He kill dem, because he can't hear dem answer him. Dat man is da devil."

Jack watched through the scope, as Marcus and his new driver dragged the bodies into the swift current rushing through the cut into the Atlantic. Jack met Neil and Elliott on the shoreline, and they returned to the boat.

Equipped with new intelligence, Neil formulated their final plan. The mission had changed, in that they would be extracting mutinous Bahamian elements of Felipe's force, as well as the two Americans. Felipe's men were fatigued and demoralized by their leader's erratic behavior and the senseless killing of the two Bahamians. The guards weren't expected to be alert and might even be asleep.

Under the cover of darkness, they would place explosive charges on the generator and diesel tank at the Beach Club, the large dock, the fuel tanks at the south end of the runway, and the barracks. They would approach the volcano house at two o'clock when the charges went off.

With two hours to prepare, they blackened their faces and hands. Jack opted for his M1, along with a silenced .22 and .45 caliber pistols. Elliott had the twelve gauge and his silenced .22. Both carried six-inch sheath knives. Claymore mines and explosives went into the Zodiac. Neil gave the brothers four frag grenades each.

At 12:15 AM, Neil gave orders to Clara to guard the boat,

and they departed for the south end of Fishmonger Cay. Everyone lay down low in the boat, and they went west first, swinging a wide arc on the bank side of the island. Arriving undetected at the south end, they pulled the Zodiac up on the beach into the grass.

The beach club was lit up, and they heard loud conversation in Spanish, broken English, and loud Bahamian accents. It was unclear whether it was a dispute or a big party.

Jack and Elliott took positions between the Beach Club and the generator building at 12:45. Neil set the timer for an hour and fifteen minutes and attached the C-4 charge to the 500-gallon fuel tank beside the generator.

They retreated to the Zodiac without being seen and navigated around the southern tip of the island to the commercial dock, where they found two men asleep against the pilings, their AK-47s in their laps.

Paddling instead of using the engine, they slipped past the guards and beached between the pilings. Elliott provided security, while Neil set up a Claymore ambush on the road to the dock from the hangar barracks with a tripwire. By then it was 1:15 AM, so he set the time for forty-five minutes and placed explosives against the 3,000-gallon tank by the dock.

Jack slipped silently through the water, cutting the fuel lines to the outboards on the two skiffs tied at the dock. The engines would start, but they wouldn't run more than a few minutes.

The three men got into the Zodiac and paddled away from the dock until it was safe to start the engine. Neil watched through the scope and saw one of the guards wake up at the sound, but he just looked around before pulling his hat down farther over his eyes and going back to sleep. That was lucky for him.

Marcus and his driver returned to the barracks after leaving the rendezvous at the north end of the cay. Gathering with their fellow Bahamians, they secured their loyalty against Felipe. They subverted the no-drinking policy by breaking into storage and getting out tequila, rum, and beer to have a raucous celebration at the club. They brought as many men from the barracks with them as they could, enticing them with the liquor.

The alcohol went straight to the men's heads. They didn't notice when the Bahamians slowly left the party until all were gone by 1:30. Marcus and his driver led the way in the Land Cruiser, followed by an open truck with ten armed Bahamians.

They drove to the volcano house and said they needed the doctor and mechanic, because a man was badly cut while trying to repair a truck. The trusted bodyguard didn't care and released the two gringos.

When the Americans joined Marcus and the driver, Marcus grinned. "Hey, Mon, I tol' you. You can trust me. Three commandos come for you tonight. You taking your boat home. Hope she ready to go. We all going wit' you."

"That's the best news I've heard in a year. What do you think, Doc?" Neil's dad, Jim, asked.

"I've already done my part."

Jim cocked his head and studied the man, wondering what that meant.

Jack had to slow the Zodiac going through the pass. The wind opposed the tide, kicking up huge swells. Neil turned on his VHF radio and said, "Mongoose, mongoose, this is Cobra. Do you have my package?"

"Ya, Mon," Marcus replied. "We got da package and more. Got a dozen men ready to do whatever you say, Mon."

"Can you meet us at the volcano house after the fireworks?"

"Roger."

The volcano house was easily visible by its silhouette against the sky atop the rock bluffs. Idling quietly beyond the breakers of a small reef, Neil located a sandy spot among the rocks where they could beach the raft. They picked their way below the rocky bluffs until they were 100 yards from the house.

At exactly 2:00 AM, the sky on the southern end of the island ignited. The concussion from the explosion rattled windows on adjacent islands. The sky filled with towering plumes of flame and smoke.

Two men sleeping on the dock at the south end of the island were blown into the water by the explosion. The mercenaries partying at the beach Club didn't fare as well. There was nothing left but scorched earth where the club and generator had been.

The two men responsible for watching the ocean approach to the house ran to the front for a better view of the fire in the sky. All four guards stood together when Neil rolled a fragmentation grenade between their legs like a bocce ball. Eight more frag grenades went into the house, one of which flew into the bedroom, where Felipe's bodyguard tried to shake his already-lifeless body awake, but he didn't move. He shielded his boss with his body in a final act of loyalty, but the doctor had cured Felipe of all pain hours earlier.

The two Americans, with two armed Bahamians for security, started the diesel engine and prepared Jim's shrimp boat for a hasty departure. Marcus and the others sped off for the volcano house in the Land Cruiser and truck. They formed a security perimeter while Marcus helped Neil clear the house. Marcus rolled the dead guard off Felipe's body and checked for a pulse, then he shook his head.

"Now we send him to hell to join da devil. We send him off with all dat poison and do it Bahamian style—wit' fire."

Neil placed plastic explosive on the door to the cistern, and the steel door blew off its hinges to reveal hundreds of pounds of cocaine and duffel bags of American cash.

Loading the money into the Land Cruiser, they tossed kilos of cocaine through Felipe's bedroom window. There was a party atmosphere among the Bahamians, as they spread five-gallon cans of diesel fuel intended for the generator throughout the house, especially around and on Felipe. It seemed likely they had partaken wholeheartedly at the party at the Beach House before leaving.

When the fire was lit, the men chanted, "Burn da poison. Burn dat devil."

In a strange twist of cultural integration, they sang, "Ding, dong, de devil's gone," to the tune of the Wicked Witch, as they drove away in the truck.

Neil got into the Land Cruiser with Marcus. One

Bahamian went with Jack and Elliott in the Zodiac to guide them through the narrow cut from the Atlantic into the pond. Going through the wrong opening in the rocks would be fatal.

Jack sat at the tiller when he saw the flash of an AK-47 from the rocks at the entry. He felt a bullet hit him and instinctively lowered his head while opening the throttle to head straight toward the opening and the shooter.

Elliott and the Bahamian returned fire but missed, though they forced the shooter to seek cover. Jack held his course through the rocks, the throttle wide open, as the Zodiac flew over the wave tops. He beached the boat just inside the pass behind a sand dune for protection. Elliott applied a bandage to Jack's chest just below his shoulder.

The Bahamian got out and used the heavy vegetation to move closer to the shooter. Elliott watched through the scope of his rifle when he heard the Bahamian call out.

"Hey, Mon! You done gone crazy? Why you shootin' at us, Mon?"

The man stood with his AK-47 ready, intending to speak. His mouth opened, but his brain never sent or received any more signals. His face disappeared with the back of his skull, as the projectile continued out over the sea. Birds would soon pick his carcass clean, and the tropical sun would bleach his bones.

The Zodiac took rounds in the front and left air cells, but it was seaworthy enough to continue at idle. Jack applied pressure to both sides of the wound with his right hand on the bandage.

The remainder of Felipe's goons, who slept in the barracks, awoke to the sound of explosions and tried to decide what to do. When they found all the vehicles disabled, they decided to go to the dock and take the skiffs up to Felipe's volcano house.

Neil and Marcus were descending the stone stairway to the pond when they heard the rat-a-tat-tat of AK-47s shooting at the raft, followed by the percussion of the Claymore mines going off at the south end of the island. No one would be loading into the skiffs after that.

Neil looked up, seeing his prayers were fulfilled. The lettering on the stern of the shrimp boat read *Betty Lynn, Dauphin Island, Alabama.* He almost floated on air down to the dock carrying his twelve-gauge and a large duffel bag full of hundred-dollar bills.

"Captain, request permission to come aboard?" he asked.

"Hurry up, whoever's coming," Jim shouted. "Climb aboard." His eyes remained focused on the charts he laid out. Somewhere in the back of his mind, he had the feeling the voice sounded familiar, but he was too busy to think about it, as he moved to the helm. He was anxious to shove off.

"Let's go!" he barked as usual. "Cast off those lines!"

Neil smiled, but Jim didn't recognize him with his face camouflaged.

"Hold on, Captain. We got three more coming in the Zodiac."

"I hope they get here before any more of Felipe's men."

"Don't worry about it, Dad. They've all been taken care of."

Jim spun around from the helm and stared at Neil.

"I said Dad, and I damn well meant it."

The two men embraced.

"You made it!" Jim said. "Thank God you made it back from Vietnam. You don't know how glad I am to see you, Son. You don't know how long I prayed for this day. Thank God!"

Elliott drove the nearly deflated raft to the side of the shrimp boat. The men handed up their weapons to waiting hands and were quickly pulled aboard.

"All aboard, Captain," Marcus said.

Jack and Elliott witnessed the reunion.

Neil turned to them. "I heard the AK-47. Everybody OK?"

"We were engaged while approaching the cut," Elliott replied. "Hopefully, there was only one of them. Unfortunately, Jack took a round through the shoulder, and the raft's shot up, too."

"Take the wounded man below," Jim said. "Doc, you've got a customer. Anyone else who's hurt, go below and see Doc. The rest of you men, hoist that raft aboard. Make it snappy. Let's go."

He was definitely a captain. Within minutes, they shoved away from the dock and motored toward the narrow passage into the Atlantic. Neil stood beside his dad in the pilothouse, just as he had when he was a small child. He used binoculars to scan for would-be shooters. The sound of the big diesel was as comforting to him as his mother's heartbeat in vitro.

The world was right again. No words could explain how he felt, as the big prop churned, pushing them through the surf into the Atlantic.

24. Sweet Home, Alabama

The doctor treated Jack for what he diagnosed as a through-and-through bullet wound that missed bone and artery. His prognosis was a complete recovery.

Neil guided his dad to where they left the *Tipsy Gypsy* with Clara on guard. As they came alongside, she ran around the deck and barked, recognizing the sound of the *Betty Lynn* long before the ship arrived. Leaping from the *Gypsy,* she cleared the gunwale and bounded into the pilot house to jump up on Neil and Jim.

"OK, Son," Jim asked, "where are we going?"

"We have to get the Bahamians to safety, then back to Alabama. Marcus, where do you want to take these men?"

"Great Harbor. Dat's where to go. No cartel dere, jus' Bahamian."

"Will that boat make it, Son?"

"We made it this far. I don't see any reason why not. I know it looks funny without the mast, but she's mechanically ready to go. I'll take Elliott and a couple of Bahamians for crew and follow you. Doc can look after Jack."

"Can you make eight knots?"

"I can probably do 6.5."

"That won't cut it. I can tow you faster than that. I've got a bridle. I'll throw it to you."

Neil attached the bridle and tow ropes, then he pulled the anchor and jumped back on the *Betty Lynn.* She was fifty-feet long, built out of Cyprus in the Mobile boatyards in the 1920s. At the start of World War Two, the *Betty Lynn* was needed as a buoy tender. Neil's grandfather, the owner, went with her as captain. The first thing they did was repower her with a powerful cat diesel that still had plenty of life. Jim eventually inherited the boat and fiberglassed it in 1968. She pulled the *Tipsy Gypsy* effortlessly forty feet behind.

"All right, then," Jim said. "Giddy-up. I heard the weather earlier. There are a few scattered showers, with east winds at eight to twelve miles per hour. It's about 160 nautical miles to Great Harbor. We'll arrive in late afternoon. We've got a lot of catching up to do, Son."

"No doubt, Dad. I need to speak with Marcus in private for a moment. We owe him a great deal."

"The Bahamians were never mean to me on the island. I have no beef with any of them. Most were fishermen or workers looking for a wage. They weren't bad people, they just chose bad employment."

Neil motioned Marcus to follow him down the companionway into the storage hold, where he secured the duffel bags of money.

"I can't tell you how much I appreciate what you did for our family. I doubt we could have succeeded without you. Your intelligence, and the actions of you and the other Bahamian men were invaluable. I don't see why you shouldn't be rewarded."

"All dese men, day promised to be paid. Maybe we can compensate dem and da families of da men Felipe killed. Nobody got to know what we do wid dat money."

"I agree. There's no point turning it over to the government. We know what would happen if we did. We should take care of all the men. How much money do you think this is?"

"I don' know. Every time plane come in wit' drugs, money go out. Could be close to one million in each bag."

"There are two duffel bags. You take one, and I'll take one. I just hope the cartel doesn't find out who to hunt for to find their money and the drugs we destroyed."

"Ya, Mon. De cartel be real mad 'bout dis. Maybe nobody left to tell what happen."

"You'd better be real careful. If these men suddenly come home with large amounts of money, someone will get suspicious and talk, especially if there's a large reward for information."

"Dat's da chance we take. Lots people make easy money wid da smugglin'. Mos' Bahamians know to keep da mout' shut or dey get killed or go to jail. I don't want da other Bahamians to know I have anytin' to do wit' da money. Maybe after de spend deres, they try to blackmail me or turn me in fo' a reward."

Marcus lifted the bags one at a time, looking a little like the scales of justice. "Mon, I tink day weigh da same, close to 100 pounds."

He set down the bags and unzipped one. It was full of circulated $20 bills in bands of 100. Neil decided to give each of the Bahamians, including Marcus, five banded stacks of twenties, totaling $10,000 each. The rest he placed in a rucksack for Marcus to carry on his back when they left. The others wouldn't know he had any more money than they did, and they wouldn't' come to him when their own money ran out.

Marcus liked the idea. He would get money to the families of the dead men covertly.

"You know much about Great Harbor? I'd like to get in and out as fast as possible without being seen," Neil said.

"Dat no problem. We don' have to go all da way dere. I can call Conky Joe, a friend, to meet us off Chubb Key. He's the dockmaster who always monitor da radio. All you have to do is get us to da beach. Dat way, nobody see dis boat in Great Harbor."

"What will you do there?"

"First thing, I quit livin' dangerously. My cousin, Antony and I, always talk 'bout buildin' a beach club. We will sell burgers, conch, and fish to da tourists. Maybe play bocce and drink rum with da pretty European women. We won't have any problem wit' cash flow."

"Sounds like you've thought this out."

"Ya, Mon. I dream up dis ting long time."

"I better fix that dingy if we're going to get you to the beach without getting wet."

They returned to the deck, where Elliott helped Neil patch the bullet holes. Clara Bell paced the deck over the sleeping Bahamians, stopping in the pilot house to be petted occasionally by Jim. She knew him since she was a puppy.

Marcus showed Jim on the chart the beach where he wanted to land. Elliott took a turn at the helm, while Jim went below. He returned with a case of C rations and distributed them.

Neil pulled out a roll of trash bags, and Marcus helped him put $10,000 in twenties in each of twelve bags. Only half the remainder would fit in the rucksack, but Marcus wasn't greedy and didn't care. He had plenty of money to start his new beach club and take care of his large family.

Jim, awaking around two o'clock that afternoon, took over the helm for their arrival. Turning into the wind so the *Gypsy* would trail behind, he shifted the engine into neutral and let them drift off Mama Rhoda Rock. They lowered the dinghy with one of the cargo davits. The Americans and the Bahamians shook hands, saying good-bye. Neil gave each man the double-bagged money as they climbed down, and thanked them. They would be very surprised when they opened their bags.

"Enjoy the raft, Marcus," Jim called, as Marcus climbed down. "You might need it to get lobsters for your customers. I forgot to ask what a Conchy Joe is."

"You come back to Great Harbor and spend time, you might become one," Marcus replied.

The Bahamians laughed and smiled, as Marcus started the Johnson and motored them away.

Jim estimated it would take them fifty-six hours nonstop to reach Dauphin Island. Neil hid the money in case they were boarded and searched. They maintained a vigilant watch, keeping their weapons at hand.

Neil spent most of his watches with his dad. He explained that a DEA field agent helped him in his search and set up the rendezvous with Marcus. They knew about Felipe, but there was nothing they could do to him on Bahamian soil. Neil, however, was free to do whatever he wanted.

He explained how he and Jack met and why the two brothers were helping. He told Jim about the prayer vigils held on the island after he disappeared. Jim, touched, quickly asked about Cat, Bonnie, and his brother. He was very excited to finally be free.

When he asked Neil about his experiences in the war, Neil said, "It was hell, Dad."

Two and a half days later, the *Betty Lynn* towed the *Tipsy Gypsy* between the watchful ramparts of Fort Morgan and Fort Gaines. Jim called his brother on the radio and told him he needed an extra slip.

Half the island population was waiting to greet them. The only thing missing was a brass band. Tears of joy ran down Cat's face, as she held her dad and cried. She hugged Neil, then Jack, who flinched.

"Oh, no. You've been hurt. Is it bad?"

"Nope. Merely a flesh wound. I told you I'd be back soon."

She kissed him on the mouth, and Jim raised an eyebrow.

"I see you got to know my daughter."

Neil looked at Jack and winked.

"Yes, Sir," Jack said. "I've become quite fond of her."

Bonnie latched onto Elliott and held him tightly, too.

"You just remember," Jim said, "this ain't California, and her daddy's back in Alabama now. Hey, Elliott. That's my niece you're holding." He wore a half-smile, as he said it.

Jim was very happy to be back in Alabama with his family.

They went to the homestead for showers and fresh clothes. Doc got a plane reservation to take him home in the morning.

That night, the island had a party like no one had seen in years. The parking lot at the Fish House was full of people rejoicing and celebrating. Watermen from the whole Mobile Bay area arrived. It wasn't often that a man lost at sea returned from the dead.

The party lasted well into the morning, and the brothers and cousins were rocking the Tipsy Gypsy when the sun rose.

Neil and Jim took Doc to the airport at nine o'clock, where Jim handed him a Dauphin Island souvenir beach bag.

"Thank you for rescuing me," Doc said. "What's in the bag?"

"Felipe forgot to pay you for your services before he left. I thought you might need a little help getting back on your feet. Open the bag in private."

"I don't know what to say. You save my life, then give me this, too? Thank you."

The three men shook hands and walked away. Neil gave Doc $100,000 neatly wrapped in birthday paper in the souvenir bag.

They drove back to Dauphin Island and found Jack and Elliott in the Land Cruiser at the fish house.

"I really appreciate you boys going with my son and all," Jim said. "You were brave to risk your lives to rescue an old man. My son tells me you might be in a little trouble where you come from. There ain't no better place for an outlaw hideout than Alabama. You can be my guests here as long as you want. No one will bother you on this island as long as we're alive. The sheriff, circuit judge, and county prosecutor are all relatives of mine. You can't get in trouble here even if you try."

"You're very welcome, Sir," Jack said. "We were honored to help. Our trouble's with the Mafia. They came after us and our dad. We killed a bunch of them, but there's no telling if they're still after us. Dad told us to stay down here through the winter unless we hear otherwise from him, so I guess that's what we'll do."

"Like Jack said," Elliott continued, "we're going to hang out for a few months. Maybe we can put the *Tipsy Gypsy* back together and really learn to sail, if Neil would be willing to teach us."

Neil placed an arm around the brothers' shoulders. "Believe me, I'll do that and more. To be more exact, there's probably half a million in cash that's rightfully yours, waiting for you whenever you want it."

About the Author

The author is a retired Army reservist, Aviator, Sailor, Carpenter, and Wood Sculptor. A self-proclaimed minimalist, he and Salli, his partner of three decades, fish, hunt, garden, and gather in Southwest Missouri and Florida. They still drive a 1970 FJ40 with a '69, 327 Corvette engine. They can venison, squirrels, mullet, and homegrown organic fruit and vegetables. Their dog, Mango, is never far away and they both almost always have a Swiss army knife at the ready.

CPSIA information can be obtained
at www.ICGtesting.com
Printed in the USA
LVHW030041101221
705804LV00005B/13